GRAVITY IS GETTING
ME DOWN

£6

GW00480505

Fred Plisner

GRAVITY
IS
GETTING
ME
DOWN

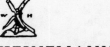

HEINEMANN : LONDON

First published in Great Britain 1994
by William Heinemann Ltd
an imprint of Reed Consumer Books Ltd
Michelin House, 81 Fulham Road, London SW3 6RB
and Auckland, Melbourne, Singapore and Toronto

Copyright © Fred Plisner 1994
The author has asserted his moral rights

A CIP catalogue record for this title
is available from the British Library

ISBN 0 434 59078 9

Printed in England by Clays Ltd, St Ives plc

'This is it,' said Sergei, dropping his stack of papers onto the saw bench. Mournfully he stroked his tobacco-stained beard. 'There's more to all this,' he added, 'believe me, Yomini, a great deal more.' He paused, chewing his lower lip. Then, impetuously, he sliced the air with his bandaged hand and pointed at the pathetic pile. 'But this is where I draw the line; beyond my bikinis I will not strip.'

Kvadratnikoff, A. F. Pliushkin

Transition

Suffice it to say comma that out of four hundred and sixteen million contestants in the first ejaculation, it was I who won the race up the Fallopian tube, thus setting in motion a succession of events and reactions which form the skeletal structure of this narration.

Suffice it also to say that, nine months later, serene and snug in my sedate surroundings, I was in no mood to leave. All I wanted was to be left in peace. But no. 'Come on in,' they cooed from out there, 'the water's lovely.'

'Anyone for tennis,' they probed when that didn't work. (My game is netball.)

'Your time is up,' they nagged. 'Make room for your sister.' I pretended not to hear them.

'Fulfil your calling . . . rise to the challenge . . . conform, damn you, everybody's got to do it.'

Nothing!

So they brought in the big guns in the shape of the no-nonsense obstetrician and his horn-rimmed assistant, wielding nickel-plated tongs and implements, and within minutes they brought about the naked arrival of the so-named Alfred, son of Sidonie Frommer and Sigmund Klausner, in polyglot Vienna. He was hauled screaming from the womb of his little mother, in the early hours of Tuesday in the autumn of 1919, the year following the end of the great holocaust when an entire generation of Europeans were deported to the river Meuse and there exterminated by gas and artillery and machine-gun.

Life being the dangerous pursuit it is, this then is a success story. It is a story of surviving, of scraping through, a story of all's well that ends well. This is a story of hanging on in the face of enormous threats. Threats and perils such as: climatic caprices, bacterial and fungal attack, automobiles, policemen, horses' hooves, shell fragments, trilby man, tram-cars, teachers, psychologists, unemployment, work, undernourishment, obesity, and the interminable ricocheting of man's hatred towards . . .

STOP! HOLD IT RIGHT THERE . . . I SAID HOLD IT!

ALFRED KLAUSNER ALIAS ALFREDO BRESNOR. ALSO KNOWN AS: G'SCHERTER, TARDURIZ, BLEU BIT, EL INGLES, TEMPRANILLO, KOREA, CURLY, LOFTY AND SHORT-ARSE; NAVVY, TOOL-MAKER, FARM LABOURER, DIESEL MECHANIC, KIBBUTZNIK, BRONZE FOUNDER, SEARCHER FOR THE HOLY GRAIL, OK? STEP FORWARD.

YOUR TURN HAS COME. ACCOUNT FOR YOUR DEEDS AS WE MUST ACCOUNT FOR OURS. GIVE US THIS DAY THE WHOLE TRUTH, AND DELIVER NOT A WEB OF LIES AS MIGHT WELL BE YOUR TEMPTATION. BUT RENDER UNTO US YOUR NARRATIVE WITH SINCERITY AND WITH BREATHTAKING CLARITY. FOR THINE IS THIS MOMENT, ITS POWER AND ITS GLORY.

GO AHEAD. AND MAKE IT BRIEF.

The umbilicus severed, I was now irreversibly on my own. Here I stood, toothless, barefooted, barefaced and bald-headed in the first quarter of the twentieth century, unprepared and vulnerable. But I got into the stride of things and went from strength to strength. The milk supply was flowing and I was putting on weight. Things, generally, began to look up.

There were setbacks. At the tender age of three weeks, I lost my foreskin to the mohel, the man with the sharp razor and the Judaic template. My rights had been violated, my liberty had been infracted. But then, as the saying goes, there is always a first time. The removal of that flap of skin marked the disposal of my choices, or so it was assumed. An irrevocable act such as no Christian baptism can accomplish. A mutilatory imposition in place of holy water.

'Once a Jew, always a Jew!' The maxim was put to me, with glee and gusto on more than one occasion, by committed Jews and pious anti-Semites.

And then I was two, and waking to the din of the sparrows in the chestnut tree below my window. And the copper pots were gleaming in the sunlit kitchen as I gobbled my morning pap. And the great inflation was galloping and food was scarce, and I was thriving on flour and water and saccharin.

In the dance halls of Vienna, Berlin and Hamburg, couples were tangoing to the tune:

> *In Nizhni Novgorod,*
> *In Nizhni Novgorod,*
> *Ist eine Hungersnot . . .* – There is starvation. –

The writers of the lyrics needn't have gone as far as Novgorod; people were starving all over Europe, only that didn't rhyme.

The song referred to the famine in the Soviet Union coming in the wake of the Russian Revolution after the Czech, the British, the United States, the Japanese, the French, the German and the Polish interventionist

5

armies had finally pulled out. The intervention failed to crush the revolution but it sowed the seed for a paranoid regime which was to see enemies in every nook and cranny, and which grew into a monster that was to devour the best and the most dedicated of its sons and daughters.

And then I was six, and taken by my ever-eager mother to the establishment up the road, to be institutionalized. The aroma of cedar wood and inflated ego reigned supreme and intimidating over me and my fellow captives. The corridors, the rooms, the podia and the blackboards reeked of authority, compulsion and prohibition. Over the entrance, carved in stone, the dictum:

DEPOSIT YOUR INDIVIDUALITY IN THE CONTAINERS PROVIDED.

And then, I was eight and, together with mother and sister Lizzi, crossed the English Channel one night and arrived in Manchester the next morning, joining father, who had preceded us in pursuit of the elusive pot of gold. Here I fell in love with Britannia guarding the approaches on the reverse of my first penny. The old penny is no more, but my affection for the aged lady has not faded. She has treated me with kindness and generosity, forever tolerant of my quirks and idiosyncrasies.

And two years later we moved to Germany. It was the first day of July 1930 and the French must have seen us coming, for they withdrew from the Rhineland that same afternoon, I swear!

And then, Tuesday, May 17th 1932, ten o'clock in the morning; the buds were erupting on the acacias in the schoolyard, and while I was reciting the congruence of triangles, 582 miles to the west in the heart of the British Empire: baby Jean was born; Jean Blanche Richardson, the girl I was to marry on her twenty-fifth birthday. The weather was bright and the airship *Graf*

6

Zeppelin could be seen from the classroom window, floating quietly past.

What a majestic sight!

And then, I was thirteen and bar-mitzvahed. And on the streets of Berlin the drums were rolling, and I was about to witness the ushering in of the thousand-year Reich, while the shickled groover was making threatening gestures in my direction.

Contemporary history was taking a personal interest in my progression, bouncing me back to Vienna and, over the following years, to Zurich, to Paris, and on to the Pyrenees.

'*Il faut partager*,' mumbled the miller as he fetched another bowl from the dresser for twenty-year-old Fred who, in the calamitous summer of 1940, was tramping south, for ever on the lookout for the consumable, one step ahead of the invincible German army that was smashing through France.

And then, aged twenty-two, I was living it up in the prison of Zaragoza. Twenty-two, and maturity as always close behind.

And then I was twenty-four, and moving stealthily through the Gibraltarian Straits, on through the Mediterranean past German-occupied Crete to Palestine. And years of danger and disillusion and desperate searching.

And, in 1955, I finally arrived at Victoria Station. The following year I duly married the young lady, mentioned on the previous page. It was around that time that I came to realize that I was neither immortal nor infallible nor invincible. Maturity, out of breath, was catching up.

And then our daughter arrived, and we have been calling her Julie ever since. And five years later Peter turned up, and I was old enough to be his grandfather.

There followed years of frustration and joy and scrimping and scraping.

And then, abruptly, without warning, I mean out of the blue, I was confronted with sixty-three candles on my cake. Sixty-three! SIX-TEE-TH-REE? What happened to 47 and 17 . . . and . . . and when was 29 and 31 and 53 and the other prime numbers? All eighteen, unaccounted for.

Forgive the outburst, friends, but I must insist on a recount!

And now comma the bitterness subsided, the decks cleared and the hatches battened down; in a final act of vanity, I am feeding it all into this microchip-motivated writing machine. I owe it to history. She has been good to me.

Thus far.

Vienna

It was love at first sight in the voluptuous sand-pit.

Marie, our washerwoman-cum-parlourmaid-cum-cleaner-cum-nanny, takes Lizzi and me to the park. She guards us with motherly affection, chinwagging all the while in sisterly Slovak with her cronies; peasant girls come to the city, offering themselves to lower-middle-class homes as washerwomen-cum-cleaners-cum- housekeepers-cum-nannies, working sixteen hours a day, with half a day off on Sunday, for peanuts and a bed in the broom-cupboard.

'My daddy's gotta big wobbly,' says to me the young lady who had found grace in my eyes.

I shovel the sand from my bucket into hers, and gape admiringly at her blue satin bow, tied to the shaft of her silky brown hair.

'Less jump,' I say, helping her up the ramp. She shrieks with excitement and delight, landing in the soft sand.

'Where is your wobbly?' she asks as I pat and compact the sand in her bucket.

'Wha's your name?' I reply, digging a tunnel under our castle.

'You can have my sweet,' she says, her brown eyes taking dominance over my senses and cautiously she adds, 'For a while.' With her sandy fingers, she transfers the toffee from her mouth to mine and we are bonded.

'Less jump,' we squeal in unison. And we leap again and again until we are out of breath.

'My name is Korianda!'

'My name is Mono Sillabik.'

She kisses me on the mouth and runs off and I never see that woman again, much as I look for her in every sand-pit in town, on every swing and slide. She has gone and left me in limbo, dangling.

Korianda, you disloyal wench! You have gone and left me when I most needed you. You have gone and left me out in the cold, exposed to hostile elements and sinister forces; exposed to the likes of Franz Kafka and Friedrich Nietzsche. You have gone and left me at the mercy of gravity and magnetic storms and Wally's bawds of euphony and his organic boomings. How am I to cope?

How am I to cope?

You bitch! You have gone and left me out in the cold, yourself living securely in the safety of my memories.

The story goes that at the height of the great inflation, when wages were paid daily, a woman, queuing outside the baker's in the town of Altenburg in Saxony, had to attend to some momentary urgency. She left her basket full of freshly printed *Notgeld* to retain her place in the queue. *Notgeld* was emergency money printed locally, almost hourly, to feed the unrelenting devaluation.

When the woman returned the shop was closed, the queue had vanished and the basket had disappeared. The bundles of money, however, were stacked neatly in its place.

On the very same day, in the Hernals district of Vienna, a man goes to the butcher's to collect his weekly ration of sausage. The butcher counts the money, $13\frac{1}{2}$ million kronen, takes the ration voucher, weighs the appropriate portion and wraps it in a used tramway ticket.

Arriving home, the man carefully unfolds the ticket to find that the sausage has disappeared.

'It must have dropped out through the punch-hole,' remarks his wife, putting back into the drawer the forks and the knives.

Promptly, one month before my sixth birthday, Mother dresses me in my best apparel and, in high spirits, great expectations and a sinking stomach, we leave the house and direct our steps towards the unassuming, lugubrious building with its crash barrier outside the front gate.

Strapped to my back is my new leather satchel. It contains a pencil-box and my sandwiches: sardines spread on buttered rye bread, lovingly sprinkled with lemon. All other necessities are supplied by the City of Vienna Education Authority. These comprise the latest in classroom equipment: two cedarwood pencils, India rubber, pen-holder, steel nib and exercise book. Gone are the days of the slate, the stylus and the little sponge. Our newly designed benches have built-in inkwells.

Now we are sat at our desks and the bell rings and our mothers instruct us to sit perfectly still and straight, with our hands gripping the edge of our desks; four fingers above, thumbs below, index fingers touching. The teacher and the headmaster come in and our mothers drift out. And my umbilical cord is severed, yet again.

. . . then the headmaster told us to stop whispering and listen carefully and . . . and . . . then Mister Teacher told us to sit up straight and pay attention and . . . and then he gave each of us our pen-holder and steel nib and explained how to put the nib in the holder and then he stuck his tongue out

11

*and . . . and he licked the nib because . . . because the ink
does not stick to a new nib and then we all had to lick the
grease off the nib and spit it in our hankies so that the ink
would stick to our pens and Kohlberg cried because he didn't
have a hanky and Mister Teacher was annoyed and gave him
a piece of paper and Kohlberg went all red in his face and he
spitted into the paper . . . and then Mister Teacher gave
everyone an exercise book and they had our names on it and
class one and . . . and then Mister Teacher sent Reindl and
Saltzinger to go and fetch Mister Caretaker with a shovel
and a broom and sawdust because Pomeranz had vomited in
the centre aisle . . . and then the bell went and Mister
Teacher said to put everything that belongs to us and . . .
and . . . put it in our satchel and then he told us to stand up
very quietly and file out of the room and line up in twos
outside the door . . . and we all lined up outside the door . . .
and in twos . . . and Schramm was still sitting there . . . and
Mister Teacher shouted and said why don't you get up
Schramm and how often do I have to tell you Schramm and
. . . and do you require a special invitation Schramm . . . and
Schramm didn't move because . . . because he was all stiff-
ened up from sitting to attention and grabbing the desk and
Mister Teacher went back and loosened him off his seat . . .
and then Mister Teacher told us to lead on down the stairs
quietly and not so much fuss and then he took us down to
the street and all the mothers were leaning on the crash
barrier.*

The following day we had our first lesson and the
teacher said, 'The coachman sits on his box and drives
his horses. What is he holding in his hand? Don't shout
. . . put your hands up if you know.'

'Please, Mister Teacher, I saw a coachman and he
was holding a stick in his hand.'

'WRONG!'

'Please, Mister Gildenkraut, he is holding the reins.'

'Wrong. Sit down and be quiet. – Quiet, you there
. . . yes you.'

'Please Mister Teacher, he is holding a whip.'

'He – is – hol – ding – a – whip,' said Mister Gildenkraut,
bending forward and sideways accentuating every syl-
lable, 'very right. What is your name?'

'Joseph Eintracht, Mister Teacher.'

'Come and sit in the front row, Eintracht. You will
be the class monitor. Now be quiet every . . . I DIDN'T
SAY FUSS, DID I? WELL DID I . . . QUIET . . . I WILL
NOT HAVE . . . now look at the blackboard and
observe carefully what I am doing. What have I got in
my hand? Quiet! You there, what's your name?'

'Anton Svobotnik, Mister Teacher.'

'Well shut your beak, Shvopnik! – You there, what
have I got in my hand? A piece of chalk. Very good.
QUIET! . . . and I am drawing on the . . . yes blackboard
with my piece of . . . you there . . . chalk. And what am
I drawing? I – am – draw – ing – a whip. *Nicht wahr?*
Here is the wooden stick. And here is the . . . QUIET! . . .
here is the rope attached to the stick. So! And this is the
number One. Now, for your homework . . . WILL YOU
SHUT UP . . . for your homework you will write number
One, twenty times on the first page in your exercise book.
Tomorrow I will teach you number Two.'

Ach so!

About one third of my classmates were Roman Cath-
olics. There were two or three Protestants or
Evangelicals as they sometimes called themselves, and
Dragomazar who was Greek Orthodox. We the Jews,
who were in a majority, situated as we were in the
second district of Vienna, were registered as Mosaics.

Mosaisch was the official and polite adjective for
those of us who professed the Jewish religion. The
French have their euphemism for *Juif*, which is *Israélite*.
Only the English have no other word for Jew. But even
here, there is a fine distinction between a Jew, and

being Jewish. If you want to be polite, you say, 'That man with the horn-rimmed spectacles is Jewish,' rather than proclaiming, 'He's a Jew.'

Don't turn your head now, but that person over there is of the Mosaic persuasion.

La famille à la deuxième étage, ils sont des israélites.

Quello scrittore là, con la testa enfiata, é ébreo.

These revelations, it goes without saying, are pronounced in a cultured, almost imperceptible murmur.

Growing up in this compact community, I was brought up to look down on the *Goyim* who, we were told, hated us. Our scorn was specifically directed at the one whose name was not to be uttered. He who had been one of us but had started his own enterprise.

The *Goyim*, I was taught, were uncultured country yokels whose main preoccupation was to get stoned on pay day, and who carried innumerable diseases. They were to be treated with the utmost reserve. Anyway, they were all anti-Semites. If there were some who showed kindness towards us, that only proved their duplicity.

'They smile to your face, but they'll stab you in the back, give them half a chance.'

Mum:	Where are you going my son?
Son:	I'm going out to play.
Mum:	Not in the street you don't. Not with those Christians, you don't. I forbid . . .
Son :	(jumps up and down): Oh Mum, why not Mum? Karl lends me his new scooter and he teaches me lots of tricks and . . .
Mum:	Go and play with with young Goldwasser at number 32. He is a nice Jewish boy and his father is an actuary, a very . . .
Son :	(jumps up and down): Oh why do I have to play with him? I don't like him. His hair is

14

> all curly and he never plays in the street.
> *Anyway, you let me play with Andi Krautho-*
> *fer and he isn't Jewish.*
>
> Mum: *That's different. His father is a*
> *Kommerzialrat . . . highly respected.*

On Republic Day, Mister Gildenkraut would tell us
about the grandeur of Austria and its spirit of
enterprise – *Unternehmungsgeist* – Austrian valour,
Austrian determination, Austrian inventiveness.
Austrian this, Austrian that, and Austrian the other.
We were being fed on a diet of past magnificence and
the dignity of conquest and hegemony. The map on the
wall showed the importance of Austria. It was the hub
of the world, its navel, if you like. All roads and rail-
lines led to Austria and in order to travel to any part
of this universe one had to pass through Vienna.

When it came to the final HURRAH, long live
Austria, hip hip, it was Freddi Klausner who cheered
the loudest. At the age of seven the spirit had entered.
The love of the Fatherland had been implanted in my
receptive mind. Patriotism had struck root. From then
on I was in the grip of a loyalist fervour. I abused my
father's atlas by improving the boundaries with lines
of graphite, taking in a chunk of northern Italy, then
returning Budapest to the fold. One moment I would
incorporate eastern Switzerland and the next I would
annex Bohemia and Silesia, moving north one day and
maybe west on another. Occasionally, my passion for
realism would demand that the odd battle be lost. Then
the India rubber had to go to work readjusting armistice lines and returning territories.

Imperceptibly and with stealth I created the most
potent central European power ever.

Father left for England when I was eight but the event has made no mark on my memory. That was in April 1928.

The previous summer a retired English couple from Blackpool, had come to Vienna in search of relations. They had mistakenly been directed to us but became friends and they offered Father a house with a shop, situated in Manchester's Cheetham district. We could have the house rent-free, on condition that Dad kept an eye on the other houses they owned in the street and collected the rent. The offer had come at an opportune moment. A few months earlier Father had fallen out with his young partner in the fur-coat business. The partner had been the workshop expert and, with him out of the way, the business had freewheeled downhill and folded.

Meanwhile, Mother had to cope as best as she could for the next six months. She was an accomplished milliner, having completed her apprenticeship at the age of seventeen. But she could put her hand to anything: dressmaking, shirt repairing, darning; she was always able to earn a few pennies where there were few on the ground. She scrimped and she scraped and we got by.

Manchester

1928 was not an unforgettable year as years go. But I'll say this for her, she wasn't a harmful year either. She wasn't bad or cruel or anything like that. She was plain in appearance and reliable. In fact, war was abolished in that year. In that year, the year 1928, the year I am telling you about, the United States Secretary of State (Foreign Minister) Frank Kellogg, and his French counterpart Aristide Briand got together and outlawed war. They arranged a meeting of the representatives of sixty-five nations and a treaty was signed that effectively abolished war forever after.

It was in none other than the unassuming year of 1928 that we moved to Manchester. Father's business consisted of a corner shop selling groceries, cigarettes and sweets. There was something essentially English about the bearded sailor, framed by the life belt displayed on the packet of Players, which made a deep and more than visual impression. Mother revelled in the new spirit and missed no opportunity to express her enthusiasm for the casualness and pragmatism of the English. Where we had come from, one followed rules. Here, common sense prevailed and things were judged by results. The tram crew, swigging tea during working hours; this was unthinkable in regulation-ridden Vienna which choked on bureaucratic efficiency. The design of the kitchen range with its constant hot-water supply and its plate-warming compartment, all built around the open fire grate, was another one of mother's much-appreciated novelties. Back in Vienna, boys played with coloured clay balls, shoving them clumsily with the index finger. Over here, they launched their flashy glass marbles with a powerful flick of the thumb. Yes, in my heart of hearts, I had to admit that dirty, foggy, grey Manchester was streets ahead of Vienna.

The restrained manner of the English, with their deliberation and composure, was impressive. The apparent absence of arrogance and emotion – except that displayed by our teachers – had a refreshing effect on me. I was eight years old and inspired by their reserve, deadpan humour and their tendency towards self-deprecation.

Elizabeth Street in Hightown, the northern and seedier part of Cheetham Hill, is where our new home was. Cheetham was the district where the bulk of Manchester's large Jewish population lived. The majority were turn-of-the-century refugees from the pogroms in the Ukraine and immigrants from Poland and Lithuania.

Many shed the names which reminded them of their unpleasant past. Thus our neighbour, the barber, whose name had been Chatskelson now called himself Davies, and the kosher butcher in Waterloo Road who, back in Kovno, had been known as Gedalye Shekhter, was now Gordon White. The Rappaports, the Grinspans, the Nisselboims, now called themselves Wallace, Gilbert and Clements but rarely Smith, Jones or Miller. Their boys were given names such as: Sidney, Martin, Stanley and Harold. James, George,

Frederick and John were avoided. With girls: Doris, Mabel, Pearl, Gladys, Olive, would do fine.

Yiddish was freely quoted but seldom spoken.

Yiddish; reputedly twelfth-century German, which the Jews had taken along to Eastern Europe in their quest for greener pastures. Interspersed with Hebrew and elements from the languages of the various host countries, it is written and printed in Hebrew characters. It is still used by the Jews of Eastern Europe and their descendants around the world, but is now in decline. It has survived for nearly seven hundred years. Its structure remains German, and to this day one can witness Yiddish-speaking Jerusalemites conversing, albeit haltingly, with German tourists.

The question arises, why had this language proved so durable? After all, it carries painful memories. Why did the Jews abandon Aramaic and Greek which they spoke at the time of their gradual exodus from Palestine throughout the three centuries preceding the birth of Christ when Hebrew had ceased to be the spoken language; elevated to *lashan kadosh*, the holy language, reserved for prayer and Torah readings.

Sister Lizzi and I were enrolled at the Jews' school in Derby Street, the day after our arrival. We were mobbed in the playground and gawked at, as a curiosity. Soon after, when the novelty had worn off, I was derided for losing the war and chided for raping Belgium and committing atrocities on innocent civilians.

'Hey German Klosna,' they would accost me with, 'who won the war?'

'We won the war,' I would counter, as soon as my English was good enough. 'We won on the sea and in the air, only on land did we lose. That's two to one.' Factually and substantially wrong, but effective. It kept them quiet for a while.

In the shifting hierarchy of the Junior School I was near the bottom rung. But most times I would give a good account of myself. I was known for my vicious kick to the shin when cornered. Thus, I would get my own back and, at the same time, my opponent was unable to catch up, pursuing me as he did with a hobble and a skip. It gave me a head start which, at worst, got me to within yelling distance of our kitchen window.

The first thing I learned in those memorable early days, emulating my new classmates, was to place my left hand on my right biceps, whilst vigorously propelling my fist upwards whenever Danziger turned to the blackboard. At the time, I didn't know what that gesture symbolized and I doubt if half the class knew. Danziger was our form teacher. She was one of the two Jewish teachers on the staff at the Jews' school. It was from her that I learned the multiplication table and from then on I always multiplied in English. Seven eights's fifty-six, forever after.

The world map in the assembly hall displayed the British Empire in all its pink glory, splashed liberally across the Mercator's projection. It revealed the importance of Great Britain and its central position. It showed clearly and to the exclusion of all irrelevant detail, how the sea lanes around the world converge on, and fan out from London and Liverpool. Around the edge of the glazed, cloth-backed map were pictures depicting: merchant vessels in dock, Sidney Habour Bridge, a captured howitzer, Battersea Power Station, the Victoria Falls and the front half of the battle cruiser *Hood*. At the apex was a portrait of King George V and Queen Mary. Topping it all were the lion and the unicorn. They stood on their hind legs, conversing in lofty Norman, one proclaiming '*Dieu et mon droit*', the other nodding agreement, declaring that '*Honi soit qui mal y pense*', universal slogans affirming that right is on *our*

20

side, and expressing contempt for the despicable
blackguard who may think otherwise

In comparison with Vienna, where anti-Semitism, even
among children, was an earnest pursuit, in Manchester
of 1928 it was part of a dispassionate rivalry. On numerous occasions, playing in Cheetham Park, the cry
went up: 'The Yoks are coming! The Yoks are coming!'
and a band of raiders, Christian kids from Herbert
Street and beyond, appeared and proceeded to beat us
up. The one that caught up with me would aim a few
perfunctory blows at my head, while making uncom-
plimentary remarks about the Jewish race. The
hostility was embryonic in its diffidence, tentative and
exploratory.
    The tables were turned when we caught three Yoks
in the clay pits riding our brick-trolleys.
    The clay pits were Jewish territory.
    We took them prisoner and were marching them off
to be executed when two older boys, skiving from
Talmitoire, caught up with our gang and pleaded on
behalf of the captives.
    '. . . 'snot their fault c'mon . . . let them go, they were
born like that. . . they can't 'elp it.'
    'They eat pork an' . . . an' they get drunk,' screamed
little Glickman from standard 2, winding up for the
prosecution.
    'Yea an' they play the gramophone,' added Sender,
'an' they . . . they . . . an' they . . .'
    He was drowned in '. . . yea an' bacon meat . . . an'
they gobble jellied eel . . . yerkh . . . an' horse meat . . .'
Accusations were raining down: smoking cigarettes on
Shabbes, carrying syphilis, wearing hobnailed boots,
pissing on Jewish boys' legs at the seaside lavatory . . .
    The older boys stood their ground. The taller of the
two pleaded.

21

'If they had a choice . . . I mean it would please . . . Shut up all of you, will ya? Will ya listen? It would please them no end, if they were Jewish . . . stans to reason, dunnit?'

Prying the prisoners from their guards, he turned to the Christians for confirmation.

'Wha' . . . ?'

'I said, you'd rather be one of us, woodn'tsha?'

'Wha' . . .?'

'Jewish.'

'Jewish?'

'That's what I said, Jewish.'

'Yea, sure,' admitted the spokesman for the captives.

In the end we relented and sent them off with a warning not to show their 'goyishe faces 'round 'ere again.'

'An' tell your cousins an' friends,' we shouted after them as they trotted off, dodging our missiles and amplifying their expletives in direct proportion to the distance covered.

True to its name, a matinee in those days really did take place in the morning. Every Sunday morning at the local cinema we were fed a diet of Wild West and horror 'silents'. Most were serialized, compelling us to return the following week and the week after. At about that time, the moving picture industry was experimenting with sound track, added to the edge of the celluloid strip. This, fed through an electro-magnet and an amplifier, induced vibrations in a loudspeaker which, in its turn, would put many musicians out into the street, musicians who had hitherto accompanied the silent movies, hammering the keyboard to match the action.

The current term 'film' as opposed to 'movie', is most appropriate because it is descriptive of the essentially superficial nature of the art.

'Hey, I saw a film yesterday.'

'Oh yarse? What film was that?'

'It was an oil film on a puddle in the lane and it displayed all the colours of the rainbow in the evening light.'

'Who starred in it?'

'Well, at night it reflected the Seven Sisters, Algol, Vega, Aldebaran and a host of minors who's names I didn't gather.'

Occasionally, Father took me to the greyhound races at Belle Vue. Belle Vue Gardens fulfilled the edifying needs of the industrious classes by providing culture on tap. Apart from the dog tracks, it had a boating lake, an amusement park, a motor-cycle racing track and football fields. At the far end, there was an array of securely caged animals for human edification. Competitions took place at Belle Vue. Championships were organized to determine the best in brass bands, dancing, boxing, wrestling, and tiddly-winks.

After the last dog race we would cross the road to watch the fireworks: Catherine wheels, rockets, bangers, crackers and Roman candles, along with the inevitable ambush of the German patrol with the inevitable German rout and the inevitable marching off of the 'square heads' with their hands inevitably in the air. This feature consisted of a mock battle being performed by two groups wearing khaki and field grey. They lobbed illuminated grenades and fired flashing bullets from mock machine-guns. England was forever reliving the trauma of the trenches and the mortars; seemingly enjoying it, ten years on.

One wintry morning towards the end of 1928, a woman charged into the shop, ruffled and bedraggled. The outfit to be seen in, at that time of the morning, was: curlers, hair net, dressing gown, slippers, Woodbine dangling from mouth. She was our foremost purveyor of titbits and rumours, but on that morning there was urgency in her demeanour. She had charged through the door, showing signs of advanced RADA, wailing about the imminence of war 'with America', meaning the United States. Even at the age of eight, the proposition seemed to me preposterous and I never gave it much thought until recently, when I came across Anthony Burgess's account – also set in Manchester – 'blaming the Pope for the coming war with America'. 1924–28 was the period when president Calvin Coolidge was holding office.

From an early age, I was taught to believe in a supervisory deity from which I could not hide, which allowed no private thought. A personalized God, universal, yet attached securely to the Jewish nation; omnipresent and all-powerful; unsmiling. A no-nonsense God who would punish me for my infringements and shortcomings as well as those of my ancestors even unto the third and fourth generation. No wishy-washy God he.

My problem has always been excessive brooding. I was continually pondering over one thing or another. And a great many issues don't stand the strain of persistent scrutiny. Still, God has not given me brain tissue to investigate and examine, but so that I may remember to thank Him for 'not making me a woman', and for commanding me to wash my hands before meals. However, doubt is not a conscious effort, rather a nagging toothache. Perplexity, in my case, turned into an inability to go on turning spiritual somersaults.

It was more than a belief that I had been expected to inherit from my father, as he had done and generations before him. It was a closed, self-supporting system with built-in safeguards and defences and labyrinthine traps for the unwary logician, on top of which it had the added attraction of its exclusivity. One can see how this package can bestow strength upon those who are prepared to trade in their critical faculties for an inflexible creed . . . how it can offer a sense of security coming from the conviction that 'right is on *our* side'.

In order to give me a good grounding in Jewishness, my father sent me to the *cheder* which is the equivalent to Sunday School, only the other way around – we had to attend every day except the Sabbath. After one year I was still stumbling over reading exercises, while others who had started later, had advanced to Torah-chanting and interpretation. After four millennia, or thereabouts, we were naturally concerned about the true meaning of the Law given at Sinai. In Babylon, wise men wrote lengthy commentaries; commentaries, it goes without saying, which necessitated annotations and footnotes, which in turn, required further transpositions and analyses. Today we are pondering over essence and gist.

In the meantime, pragmatism ruled. It consisted of circumnavigating the Law by making one's wishes known by indirect means as in the case of the Jewish housewife who was forbidden to light a fire or flick the electric switch on the Sabbath, nor did the faith allow her to order her maid to do so; but there was no law to prevent her from remarking to her husband, within earshot of the parlourmaid or the chauffeur, how nice it would be not to have to sit in the dark.

'Would madam like me to switch on the lights?' enquires the servant who happens to have overheard the expression of desire for illumination.

'That's entirely up to you, my dear,' replies the *balabusteh*, piqued by the girl's failure to take the hint. 'You must be the judge of that.'

If the servant is too dumb or inexperienced in the intricacies of the Jewish household to understand a request couched in a casual remark, or if she just likes playing silly buggers, then she mustn't be surprised if she finds herself out on her ear the following Tuesday.

The Law ordained that a girl cut her hair when she got married, as indeed her mother had ever since she was married. But there was no law to prevent her from having a box full of wigs to wear on various occasions. Neither was there a law forbidding her to have her beautiful hair shorn by the wig-maker on the Thursday prior to her wedding and have it back on her shaven skull in time for the party.

The circumventive approach is not, of course, confined to the Jewish housewife. 'We can get hold of a million dollars to keep them quiet; no problem,' says RMN on his magnetic tape, nodding and winking. 'But it would be wrong.'

'Dad! Why don't we send out missionaries, like the Christians, and make everybody Jewish?'

This proposition has an alluring appeal. Not only is it seen to be altruistic, but it could mean an end to Jew-hatred.

'Make everybody Jewish? Listen son! We don't want them. WE ARE SPECIAL. We are the chosen people. If we really . . . let's assume for one moment that we might succeed in converting them. Then what happens . . . I mean what happens? Everybody, but everybody will be special. And when everybody is special then nobody is special. Geddit? Impasse! Paradox! Who wants paradox? You want paradox like you want a broken collar-bone, ora . . . ora . . . or a hole in de head. I mean . . . Finish your noodles.'

Klausner or *small is smart*

> In the life of every person there are three provinces. Mind, body and articulation.
>
> *Illyrian saying*

When the inches were handed out, the Klausners were short-changed; and the Frommers, my maternal ancestors: they were directed to the wrong queue.

Shaking the genes about, making the best of a bad job, I stopped growing bodily in the year 1934. It was the year in which Engelbert Dollfuss the Austrian chancellor, a fellow-sufferer from arrested growth, was shot dead in the abortive Nazi *putsch*.

Considering the malnutrition I had been subjected to, due to circumstances prevailing at the time of my early childhood, I did relatively well winding up five feet tall with half an inch thrown in for good measure. It means that, wearing my hobnailed boots, I would be as tall as Queen Victoria was when *she* wore her hobnailed boots.

Why is it that a nasty man is called nasty or obnoxious, so long as he is over five feet and four inches tall?

Why?

For, make no mistake, below that height, he is known as a nasty *little* man. Have you ever heard of a nasty tall man? Or a nasty man of middling stature? You can be stupid, dirty, greedy, disgusting, horrid, but when you're short, you've got yourself an additional adjective clothed, might I add, in a derisory mantle.

27

I have had to provide amusement for people who have nothing to offer but their corpulence.

'Hi Shorty, my top drawer may be full of cow dung but I stand five feet, five and a half inches in my socks.'

People of all walks of life can add to their sense of achievement, simply by accosting Klausner and measuring up to him. After all, in this world it's bulk and appearance that counts.

They look down on you. Your face is level with their elbow. 'Stand up,' they blurt at you. 'What's the weather like down there,' they jovialize.

I have not been endowed with the wherewithal to cope with, or to compensate for, the impediment. I have never been able to come to terms with it. Why can't I live in a world where the top row of the magazine racks is accessible to the likes of me; a world where small is smart?

I am being hysterical, am I? Well you try walking around on five feet and half an inch or one meter fifty-three. See how you like it.

ENOUGH OF THIS TIRADE FREDDI. SHE DOESN'T SELL BOOKS. THIS IS ONE DICKHEAD WAY OF LOSING YOUR READERS.

OK! I am all right. Once more, small is smart – small is smart– small is smart – I feel better already – small is smart – small. . .

I said I am all right! All right? You do go on.

Small is smart, and apart from the obvious drawbacks, miniaturity carries advantages. You tend to be under-assessed. Smallness is equated with cretinism and looked upon as an aberration. This is a world where smallness is treated as laziness; contemptible and inexcusable.

Out of this comes a miscalculation, a refusal to credit the below-average-sized person, with the ability to think and scheme; to retaliate. All my life I have been taken for an idiot. And when I responded to their at best patronizing stance, they didn't know what it was that had stung them. I would have trapped their queen before they could even utter 'Sicilian defence.'

They are disorientated by the unexpected. Small is smart!

Take heart, you mighty midgets. You present a smaller target to machine-gun bullets and whining shrapnel. Have you ever thought of that? You spend less on food and, although maybe half the weight of the next person, your vote cast in elections has an equal lack of impact. Have you ever thought of that? In the population statistics your height, unlike your age, is of no import. You are counted as if you were full size. Did you ever consider that? Your tailor must charge you half price, for is it not a fact that he needs only half the thread and takes half the time for half the stitches? Not to speak of half the amount of cloth and lining.

Small is indeed smart!

You provide succour and reassurance for a great many people. Imagine a five-feet-three-and-a-quarter-inch hombre walking past you in the street. Once out of earshot, he turns to his consort and murmurs:

'Garsh Razzlyn, a'm sho' glayad a'm nart as short as heyum.'

Spare a thought for the poor slob clearing six feet two inches who, on a winter's night, is issued with a standard blanket, no bigger than the one supplied to you. His palliasse is not an inch longer than yours. Is that justice, or is it justice?

Galicia, the home of the Klausners, constitutes the western part of the Ukraine and is in no way related to the Spanish province of the same name. Whereas, in Spain, the name relates mainly to the Gaels, the name in the Ukraine remains the latinization of the Duchy of

Galish, which the territory was known as, around the turn of the millennium.

Since the beginning of the twentieth century, the people of the eastern part of Galicia have sailed under seven different flags.

How so?

Suppose you were born in that province at the beginning of 1914, you would have been a citizen of the Austro-Hungarian Empire. At the age of one, you would have found yourself under Tsarist Russian occupation, followed a year later by that of the Imperial German Army. At the age of five, you would have been taught to sing the Polish anthem (affirming that 'Poland is not yet lost'), in a classroom dominated by a portrait of General Piłsudski adorning a map showing Poland as the centre of the world and as its most important component.

Come 1939, you are now twenty-five and in the middle of the celebrations of your first wedding, the Red Army occupies your town. Two years later, the panzers of Nazi Germany race east leaving the swastika hanging limp from the town hall balcony, in the summer heat.

Having survived three and a half years of hardship and danger and domestic woes, you witness the German forces rushing through your town with the same urgency as in June of 1941, only this time in the opposite direction, hotly pursued by Soviet advance units who promptly incorporate you into the Ukrainian Soviet Socialist Republic, in time for filing papers apropos your first divorce.

Seven administrations in the space of thirty years? Have I got this right?

Father was always one step behind his ambitions. He never fell on hard times, rather the hard times fell on him. He always had a tough time, most of all with himself. Success was around the corner and when that corner had been turned, another corner, the last one, beckoned. He became a frustrated man. The whole world misunderstood him and he had been left standing with his expectations and visions playing kinetic tricks.

He was assertive and given to histrionics. Being a benevolent despot, he continually felt the need to justify his case and endow it with a pragmatic-moralistic quality. He would deny us the right to keep money, including of course the money each one of us was earning, telling us that as every government needed a finance minister, so did the family unit. And he was the one with the qualifications. Had he not handled thousands of Austrian schillings and hundreds of dollars over the years? If we needed anything we only had to ask, was Father's reasoning. He would then appraise that need, analyse it, evaluate it and advise us on ways of overcoming it without recourse to spending hard earned money, 'in times such as these'. Or indeed he would show us that the need, in reality, didn't exist.

I was well into my third year at work, seventeen years old when, on a courageous night, I managed to *tell* him I was going out instead of asking for permission. I even disregarded his express order, hanging out with people of whom he disapproved. Oh yes, he was Minister of the Interior and Public Order as well.

He himself had left home at the age of seventeen in 1905 to seek his fortune in the United States. That was the year when the mighty Russian Empire ordered its fleet, from the Black Sea and the Baltic, halfway around the world to the Yellow Sea, to teach the up-and-coming Japanese a lesson in the European superiority. In the event, the Japanese navy surreptitiously hid behind the island of Tsushima and sank the Russians as they proudly entered the Sea of Japan.

I never found out exactly what Father had occupied himself with, during the nine years he spent in Boston, Massachusetts. At the outbreak of the First World War he decided to return to his home town, in time to witness the Russian 'steamroller' push the Imperial Austrian forces out of Galicia.

'Lemberg probably still in our possession,' ran a headline at the time. My mother found the wording noteworthy and missed no opportunity to bring it up when the occasion arose.

In 1917, with the Russians expelled from Galicia, Father moved to Vienna.

My parents married on Christmas Day 1918.

Without experience but with a skilled partner, Father started a fur business which folded after five years. Around that time he brought his parents from Galicia and established them in our home. It exposed an unbridgeable culture gap. Theirs was a patriarchal order in which the daughter-in-law occupied the lowest rung in the hierarchy. Father's parents were something out of the Stone Age and to the young Viennese housewife, brought up on a diet of enlightened 'modernism', they seemed crude and uncouth. They spat on the floor, and screamed *Lingenentsinding* (pneumonia) whenever a window was opened. The marriage suffered irreparable damage and mother left years later, having bided her time until Lizzi and I were old enough to fend for ourselves.

Father perished in the great conflagration of 1942–44. Together with millions of Jews, Gypsies, Slavs, Germans and other victims of a depraved concept, he was murdered in an orgy of arrogance and madness; a sickness that has plagued mankind since the beginning of time.

The last documentation of Chayim Pesach Sigmund Klausner is the notice in his registration form. It reads: '*Abgemeldet nach Minsk.*' In keeping with Austrian procedure, all changes of address had to be logged with the police. Deportation to the death camps, it appears, was entered as departure to Minsk or Riga.

He had been denied the dignity of old age and the joy of grandparenthood. Like millions of other Jews who were destined to perish, he had donned his *tefillim* every weekday morning since his childhood, recited his prayers twice daily and blessed every piece of bread that passed his lips, thanking him who provided. And yet his God had forsaken him. All his life he had worshipped a male deity of fair complexion that was to let him down when the crunch came.

Berlin

Triangles are congruent when you are thirteen and education has gone off the rails.

A. Barbés-Rochechouart

The corner shop in Manchester had turned out to be another one of Father's disappointments. His younger brother Ralph, however, whom he had always treated as a nincompoop, had settled in Berlin and was doing well. Ralph was plying the provinces as a pedlar.

Once again Father packed his bags and left, this time for Berlin, to set up yet another home. There he joined the band of *Keilers*, a slang name depicting hawkers; one-man firms calling their operation mail-order enterprise – *Versandhaus*. They roved the countryside of the Mark Brandenburg taking orders for bed-linen and tablecloths.

It was left to Mother to manage as best as she could and wind up the Manchester operation. Three months later, we crossed the English Channel or La Manche – depending on which side of the water you are – and proceeded via Ostend and Cologne eastwards to Berlin.

Wall Street had crashed several months earlier and the economic calamity was racing across the Atlantic Ocean making its entrance into Germany with headlights blazing and hooters blaring.

The paving stones were hot as we went out to play in the summer of 1930 in Berlin's Skalitzer Strasse. Down the road, an old cart-horse had slipped and fallen. – My German language master corrected my composition. 'The horse', he said in red ink, 'had not *umgefallen*, it had *hingefallen*.' Here was an acute case of disparity between Prussian diction and Austrian parlance.

I was nearly eleven when I enrolled in the Sexta of the Luisenstädtisches Realgymnasium. In Berlin, one progressed from the Sexta through the Quinta and Quarta to the *Abiturium* class, the upper Prima. Likewise, the marks worked from back to front. The highest mark would be one, which denoted very good, and in descending order: two (good); three (satisfactory); four (deficient) and five (plain unsatisfactory).

School term, in Berlin, began at Easter and, since we had arrived in the middle of the summer recess, classes had already been in progress for three months. The headmaster took me around to the first-form teachers, who wrung their hands, lamenting that they were bursting at the seams. Only when Dr Michaelis was told that I had spent two years in England was I found a desk in his class. The *Doktor* was the English language teacher.

> *Look. This is a book.*
> *The book is full of pages.*
> *The boy is reading the book.*
> *The book is on the table.*

The *Herr Direktor* ran the school with an iron rod of friendliness and understanding. To him, diligence came before discipline, and achievement before performance. His office was a hotbed of moderation and *laissez-faire* and Mother called the establishment approvingly a 'Bohemian school'.

However, tolerance and broadmindedness, by their very nature, are unenforceable and there were, as in the best of establishments, a generous allocation of teachers to whom school was a place of discipline and inculcation, who didn't go along with patience and kindness, teachers to whom kindness was weakness and shameful defeat; teachers with a military past in their bones.

We were fed on a diet of myths and legends, dished up as facts: Diogenes had lived in a beer barrel (Ha Ha). He had been contemptuous of the paraphernalia of civilization, and discarded his beaker after observing a boy drinking from his cupped hand. Here I challenged the teacher. How could this apparent contradiction be explained. Namely, on the one hand, Diogenes's opposition to gadgets and on the other, so the story goes, his walking about town with a lamp in broad daylight.

'A lamp', so I argued, 'is a gadget; why then had he retained it when he had smashed his drinking mug?'

'Lamps in those days, dear boy,' explained Dr Stiehl, 'were very primitive articles. They consisted of a clay receptacle and some oil and a piece of string for a wick.' He smiled and waved me on.

'But *Herr Doktor*, the drinking vessel he smashed was even more primitive. That too is made of. . .'

'Don't be so silly Klausner. *Sei nicht so albern*. Sit down and open your book on page 78. *I SAID SIT DOWN!!!*'

That year, most of our history lessons consisted of being told to sit absolutely still and read set pages, while the *Herr Doktor* would busy himself going through stacks of exercise books.

It is still done today.

In fact, the reason why juvenile regimentation is stretched over so many years is to provide time for teachers to go over their exam-classes' work while in charge of the younger grades.

The world map displayed in the *Aula* stressed the importance of Germany and its central geographic position. Roads and rail-lines led to the far corners of Europe and Asia. Sea-lanes were fanning out from the estuaries of the Elbe and the Weser, servicing the continents of Africa, America, Australia and the islands of the Pacific Ocean. Travelling from the Cape of Good Hope to the Yucatán, one would have had to pass through Bremerhaven or Hamburg.

The map also highlighted the pre-1918 borders, dotted lines cutting into Lithuania, linking East Prussia to the mainland, and caressing Alsace, Lorraine and Malmédy in the west.

And there were of course, our ex-colonial territories of South-West and East Africa, as well as the Cameroons, and Togoland, which we had been robbed of, as we were taught in our physics lesson, by the deceitful English and the insidious French, not to forget the Marianas or Ladrones, Pacific islands grabbed from us by the thieving Japanese.

A bank of pulleys had got hopelessly tangled as Dr Posner reminisced on past glory. He was struggling and clawing at the ropes impatiently. The mechanical device, designed to show relationships of forces and distances, resisted his endeavours and in desperation he slung them into a corner and shouted:

'Deutschland will get them back! We will return.'

Towering over tiny Freddi, he donnered: *'Nicht wahr, Klausner?'*

The answer came crisp and unequivocal, *'Jawohl, Herr Doktor!'* I thundered back at him with utter commitment, as my first came crashing down on the desk.

However, on other occasions, we were to learn that what we had lost hadn't been prime land in the first place. The juicy parcels had already been taken by the time we arrived on the colonial scene. Dr Falke, the maths teacher, told us how, in the nineteenth century, 'good-natured, trusting and trustworthy but slow-witted *Michel* (Germany)', had been outwitted by the sharp-witted and perfidious British and the quick-witted and devious French and Portuguese. Germany had arrived late on the colonial scene and 'we had to make do with the leftovers'.

During the days of the great inflation, which lasted from 1919 into 1923, one US dollar would have bought 4,200 000,000 000 reichsmarks. Over four million million. Industrial output had dropped to half of what it had been in 1913.

In the mid twenties things were beginning to look up and the employment situation improved steadily. By 1928 Germany was well into recovery. With this came contentment and a modicum of political stability. But when in October 1929 the New York stock exchange crashed, the repercussions were felt in Germany more than in any other country and unemployment returned with a vengeance. It drove the ever increasing army of the destitute into the arms of the Nazis. Hitler had become the last hope of the impoverished. He increased his standing in the Reichstag elections from 800,000 in 1928 to over six million in 1931. The Nazi party had arrived, riding on the back of renewed misery and stagnation.

Increasing numbers of the middle class lost all they had and joined the soup-kitchen queues. They begged, some in their First World War uniforms, or scratched a living playing instruments, singing, dancing, juggling, tumbling.

The popular tear-jerker at the time was 'Waldeslust', 'Woodland Joy'.

Hand-cranked pipe organs would be wheeled from courtyard to courtyard. They all vied for the attention of the housewife, inducing her to wrap a few pfennigs in newspaper and drop them into the yard.

Waldeslu-hu-hust,
Wahaldeslu-hu-hust,
Oh wie einsam ist die Brust. (How lonely is the
heart.)
My father knows me not
And my mother loves me not
And die, I will not
I'm much too young.

The undercurrents were swirling and Berlin's streets
were noisy with confrontation and animosity and the
Nazis were making hay while the sun shone. And shine
she did. Germany's political activity invaded every
corner of daily life, reaching its peak in the summer of
1932. Political topics permeated conversation, radio
and newspapers. Most of the people were being
deluded by most of the parties, most of the time. And
while one can argue that not many people allowed
their reason to rule their emotions, in those days very
few could be accused of apathy.

Political parties were prominent in the High Street
just like banks and chain-stores. *Parteilokale* were situated in premises among the shops, and in the
courtyards. They served as the nerve ends of the respective parties. Political creed was being sold in a
highly concentrated form. The Nazis were the ones
with the most resources in permanent staff, meeting
places and ready cash. The 'Hitler movement' was now
numerically the second largest political party. The parties were outdoing each other in the art of outdoing
one another. Songs of struggle, *Kampflieder*, were
charged with pride and self-righteousness and sentiments calling to 'wipe out the enemy' and 'fight to the
death'.

More than any other right-wing party, the Nazis had
from the very beginning targeted the workers. Back in

the early nineteen-twenties, when the party was formed from an amalgam of right-wing splinter groups, the name chosen was the 'National Socialist German Workers' Party, (Hitler movement)'. They had hijacked the red flag, adorned it with an ancient Persian symbol, the hooked cross, and proceeded to make inroads into the working class from the lowest stratum, the unskilled and the unemployed, the 'lumpenproletariat' as the communists called them. Any person signing on received a brown shirt, breeches and riding boots. They were given three square meals a day but above all a sense of belonging and purpose. The Nazis imparted a proletarian mythos to their movement. They retained the first of May, International Labour Day, renaming it: Day of German Labour. They adopted the communist address of *Genosse* (comrade). They displayed shrewdness and perspicacity in that they bestowed self-respect on those who had been neglected by society, imparting a sense of dignity to the most menial and soul-destroying occupations by stressing their importance.

In my thirteenth year, I was making myself heard, prominently and affirmatively, to the strains of the national anthem, and each time the occasion arose for *Deutschland* to be held *über alles*, it was I who sang the loudest, shivers running down my spine.

This song of which the first line proclaims, 'Germany above all [else] in the world', was written in 1841 – not 1848 as erroneously stated in the *Encyclopaedia Britannica* – in the heady days of rising hopes for a free and fraternal world.

With Voltaire and Rousseau still in people's minds, with Napoleon and his radical reforms a living memory, with the manufacturing revolution in full swing throughout Europe, with Karl Marx in the wings, libertarianism and radicalism were threatening the established order.

Heinrich Hoffmann von Fallersleben wrote the song in exile, on the run from the Prussian police for his support of the seditious ideas of liberty and equality. He adapted the song to a Croatian folk tune which Haydn had rearranged forty-four years earlier for an anthem grovelling to the Austrian Kaiser.

At the time, Germany was a loose collection of bickering and warring duchies and kingdoms in the shadow of mighty Prussia. The concept of a united Germany was a revolutionary one and was opposed by the princes and kings and dukes. They saw in it the end of an era; a threat to their privileges and opulent lifestyle. No mistake, the song was placing 'above everything' the utopia of a supra-national Germany, in which every citizen had full rights. A Germany with equality of opportunity and social justice.

The song has been misunderstood, misinterpreted and mishandled by nationalists from the day it was written. It was elevated to the national anthem by the Weimar Republic in 1922, replacing the obsolete 'Hail to you, in garlands of victory'. Throughout the most repressive days of Hitler Germany, a libertarian song was heard on state occasions.

The third verse, *Einigkeit und Recht und Freiheit* – Unity, Justice and Liberty – echoed the sentiments of the French Revolution. This stanza has become the current anthem of the Federal Republic of Germany.

Not bad!

My bar mitzvah took place in December 1932, two months after my thirteenth birthday and one month before the handing over of the chancellorship to Adolf Hitler, on a plate so to speak.

Many people believed that the appointment would

cut him down to size and show him for what he was; a semi-skilled house-painter and lime-slaker.

'He won't last long now, ha ha ho!' they said. But he had different ideas. His boys set fire to the Reichstag, the building housing the German Parliament, or so the story goes. Some say that the fire was started by a half-blind, dim-witted Dutchman without help or prompting by the Nazis. Whichever is the truth, the communists were blamed and the brownshirts took over the streets. The terror began in earnest. The fire was the excuse for terminating what was left of the democratic process. At the Kroll Opera House, where parliament was now sitting, half the delegates had been sent to Dachau in Bavaria, and the remainder wore military or Nazi uniforms.

The secret of Hitler's success, it seems to me, lay in his opportunism. He was more a 'grasper of the nettle' than a schemer or planner. He may not have had the brain of von Papen or even Goering, but his intuition didn't let him down until years later and then, characteristically, in the last days, he blamed the German people for the defeat.

At school, my patriotic passion did not detract from my academic shortcomings and my marks were forever hovering in the threes and fours and I fell behind more and more. And had we not left in the summer of 1933, my parents would have, probably, been politely asked to find for me a more suitable establishment.

As it was, the Klausners sold up and bought their train tickets. Completing the round trip, we returned to Vienna as refugees.

Drimmer

a+a=b, b+b=b, a+b=a
Pliushkin's mathematical marvels

If you've ever been thwacked across the head unex-
pectedly by a rolled-up carpet, swung clumsily from
the shoulder of a ham-handed handler, stunning you,
sending you flying, then you might understand. Then
you would have a taste of how I felt on that unforgettable morning of my first day at the Jewish High
School, where I had been found a place following our
return to Vienna.

It was the Drimmer girl.

She sat, gracefully slouched, at her desk in the front
row, looking at me from the other side of the aisle, as
I stammered my name and address to the form teacher;
her head resting in her cupped hand, her short sharp
shock of shiny black hair hanging heavily over the
inkwell.

I was sticking out like the proverbial sore thumb,
spluttering and blushing, as I replied to the queries
from the podium. I wanted to crawl into a hole.

Gradually, in those memorable minutes, everything
faded but her presence. Between furtive glances in her
direction, I scrutinized the initials carved into the
desk-top. In the staring game, no one was her match.

At the end of that first day, as I stood casually at the
school gate pretending not to be looking out for her,

43

she emerged quietly, radiant, among the rushing crowd. Faking indifference, I ambled off confused and tormented.

'Hi Klausner, you going my way?' She had drawn level, tapped me on the shoulder.

At that moment Vierkant, the king of the roost, who had been casually talking to some of his cronies, pretending not to be looking out for her, detached himself from the group.

'. . . You comin' Drimmer,' he bellowed.

It was the kind of thing I expected to put up with, having sand kicked in my face.

'No,' she replied softly, withdrawing her arm, 'I am with Klausner.' And she walked off with me in tow.

Oh Boy!

I was thirteen and a half; my sex life had begun a few months earlier. I was having it off with cigarette cards depicting portraits of actresses from the UFA movies of the day. Introverts and loners, who discover masturbation for themselves, might go on for years as I did, in the belief that theirs is an unprecedented endeavour, that they are freaks, unique in their solitary pursuit and alone in this world with their awesome formula. I spoke to no one about this, brought up as I was not to discuss matters relating to areas below the navel, be they urinary, excremental or sex-related and, if at all, only in whispers and blushings and euphemisms. Fully-fledged introvert that I was, I never took part in the titterings and evocations of my contemporaries. Sex was an underground subject, confined to lewd chuckles and innuendoes, and hinted at graphically, chalked on walls and carved on to desk-tops. To me, sex was murky, mysterious and menacing.

Creaking bed-springs and stains making the sheet look like a map of the Cycladian Archipelago; Mother put two and two together. She took me aside and told me, *sotto voce*, how the practice of 'tossing', as she called it, was unhealthy and reduced one's life span.

As the spring gave way to the warmer weather and vestments became lighter, so more and more her neckline opened out, revealing the enthralling presence of her jugular depression – fossa suprasternalis – the centre of my universe. That concavity, that rapturous thumbprint, convergence of the twin columns A and B, the sternomastoids, leading from her earrings to the breastbone; that, and the alabaster of her sculpted clavicles permeated my mind in those spring days.

But to me, Jenny Drimmer was not a sex-symbol. She was an ideal, an image of purity not to be besmirched with the lower parts, nor fantasized over in any way other than platonic and never below the neckline. She never got anywhere with me. What she saw in me, what she derived from the 'relationship', I shall never know. She would gaze at me in amazement and shake her head imperceptibly. She would only have had to beckon, and any one of the incumbent heart-throbs, hair-oiled, wrist-watched, and beringed, would have come a sprinting.

Hers was undoubtedly a singular taste.

She said 'Tzitzero' and I said 'Kikero'. Apart from that we disagreed on almost everything, and when I got into a heated argument with her over matters relating to the Roman orator or questions concerning physics or geography, it alleviated my intense self-consciousness in her presence. – Tzitzero. How much innuendo there was in her insistence on that pronunciation, who knows? As the shrink once mused in an unguarded moment, '. . . who can tell what goes on in the mind of a fourteen year old girl?'

45

'Tzitze' was Viennese slang for breast. But no! She wasn't that indelicate. Never! She was subtle, she had class.

In the morning, I slip into school half an hour early. I sit in her seat listening intently, for she too turns up early. Amid the cleaner's to-ing and fro-ing in the corridor, I can discern her steps and my heart starts pumping as if there was an emergency. Then the game begins. The moment I see that door handle swivel, I am back at my desk burying my head in a book, pretending to be immersed in revision. I am revising all right, but not Klopstock's *Messias*, nor the voltaic cell, nor am I swatting up on the Hanseatic League. No, I am racking my brains as to the rules of this sodding game. And while I am making out I hadn't turned up early for her sake, I am not sure why I am sitting in this crummy classroom, ignorant of the procedure.

'Servus Klausner,' she opens.

'Servus Drimmer.'

Servus is the intimate Austro-Hungarian greeting, used by all who address one another in the informal second person singular. We ignore each other and pretend to be working. I look across furtively and drop my eyes as soon as she glances at me. Her game is on a higher level, and she plays it with ease and poise.

As the weeks pass, I leave home earlier still and, surreptitiously, hang around her street. The shop window from which her house could be unobtrusively observed, displays embroidery frames, yarns and pattern-printed materials. 'Today,' I say to myself, 'today is the day.' Today it is going to happen like in the movies. Effortlessly. Once that first step is taken, I will be coasting from there on. But how. . .?

The moment she appears I walk on slowly, trying to

46

whistle casually. Have you ever tried whistling while the adrenalin is flowing and the pulse is racing?

'Hi Klausner.' She pretends to have fallen for my pretence. Innocently she asks, 'What are you doing in the Große Mohrengasse?' The Great Moor Lane – Moor was the collective name for Muslims. It had traumatic connotations for Vienna which had nearly become part of the Ottoman Empire two and a half centuries earlier, relieved by the Poles in the nick of time.

Silently I walk beside her, my mind scanning for an opening. She waits. We walk at a slow pace through the Augarten getting soaked in the tepid rain. Finally, I break the silence.

'Do you understand the Leidenfrost Phenomenon, the droplet hovering . . . the steam. . .?' She nods with interest.

'Have you worked on your adverbs?' she enquires. 'Reifeisen gave you such a nasty look last week, when you didn't manage your *Konjugationen*.' She shakes her right hand as if to rid it of water: a gesture I was to perceive years later, in France.

As usual we are first to arrive in the classroom. She gets me to do my German homework, dictating, leaning over me, breathing at me. Her short-sleeved dress exposes the soft contours of her cubital fossa, that silky mollience inside her elbow; the blue of the pulsating median faintly branching into her forearm. It makes my eyes swim. It pierces my mind.

Werther oh Werther! I have never read your 'Sorrows', but how deeply I understand them; how I understand.

At the end of term, the headmaster handed me a note for my parents in which he suggested, in the most tactful turn of phrase, that another school, a more appropriate one, be found for me.

That summer, Jenny Drimmer's family moved to Havana where her father had been offered a chair at the university. They belonged to that astute group of intellectuals who saw the writing on the wall, grabbed their money and ran. They had desperately tried to get into the United States, but had to make do with Batista's Cuba.

Anschluss

It wasn't to be, it wasn't to be, IT – WAS – NOT – TO – BE!

The people, having been given democracy, had displayed a singular lack of responsibility. Having tasted freedom, they started making unreasonable and wild demands. They took to re-examining established and proven values. Indiscriminately and irresponsibly, ideas of social justice were being bandied about. Dissent was being preached from the pulpits of the Social Democratic Party. Barely fifteen years old, the parliamentary republic had proved an unnecessary and unaffordable luxury to be disposed of, once and for all. Ever since his inception as *Bundeskanzler*, conservative Dr. Engelbert Dollfuss had been stealthily nibbling away at the democratic institutions and the accomplishments of recent years.

On the 4th of March 1933, the speaker of the house, a Social Democrat, impulsively resigned in the middle of a heated debate, on a point of procedural trivia. He stormed out of the chamber taking his two deputies with him.

Bingo!

The astute Dollfuss was not slow in recognizing the

potential of this situation and the promise it held. Parliamentary sessions could only be convened by the speaker and of course the speaker was elected by Parliament. No speaker – no session. No session – no speaker. And Joseph Heller was only eleven years old at the time.

The socialist speaker had put a noose around the neck of democracy, and young Engelbert lost no time kicking away the stool. He padlocked the gates of the Greek temple that had housed the deputies of the people. Now, with little hindrance, he could pursue his mission of taking Austria back into the past. Back to the glorious days of imperial grandeur. Censorship was introduced and trade unions were constrained.

Throughout 1933, what was left of post-war freedom was rapidly whittled away. Workers' rights were curtailed more and more until inevitably, in February 1934, the socialists made a final stand and lost the ensuing fight. It was a knee-jerk reaction. It was the lashing out of a desperate man, cornered, not able to take any more provocation. Spontaneous rather than planned, the rebellion was fraught with snags and poor leadership. From the start the workers took up defensive positions, fighting as they did from pockets of resistance centred on the housing estates. These had been built by Vienna's Town Council in the twenties and thirties, raising the quality of life for the hitherto neglected sections of the population.

In criticizing the construction of these huge estates, the opponents of Vienna's 'red' Town Hall had described the effort alternatively as 'luxury palaces for the workers' and 'council rent barracks'. According to some critics, they were jerry-built and falling apart. And now as those tenements were standing up to shelling, the accusation was made that they had been put up as fortresses in preparation for the 'revolution'.

The population at large watched, partly helpless, partly apathetic, as for four days, field artillery, machine-guns and armoured cars were used in the re-establishment of the old order. The time had come to turn the clock back. The church, the industrialists and the landowners retrieved their rightful place at the helm of the state and their God-given privileges. Political parties and the opposition press were banned. The dual head was restored on the national eagle and the symbols of toil, the republican hammer and sickle, wrenched from its claws.

Res Publica, had proved too strong a term, encouraging the wrong elements.

My last compulsory year of education was spent at the Upper School in the Weintraubengasse, the Lane of Grapes, where we shared the sidewalk with the local hookers.

Pupil: *Why do we have to learn about sodium and acids. . . and. . .*
Teacher: *Because it's good for you.*
Pupil: *How so, sir?*
Teacher: *Because we teach it to you. If it wasn't good for you we wouldn't teach it. Now would we? Would we Havlicek?*
Havlicek: *No sir, you wouldn't sir.*
Pupil: *But sir. . .*
Teacher: *Besides, you never know when you might be needing it and furthermore . . .*
Pupil: *But sir . . .*
Teacher: *Shut up and don't interrupt. . . furthermore, it's interesting, isn't it, Havlicek?*
Havlicek: *Yes sir, it is very interesting, sir.*

I remember well the chemistry lessons which I could not follow, and preparations for the serious tasks ahead – *der Ernst des Lebens* – and exhortations not to be ashamed of being Austrian.

'There are those that say Austria is on the wane. I say, what nonsense. Austria was great, is great, and will always remain great.' And so on. Well-meaning teachers extolled the virtues of love for the fatherland, of diligence and industry.

'Don't be taken in by radical ideas,' we were told, 'Karl Marx won't get you a job. That's for sure.'

'A bicycle will enhance your chances of finding work.'

'Show respect and goodwill towards your employer. Turn up early. Start work before the bell. Keep your workplace tidy.'

All this wisdom was proffered extempore and haphazardly by the various subject teachers. But it left no scars.

All in all, I have been subjected to eight baffling years of compulsory enlightenment in three different countries. I suppose I have to be grateful for having been initiated into the art of deciphering nameplates, signboards, messages such as 'Out of Bounds' or 'Strictly Interdicted', as well as notices of military call-ups. That and the intricacies of adding up and taking away and multiplying and squaring.

'If three men take two hours to dig five trenches, how many men will it take to dig seventy-two trenches in one and three quarter hours? Round off to the nearest third decimal.'

I have never seen anyone in tears on the day which ended their enforced institutionalization, but I am certain that there are those who regret the passing of their time of mandatory instruction and inculcation. There must be. Come on, it stands to reason!

On a sunny day in July 1934, I, together with a group of classmates, left the grey building for the last time with no regrets and no backward glances. Arrogantly and in high spirits we walked down the road that day; the world at our feet. Twelve invincible fourteen-year-olds, walking the wide pavement of the Praterstrasse, four abreast. We were ready to take on the world. The fact that the world wasn't ready made little impact on us. There was chronic unemployment, and choosing your vocation may have been a laudable idea, but in reality you were thankful for the job that turned up and you made the best of it.

I obtained an apprenticeship with a manufacturer of gas-fired boilers and bathroom fittings. Offering apprenticeship was cheaper than employing unskilled labour.

There followed three years of excruciating monotony and slow physical and mental growth. I could see my future mapped out as I travelled to work at a quarter to six in the morning. There, in the clammy, semi-lit tram were the manual workers travelling to their stations. Dark dank morning after dark miserable morning they sat in that crummy carriage with no promise of fulfilment nor hope of better times. Drugs such as nicotine, as well as alcoholic beverages of varying degrees of potency, provided a way out for some.

On a frosty Friday evening, it was the 11th of March 1938, I was sitting in a classroom at the evening institute, grappling with logical formulas and fallacies – Mother had insisted that I study formal logic. One of her favourite quotations was Faust's Mephistopheles urging a passing student to take up *collegium logicum* for its 'conditioning and controlling of the spirit' – Halfway through the evening, the lights failed. Someone with a candle walked along the corridor advising lecturers that a fuse had blown and that the fault would be rectified in a few minutes. It had happened before. Barely had the light been restored, when the caretaker entered and told us he had just heard on the radio that Schuschnigg had resigned. Schuschnigg was the appointed successor to

Dollfuss, who had been assassinated in the course of a foiled Nazi *putsch*, four years earlier.

For the last few weeks, Austria had been in turmoil. Schuschnigg had been coerced by Hitler to appoint German surrogates in key posts in the government. Schuschnigg complied but it did him no good. Having been brought out of hiding and having tasted triumph, the Austrian Nazis increased the pressure exercised by Germany. But the socialists had also come out into the open. They were supporting the government. There were noisy and peaceful demonstrations and counter-demonstrations, increasing in intensity as Schuschnigg announced, on 9th of March, that a plebiscite would be held in three days, 'for or against, a free and independent Austria.'

Hitler had been caught on the hop. He had to move fast. He knew only too well how a plebiscite resulting in a 99% yes-vote can be achieved. He was an expert on that. He also knew that the present Austrian regime had the will and the means to accomplish comparable results.

The invasion of Austria took place on the 12th in prevention of the referendum. It was swift and met with no resistance. Not one shot was fired. On that day, Austria was joined to the Reich.

Locked on. *Angeschlossen*.

In the secluded and sedate halls of the League of Nations in Geneva all was quiet. Mexico protested.

The annexation could quite easily be presented – and was, even by some socialists – as historically justified. The German-speaking family had been reunited. For many people those were intoxicating days. Germany, and by implication Austria, walked tall again. It was a time for the hurrahs and the *sieg heils* and congratulatory rhetoric. People who had never amounted to much were drawn into the 'revival' and made to feel part of a reconstituted 'brotherhood'. A positive change of direction was taking place. For the destitutes, the attainment of racial superiority was like winning in the state lottery. Anyone who could produce four certificates of baptism, one for each grandparent, was automatically a member of the master race. Christian baptism, two generations removed, was adequate proof of racial purity.

The *Anschluss* had the making of a social earthquake. Everybody had been promoted at the expense of the impure. Yesterday's downtrodden had now become *Volksgenossen*. They had been promoted to ethnic comrades regardless of social status. They could shed the mantle of social inferiority, exchanging it for that of equality within the superior race. The class struggle had been terminated. Attitudes to work were being changed. People were made to feel important in what they were doing for the grand scheme, however vaguely defined. The German beehive had come to stagnant Austria. This was no invasion. Not at all! Germany had come as a brother, a big brother, with its arms outstretched.

New greetings and new terms came into being. The old Austrian alliteration *Grüss Gott*, was replaced with another, *Heil Hitler*. Workers worked no more; they created. Everybody was in on the creating game. Reconstruction, the eternal favourite of usurpers and politicians, had become another weapon in the revolution of words. And yet, the apparatus of welfare, health and education, fought for and improved by Vienna's socialist administration, having remained intact throughout the years of the Dollfuss/Schuschnigg regime, was never tampered with by the Nazis. All health and social services survived the German occupation and the war years. Medical help was free to workers and the unemployed many years before England had even heard of the Beveridge Report.

In Austria in the spring of 1938, Adolf Hitler provided hope; illusory maybe. You can't fool all of the people all of the time, but you can keep a lot of people happy for a very long time on a diet of false expectations, graphic symbols and hype. Anything was better than the stagnation and utter hopelessness of recent years. The weather did its part; those were the first days of a particularly early and warm spring. History was on the move and things were getting done. Had I not been on the wrong side of the racial divide, I might have been sucked into the euphoria. Had I not been excluded for reasons of my amputated foreskin, I might easily have become a Nazi supporter myself in those heady days. It was so tempting.

Those were the days when Austria's vehicles drove on both sides of the road. Vienna, Lower Austria, Styria and Carinthia, travelled on the left, whereas the western part of the country, on the right, just like the rest of Central Europe.

There had been no disagreement as to the necessity of ending this anomaly. For years the argument went: When and how? What will it cost? How are the Viennese trams going to cope? What about the motorists? Will the horses adapt? Questions and doubts at every juncture.

The Germans tackled the problem their way. 'Two weeks from today all vehicles will travel on the right on all roads,' they decreed. And that was the end of it.

Austria, the latecomer in European history, starting as an outpost on the eastern approaches of the German Empire at the turn of the millenium, had become a superpower in the nineteenth century. Now, she was a province once again. She had reverted to the old concept of the eastern march – the *Ostmark*. But who would be hankering after sovereignty when they can be part of a greater framework, when they can be slotted into a higher design? Independence in this context becomes a mere intellectual exercise.

In one of the national dailies an article appeared which attempted to cope with the indignity of Vienna having lost its status as a European capital. With substituted pride, it pointed at Vienna's transition from being the capital of an insignificant country to the prominent position of second city in a greater Germany.

'Not so!' was the response in a terse letter published a few days later. It stated that the population of Vienna – 1,900,000 – had been inflated by irresponsibly including nearly 200,000 Jews. Hamburg by contrast had been cleansed of non-Aryans. It was *Judenrein*. That way, Hamburg with its 1,800,000 Aryan inhabitants beat Vienna into third place.

Overnight, we, the Jews of Vienna had ceased to be second-class citizens.

The Ballot Paper for the all-German referendum on the 10th April 1938, inviting affirmation of the *Anschluss*, translated word for word reads as follows:

Plebiscite and Greater German Parliament
Ballot Paper

Are you with the, on the 13th March carried out reunification of Austria with the German Empire, in agreement, and do you vote for the list [of candidates] of our Führer Adolf Hitler?

YES ◯

no ◯

The day after the referendum was held was the day I contributed to the propaganda efforts of the new order. It was the day

57

the results had been declared, showing that 99.75% of the Austrian and German peoples were in favour of Austria's 'homecoming'. A few months earlier, Schuschnigg had been denied the same exercise to prove the opposite, namely that Austria wished to remain independent.

The story goes that on the Sunday of Schuschnigg's aborted plebiscite, several rural villages came out 100 per cent in favour of Austrian independence, the cancellation of the voting had not reached them in time. Yesterday, the acceptance of the Anschluss had been just as solid in those places.

Anyway, on that day, I was walking along the Donaukanal, proverbially minding my own business, when a middle-aged lady, panting under the load of her shopping, begged me to give her a helping hand with her bags. She lived on the third floor of a nearby tenement.

I reached her door and deposited the bags while she was catching her breath on the half landing. She rummaged in her purse but I declined with a youthful wave as I passed her on the way down. That was when she started singing. That was when she called after me, praising the new spirit in the land, extolling the youth of today and the goodwill the Anschluss had brought about. Had I told her that I was Jewish, I don't know what she might have done. She would probably have accepted the fact with magnanimity and composure, conceding that none of us was perfect.

Her praises, applauding the new order, accompanied me as I made my way down the sombre stairway and emerged into the bright sun. The sun that doesn't discriminate, that shines on Jew and Gentile alike, everybody and anybody, except of course dissenters and non-conformists, who manage to get themselves locked up in windowless cubicles, in the cellars of police stations, around the world.

Two weeks before the completion of my statutory three-month stint as a journeyman, following the conclusion of my apprenticeship, I was duly kicked out by the new management to make room for cheaper talent. Being on the dole was a welcome break after those dragging years of dreary drudgery. Every day felt like a holiday. At the employment bureau, I met a new class of people. I was among equals; a welcome change from the stuffy caste system at the geyser factory. The Nazis introduced themselves to the Austrian unemployed with the promise of work and the Hermann Goering gift, an appreciated gesture consisting of a one-off ex-gratia payment of ten schillings, the equivalent of about two-thirds of our weekly handout. Of this, I was a direct beneficiary since my father didn't know about it. And what the eye doesn't see, the mind doesn't grieve after.

And while, in the years following 1933, the Gestapo and their Soviet counterpart the GPU were competing in who could torture and kill more of their respective citizens in a given space of time and were lambasted for it by the 'Western' press and radio, in the United States of America citizens could be lynched with impunity, and in Indo-China and Madagascar, as well as in North Africa, the French were pillaging and raping and murdering.

Queues

The acceptance of asylum-seekers is seldom a humanitarian act. All too often the granting of a safe haven constitutes condemnation of the country of origin of the refugee. However, we the Austrian Jews lacked the necessary political capital. Nazi Germany was not the kind of regime the empires – Britain, France and to a lesser extent the United States – were eager to discredit. Anyone with anti-communist credentials, such as Hitler's, couldn't be all bad. The prospect of active conflict between Hitler's Germany and Stalin's Soviet Union appealed to the pragmatists in London and Paris. Those wily politicians presenting their countries as the *entente cordiale* were scheming to play one side against the other, while stabbing each other in the back in the 'Middle East', in Africa, in the Caribbean.

The USA was sitting on the fence biding its time, angling in troubled waters. Franklin D. Roosevelt, fearing the Nazis for their dynamism more than he feared the Soviets for their threat to the capitalist establishment, was an outspoken opponent of Hitler's Germany and critical of the inhumanity of its regime. Under his presidency employers were empowered to hire armed teams, paying them good money for their services which consisted of terrorizing workers who tried to organize themselves in their struggle for a living wage.

And the persecuted in Austria and Germany? They got publicity. And sympathy. A place to go to, they didn't get. A country to settle in, free from fear? Not a chance. The acceptance of refugees does not depend on whether you are persecuted or not. What matters is where you emanate from. For if you flee from a repressive regime other than a communist one, then God forbid you're a fugitive from poverty. You're seeking the easy way out. Yooran EE KO NOMIK REF U GEE!

In our case, no government would help. Couldn't help, they said. With the best will in the world, they said. Come on be reasonable, they said. The USA had a quota for each country. And the quota for Austria was filled, three years ahead, they said.

And the waiting list was getting longer!

It wasn't much of a geography lesson to visit the representatives of different republics and kingdoms. One morning I would be lining up outside the Federal Republic of Brazil. In the afternoon, I would be doing the kingdom of Siam and the Soviet Union. The next day I might be trying the Estados Unidos de Mexico, Liberia and the taciturn doorman of the consulate of the Emperor of Abyssinia. Yet another time it would be King Zog's Albania, Tibet, and the bolted door of the embassy of His Royal Highness, the Sovereign of the Persian Empire.

Most of us asylum-seekers didn't know or didn't care where these countries were situated, what language was spoken, what political system their people were subjected to, nor which God they lived in fear of. Had they offered us a visa, we would have gone there first and asked questions afterwards.

Day after day we joined the ritual, harrying harassed embassy officials. Admitted in groups of eight to ten, we were conducted into some antechamber or billiard room where polite information was imparted and regretful refusals rendered.

'Yes, an Austrian passport requires a visa.'

'No, unfortunately we cannot give you a visa . . . send in the next group please.'

We were hanging around the US embassy queuing for information in the hope that something new had come up. In those days, 'Something might come up', sounded sufficiently promising to set us off on a self-deceptive chase across town.

Here was this embassy official admitting us in groups of twenty into the inner courtyard. There, he would repeat for the umpteenth time the requirements for obtaining entry into his, the most desired of countries. He would probably recognize familiar faces who had come once again to satisfy an imaginary need.

Having delivered his address, the consular official would ask us to 'step this way please' to make room for the next batch. On that occasion I crept up on him, catching him off balance. He turned to me, and with a sad expression listened to my query, whether there was a shortage of geyser-fitters in his country.

Yes, you can laugh. I was only eighteen years old and maturity not too far behind.

However, whether one did get hold of a visa, or decided to breach some unguarded point into a neighbouring country in the deep of the night; either way, it was imperative to obtain clearance from the Nazi authorities and that wasn't made easy.

For the onrush of thousands of 'Non-Aryans' of all ages, prepared to sever their roots, to leave everything, without knowing what to expect at the other end, the authorities didn't lay on extra staff. That meant queuing. Queuing on a colossal scale. Those were the longest lines one can imagine. And the slowest ever.

Middle-aged women, pretty girls, intellectuals, artisans, tall people and short ones, bald-headed men,
curly-haired, clean-shaven, and bearded, all types of
people were standing in line. And most of them would
have merged unnoticed into a crowd of Gentiles, being
Jewish only by accident of documentation.

People who were habitual talkers had a ready and
captive audience. Some were relating their woes, others
were exchanging jokes, others again were day-dreaming
talking about the time they would finally reach Tel Aviv
or Mexico City or . . . Celebes, for God's sake.

One drizzly morning, just behind me, a group of
young people were in deep conversation. I could over-
hear them and catch the drift of their discourse. Here
were three lads who had found a common interest to
while away the time. Absorbed and oblivious of the
despondency around them, they were discussing the
merits and flaws of various translations from tenth-
and eleventh-century epics into modern High German,
quoting from ancient Germanic and Icelandic texts. I
tried to join in, reinforcing a point with an approving
grunt in one instance, nodding vigorously in another
and chuckling at their witticisms when appropriate.
But try as I might, they kept me at arm's length and
largely ignored me. In the afternoon, they discussed
girls, but soon they drifted back to alliteration and
Lautverschiebung.

Scant information was available, and what could be
gleaned was incomplete and misleading. The queues
were very often the originating places – the primal
brew – giving birth to myths and rumours. Rumours
have to be incredible in order to qualify for acceptance,
and they range from the improbable to the fantastic.
The plausible and the conceivable drag on for a few
minutes, shrivel up and peter out. Rumours may be
subjected to scrutiny and doubt, but they are passed
on, none the less. They spread rapidly during their

63

short but intense life which can last from a few hours to several days. Some are stillborn. Seldom do they attain the ripe old age of two weeks. They travel, dependent on circumstances, a few metres to a few hundred kilometres. Sometimes they advance on a broad front and at other times a rumour may depend for its survival on a single person providing the vital link. Mostly, they are void of substance.

'*Psst! C'm'ere. Did you know about the Brazilian ship?*'
   '*What Brazilian ship?*'
   '*Promise you won't blabber.*'
   '*Not a word. I promise.*'
   '*There is this boat. It's due to arrive in Trieste in three weeks. It will pick up all those who have been accepted and take them to either Madagascar or Dutch Guyana . . . or maybe Colombia.*'
   '*How can I get my name on to the list?*'
   '*I can't tell you that, I'm sworn to secrecy.*'

Rumours thrive in situations of heightened tension, in times of emergency, in times when confidence in government has eroded. They sprout arms and legs and various appendages as they progress, and can change beyond recognition once around the marketplace. They play on hopes and fears and can be powerful weapons in war. They can originate through misinterpretation of facts, through misunderstanding and through malice, but mostly they are the result of fear or wishful thinking. They can become instruments of misinformation, deliberately put out by interested parties such as government agencies, political groups, or other sinister factions.

   In the early thirties, an unconfirmed and unfounded story went about claiming that leprosy had broken out in Vienna and that it had been traced to bananas which were flooding the market at the time. As a direct result of the scare, the apple-growers were able to unload their wares as before, without the encumbrance of foreign competition which had been threatening their livelihood. By the time it had been confirmed that no cases of tropical disease had been registered, the bananas in the warehouse had rotted away quietly.

Now, at a time of intense anxiety, rumours were tuppence a dozen. Like the many topical jokes that were breeding, rumours were proliferating at a brisk pace.

* Hitler was being pressured by General Franco to ease up on the Jews.
* Hitler was being pressurized by the Gestapo to ease up on the Jews.
* Hitler was pressurizing the Gestapo to go easy on the Jews.
* The Brazilian steamer was now in dock in Casablanca, taking on supplies.
* The Brazilian liner had been sighted off Tangier as it was passing through the straits into the Mediterranean.
* Roosevelt was making efforts for a safe haven to be provided for us refugees, in Argentina.
* Britain was making efforts to have a safe haven provided for Viennese and German Jews in Argentina.
* Argentina was showing genuine interest. She was pulling out all the stops to have the Jews sent to Uganda.
* All those prepared to be baptized into the Catholic faith would obtain travel documents to Macao.
* If we were to go in small groups to the Soviet frontier and sing the International, the border-guards would admit us without visas.

Anybody could start a two-liner.

Alongside the spreaders of rumours of varying kinds, there were the purveyors of mysterious entry

65

certificates to obscure and exotic places with names such as: Moreno, Atlanta, Yucatán, Shangri La. Then there were the route-mongers. These were people selling escape plans. The commodity ranged from the simple mention of placenames near borders, to complete systems which combined geographical locations with the names of guides, the use of passwords, detailed instructions of where to spend the night and timetables to be strictly adhered to. Few schemes were genuine, many were outright dishonest and highly irresponsible fabrications, others were the result of wishful dreaming; most were a combination of all three, and none catered for the unforeseen.

There was little camaraderie among those lining up. It was every man or woman for themselves. The length of the queue was deceptive. 'Families' or conglomerates of as many as thirty people, would have one 'representative' queuing at any one time. These then turned up within half an hour of getting to the entrance of the building, creating bitterness and resentment. At times scuffles broke out, watched gleefully by the guardians of the peace.

I don't remember how I finally did obtain all my papers. It was only after reaching the office numerous times and being sent back for want of one document or another, that I eventually got my passport and exit visa.

Ask me today what I consider to be the most odious and soul-destroying pursuit and, quick as a flash, I shall reply, 'Queuing up!'

Engadin

Of all the accounts of possible border crossings that abounded, one could have compiled a consumer report and, considering the pros and cons, one might have arrived at a 'best buy'.

Preferring to brew my own, I selected a point which looked good on the map. It was the easternmost section of the Austrian-Suisse border. There, I would be following the Inn river valley, up into Switzerland. This one had never come up in those endless discussions and speculations. Thus it had the advantage of keeping me away from the mainstream and was the type of countryside favoured by hikers.

Dressed in 1938 rambling outfit: *Lederhosen*, hobnail boots, rucksack and mandolin, I set forth from Vienna's Westbahnhof into the unknown; palpitating and eighteen years of age.

All went according to plan and there where no surprises as I got into the border region. I crossed the river before reaching the customs house and ambled along the high ground from where I could look down on to the main road and the guardhouse. The terrain was uneven, partly wooded, partly rock-strewn, and I maintained a respectful distance from the river/border without, however, losing sight of it. The sun was setting when I passed the area where, according to my map, the unmarked border on my side of the river would have been.

It was then that I ran into problems. I had come upon a ravine where, in the spring, torrents of melted snow would be gushing down. Seeking a place to cross I eased myself on to a lower position from which I was unable to extricate myself. I was stuck, unable to go back, forward, up or down, I was immobilized on a ledge five hundred metres above the rushing waters of the Inn. And it was getting dark.

I thought this sort of thing only occurred in legends. Wasn't it old Kaiser Maximilian who had to be rescued by a guardian angel from some similar situation? Or was that young Leopold?

It had been a long and hot day, my rucksack was weighing me down and I was too tired to cope with the situation. There was only one thing for me to do. I tied myself to a tree, conveniently provided, giving the rope sufficient slack to be able to settle down for the night. I had been looking for a rest place and this one had to be it. In spite of the discomfort, I slept intermittently, dreaming of Swiss rescue teams making their way up the slope, waving and smiling, carrying ropes, pickaxes, buttered rolls and thermos flasks full of hot coffee. The night was warm and dry. The August weather was in my favour.

As always happens in situations of complexity and anxiety, the morning's colour and mist brings good spirits and renewed vigour. The dilemma of the night before had disappeared. I lowered myself into the ravine which provided a clear route to the river below.

The good old Austrian *Lederhosen* stood up well to several hundred metres of sliding down the sharp gravel and boulders. It is said that one pair will last for generations and people take pride in the age of their trousers, recognizable by the increased shine and darkened coloration.

Apprehensively, I entered Schuls that afternoon. Schuls-Tarasp-Vulpera, to give it its full-bodied, treble-barrelled name. This small town with its huge hotels, outpost of the better known St Moritz, is a skiing resort in the winter and spa during the rest of the year. No travel guides have been written for the sort of excursion I was on, nor had my schoolmasters ever attempted to equip me with the ability to cope in situations such as this one.

Earlier that day I had stopped at a farmhouse asking for a glass of water. I confided in the lady who had brought me a slice of bread with my drink. Commiserating in broken German, she assured me that once safely beyond the border zone, I was unlikely to be sent back by the authorities. I believed it. I wanted to believe it.

Walking aimlessly and pointlessly along the promenade, I saw a Jewish-looking couple coming towards me. With trepidation, I approached them and stammered excitedly that I had just escaped from the Nazis.

I needed help with a capital H but didn't know exactly what form it would have to take nor how to express that need. What I wanted was for someone to relieve me of the burden of having to make decisions. Crossing the border had been easy compared to this. What I needed was a fatherly embrace; a 'leave it to us, your troubles are over' kind of thing, and not the two francs the man now handed me.

I held the coin and stood there agitated and disappointed, not knowing what I really wanted. 'I don't know where the Post Office is.' I blurted out, tears streaming down my face. The lady mumbled, inducing her husband to retrieve the coin I was still holding, exchanging it for a fiver. They had fulfilled their duty and pushed on, enjoying the view from the parapet.

It was well past lunchtime, and I went into the baker's and bought a couple of rolls, paying with my newly acquired Swiss currency. They were nowhere near as tasty as Austrian rolls.

With mixed feelings and trepidation, I rang the bell at the *Landjäger* residence. *Landjäger* is what they called the country constable in those parts. The house was at the edge of town, facing the magnificent range of the Engadin mountains. A young lady answered the door and informed me that Papa was out, but would be back presently. This was my first encounter with the Swiss police.

Waiting for the law, I struck up a conversation with the cabinet-maker next door who dispelled what fears I still had. The fine view he enjoyed from the workshop aroused in me feelings of admiration and envy, and I didn't mind telling him that. Although the local idiom was Romansh most of the townspeople could converse in German.

'Without that', he said simply, 'I wouldn't be able to create.'

Back in Vienna, 'creating' had become the 'in' word. The Nazis were flogging it to death, with the laudable object of imparting dignity to manual work.

The jovial *Landjäger* arrived as my conversation with the woodworking philosopher was running dry. When he had finished taking down my particulars and a detailed description of my crossing, he escorted me to a nearby inn where I was to have my evening meal and a room for the night. In the morning he was going to put me on a train to Chur, the capital of Graubünden.

In Chur I was once again quizzed, this time by a stern old official, who extracted from me the details of my escape. I was probably instrumental in helping him plug another hole in the fence. Two things he impressed on me. One: in my letters home, I was not to tell how and where I had crossed – and two: not to speak to anybody in his town. Nobody, you hear? Once again the police arranged for me to be fed and housed for the night, and I was to be put on a train to Zürich the next morning.

After a generous evening repast, I went for a stroll about the town square and treated myself to a park bench where I was promptly addressed by one of the local characters. He talked critically of the burghers and the town establishment, accompanied by approving grunts from me. The next morning, I was told off and given a stiff warning for flouting the 'talking to nobody' rule.

'New arrivals report to room 4b', said the handwritten notice at the support committee in Zürich. I exchanged greetings with some Viennese acquaintances who had preceded me, and went off to register. In the office there were six new arrivals sitting on a long bench waiting to be processed.

'Next!'

The man at the end of the bench got up and approached the taciturn official who was busy putting the final touches to the preceding application; rubber-stamping, initialling, clipping and filing. He pulled out yet another form and, without looking up, held out his left hand. Since nothing happened he opened and closed his hand several times. The man turned around, looking to us as if for help.

'Your papers,' the long bench whispered with urgency. 'Give him your passport.'

'I haven't got any papers,' the man replied with his back to the clerk.

'You haven't any papers?' said the man with the fountain pen, 'So how we know you're Jewish? Answer me that.' The manager was called. They conferred, drawing into the discussion two other officials, arms awave. Then the manager's

*face lit up and he invited the man to follow him. Meanwhile,
our clerk continued sorting his papers.*

*'Where is he taking him?' I asked my neighbour on the
bench.*

'To the lavatory, of course,' answered our official casually.

*'What does that prove?' remarked my neighbour on the
bench, trying to be helpful.*

The manager with our man in tow didn't take long returning.

'He's all right,' he said winking at the official.

*'What does that prove?' retorted the official sourly, for he
was consumed by ambition. 'Many goyim also . . . I
mean, I once knew . . .'*

*'It proves absolutely nothing,' interrupted the manager,
who had to tread wearily for he had a distinct feeling that
the official was after his job. He turned to the man.*

*'Say something that will prove to us that you are indeed
Jewish.'*

*The man turned around once more for further prompting
from us. Then he looked up at the ceiling and remained
silent, grinning with embarrassment.*

*'Say something Jewish,' the official repeated, prodding
the man with his fountain pen.*

'Say something Jewish,' echoed the bench.

*The man stopped biting his fingernails and opened his
mouth. He grinned sheepishly and uttered something which
Jews say, as often in jest as in anger:*

'Kushts mir in toukhes!'

*It was the Jewish invitation to someone who is annoying
or just teasing them, to 'kiss my bottom'.*

*The laughter abated, the problem of proof of parentage
and pedigree had vanished.*

Next please!

Walter

'*Excusez monsieur, s'il vous plaît, pardonnez, où est passage Violet? Merci beaucoup.*'

With that I thrust my piece of paper with Uncle Walter's address into the visage of my first Parisian. In France I was told, you've got to be polite. Hence the sickening effusion.

Two weeks earlier, the tremolos at the Zürich support committee had been throwing their hands in the air, wailing at the steady influx of fugitive Jews. So much so that they used their powers of persuasion to get people to toddle off into France. The method was simple. You went to Geneva, took the tram to the suburb of Annemasse which was on French territory, and caught the midday train to Lyons.

In Lyons, fellow-refugees were adamant that one couldn't get to Paris at the drop of a hat. One had to wait one's turn, apply for a residence permit and so on. It was a preposterous assumption that one could just travel to Paris at will. They were annoyed at young whippersnapper Klausner who was dissatisfied with the lack of hard evidence.

'Everybody has an uncle in Paris,' they said, laughing angrily.

After several days, I went to the committee and asked for a ticket to Paris which was refused. They gave me the fare to Dijon and I had to make my own arrangements from there.

From Dijon I hitched to Troyes and the next day took the coach to Paris.

Walter Frommer was my mother's brother. Born on the 2nd of January 1900, he was one of those fortunate people who could calculate their age, simply by deducting one thousand nine hundred from the current Gregorian calendar year. Short, lean, keen on swimming and snow-skiing, teller of jokes, intelligent observer of people and the fine points of language, a lover of chess, he was generous with advice and held in high esteem by his three sisters. He was a health-food freak long before the concept was fashionable. He never ate meat except when invited.

'Cheap is beautiful' was his maxim and he could spend hours shopping around for food, saving more in the process than his added expenditure on shoe leather. – Shoes, that was another thing; whenever he passed a taxi rank, he made a beeline for the oil-blobs on the ground. Gear oil to be precise. With that he saturated the soles and heels of his shoes. He swore that it increased the lifespan of the leather. When he centred on to one of those blobs, he was doing the Charleston and if I happened to be with him on one of his jaunts, he would assign a blob or two to me.

'Here Freddi, take that one,' he would urge benevolently, 'rub well in.' He was *giving* them away.

His purse-strings eventually killed him. Bargain-hunting for food, he was not averse to consuming bread and cheeses that were cultivating moulds. At the hospital, the tests they ran on him yielded nothing. His seemed to be an unknown disease. The medics tested

74

and retested samples of blood, urine, bone marrow, toenails and the like, until they reached an impasse. Then, the lady pushing the tea-trolley took it upon herself to take a test-sample to the tropical research laboratory. There they recognized the ailment as one occurring in the slums of Third World countries where spoilt food is far from uncommon.

From the day Walter left school, he never took up employment and was never going to. He kept his ears and eyes open as to who wanted what and who was selling. He dabbled in real estate and furniture and furs. Eventually Walter found himself a niche. From his previous diversity, he arrived at a *modus operandi* with the Viennese furriers. He had got to know every trader and artisan and knew what they were working on at any given time. Thus, he was aware of who was short of what, and who had what to spare.

Those were the days when coats were made from exquisite rodents and cats, slaughtered to adorn ladies of the upper strata and their husband's tarts. The chemical industry was not yet capable, as it is today, of producing materials indistinguishable from furs; lighter, cheaper, warmer and vermin-free. Nothing was thrown out. In the making of coats and stoles, sometimes pieces as little as five square centimetres would be used and the seam never showed. Any furrier whose join was not totally invisible would be out of business before he could so much as utter 'Persian lamb'.

Uncle Walter's method was infallible in that he never paid for anything until he had sold it. Nor did he suffer from overheads. He had no premises and people would ring him wherever he was most likely to be. Each morning he did his rounds, picking up the leftovers, more often than not already knowing who would be interested in that particular merchandise. And what he carried around town under his arm, wrapped in crumpled brown paper, could be worth a few hundred dollars, which in the nineteen-thirties constituted a little fortune. And if that parcel wasn't brown or if it wasn't crumpled, then it wasn't Walter sauntering down the road. Anyway, Walter didn't saunter. His was a springy, but carefully measured gait. His body swung forward with every step, and his foot came down with sole and heel touching the ground simultaneously, thus further undermining the survival of the cobbler's trade.

Carrying a few hundred dollars' worth of merchandise around was a risky business even in those days, but no self-respecting Viennese mugger would have accorded Uncle Walter a second glance.

He was respected in the trade, for he was regular, reliable and trustworthy.

In 1935, Walter and his girlfriend Rosi went off to Paris for a holiday. Two days later a telegram arrived saying: 'We have married stop letter follows stop kisses stop'. A sour reception awaited the pair on their return. They had deprived their respective parents of the fun and honour of a conventional wedding. Walter's and Rosi's parents had little in common. But that 'slap in the face' brought them together and from then on they were on cordial terms.

The new ménage set up house in Vienna. Rosi, a dynamic girl, started a unique enterprise. She retained the services of two cabinet-makers and opened a workshop where she redesigned and modernized old furniture. It caught on in a big way. But a chill wind was blowing from Bavaria and Prussia. In a few years, the racially impure were going to lose everything.

West it was, for those who had the acumen and foresight. Paris, London, New York were the general

76

aims. Some went east to Palestine. For Walter and Rosi it was Paris. From there, once again a telegram arrived. This time telling all that they had split up. Exit Rosi south-west to Brazil. I never saw her again. She had always been good to me. She frequently gave me money and showed kindness whenever the occasion arose.

When Walter came to Paris back in 1936, he didn't lose one day's work, continuing trading from his small brown paper parcel. He was a useful contact man two years later when, in the wake of the *Anschluss*, half of Vienna's furriers turned up, and when the faubourg Poissonière had become the Viennese furrier HQ in exile. Business picked up where it had left off in Vienna. Newcomers were welcomed and integrated with no apparent problems.

Walter lived modestly in a small room in an inexpensive hotel, appropriately called Windsor. He cooked his own meals on an Italian army stove which consisted of a small tin can filled with methylated spirits, and a stand upon which an aluminum saucepan would fit. The meals consisted of fresh peas and stale bread for the main course, and for desert it was sugared scrambled egg, day in and day out. He bought the spirits in what looked like a half-litre bottle, but in reality held a couple of spoonfuls more. The shopkeeper being fooled by the size of the bottle didn't bother to measure the liquid and Walter, regularly, came out smiling.

Rapidly, the faubourg became an established community. Business was a leisurely, informal and social affair. People were joking and poking fun at each other and worrying and enquiring about each other's relatives back in Vienna or Frankfurt. They were friendly and helpful. One day the hat was passed around at the local coffee-house, in support of some recently arrived refugees. Everybody contributed to the best of their capability. Gurevitch, who was collecting, got around to Friedman, who patted his jacket saying that he had no money on him. '*Dee konst nor grebetzen*. All you ever do is belch,' remarked Gurevitch without malice, not having expected a contribution. It was said in a light-hearted way and that was about the limit of contention.

The current gossip among the refugees constantly updated people's wealth as a matter of course and dollars were the stable currency. Walter's rating stood at a staggering 40,000 dollars, as was revealed to me years later by Bienstock, one of the furriers whom I was to meet in Miranda, the Spanish internment camp. This sum was probably a gross exaggeration as these estimates usually are, but with his modest lifestyle he probably had more than enough to live off the interest of his savings.

It was against this backdrop that, one day, a group of his cronies, sitting in the coffee-house, plotted to test Walter's golden rule to the ultimate. Test to destruction, as this is known in engineering labs. They decided he was to be offered a piece of merchandise for a fraction of its worth, on condition that he break with his golden rule and pay cash on the spot. Some said he would not let a good opportunity pass by, others were adamant that Walter would remain true to his principles. Bets were taken.

The next morning a fine ocelot coat, worth several hundred dollars, lay spread casually across a chair at Grünbaum's where Walter usually started the day. It immediately caught his eye and, fondling it, he enquired what it was about, incoming or outgoing? It belonged to Kagranian who needed some cash quickly, he was told. Kagranian was the only non-Jewish Viennese furrier in the faubourg.

'How much?'

'To you, twenty-eight dollars,' said Kagranian, keeping a straight face.

The buying and selling ritual was such that one never let on about one's feelings and Walter wanted the coat like a pilgrim wants salvation, but he hummed and hawed and stroked the sleeves and the collar, blew on the fur expertly looking for bald patches and seams. He shook the coat and put it down again, hiding astutely his eagerness and astonishment.

'I'll take it,' he said finally with an air of indifference and painful surrender.

'Money up front,' said Grünbaum, Kagranian's partner, without taking his eyes off his sewing-machine.

This was a new situation for Walter. 'I'll pay you in the afternoon. Four o'clock at the latest.'

Everyone knew that Walter was as good as his word. There was no question of not trusting him.

'No can do.' Grünbaum was adamant. 'He needs the money straight away.'

'I haven't got the money on me.' With both hands Walter was patting his chest to prove it.

There was silence. The comedy had ground to a halt.

'OK. Frommer, I'll lend you the money,' said Katz, one of the gang. Everything went still. Even the sewing-machine stopped. This was not in the script. The others were alarmed and, in desperate sign language behind Walter's back, indicated their concern. They needn't have worried. Walter was not going to be reckless. His principles were not going to be breached. Long ago, Walter had ceased thinking in terms of buying and selling, rather selling an item first and purchasing it afterwards.

Anecdotal Interlude
Walter, on a visit to New York, goes to the Austrian Konditorei, *and addresses the sales-girl.*

'Where are your Manners?' he says sharply, ready to burst into hilarity.

The girl stiffens and presses a button which rings a bell backstage, whereupon a small door bursts open and two heavies tumble out nearly overturning a plaster model of a wedding cake.

They look at the girl and the girl points at Walter and Walter retreats with incomparable agility.

What Walter hadn't known, was that the store had been raided the previous week, and a diversion had been arranged by one of the thieves talking sharply to the very same girl, drawing attention away from the felony in progress. Apparently, the robbers had managed to heist two boxes of newly flown-in Hungarian truffle bonbons and pralines, and a jar of Turkish candies.

Walter wrote a stinging letter of complaint to the management telling them of the treatment he received following his request for Manner Schnitten, the famous Viennese wafers, renowned for their logo and their prestige. The management replied by return of post, apologizing and begging him to accept a box of Manners with their compliments. From then on the catch phrase was 'Free Manners (Freeman was the name of one of our relations) geddit, Freeman-ers?' And those who didn't fall about laughing, got the sharp end of his elbow thrust into the lower part of their ribs. 'Good Manners! Hee hee haa.'

Here is one of Walter's jokes.

A man goes to the doctor complaining of aches and pains. The doctor examines him and finds nothing wrong other than a dietary deficiency.

'You must eat plenty of fruit, unpeeled mind you, and take more exercise.'

The man comes back two weeks later, a shadow of his former self.

'What happened to you?' wants to know the doctor.

'You told me to eat plenty of fruit and not to peel it.'

'Yes? Go on,' said the doctor.

'Well, apples and pears, fine. Oranges and bananas, eh
. . . takes some getting used to. But the walnuts Herr
Doktor, the walnuts they are killing me.' . . . die richten
mich zu Grund.

Not bad as jokes go, but the painful part was the
constant reminder of the walnuts, whenever we met,
throughout the autumn of 1935 and well into the new
year.

Walter got out of France at the time of the débâcle. He
made his way to Bordeaux where in the scramble for
space on the last boats to England he succeeded as a
mid-European civilian where many French and even
some British military personnel had failed.

He joined the British army and distinguished himself as a store-keeper's assistant at a secret location in
the south of England. He took British citizenship and
with Trude, his new wife, moved to Montreal at the
end of the war. There, at the earliest opportunity, he
became a Canadian citizen in order to finally move to
New York. The scheme didn't work and he returned to
England around 1960, moved to Frankfurt, and seven
years later set up home in Lausanne, where he died of
a tropical disease aged seventy-two.

On the line . . .

. . . a midnight ramble through the presumed requirements and anticipated pitfalls in relating one's passage, as well as numerous deplorations and exhortations.

He who knows, natters not.
He who natters, knows nowt.
Tao te ching

Suffice it to say that the state of the art can be described as the ability to sell one's hang-ups, without producing in the reader a pain in the you-know-what. All the writer can do, is call attention to a succession of images. The effort will have been in vain, if the recipient were to become engrossed in the pointing finger.

At the same time, like a competent guide-dog, the writing expressionist must be aware of the things she or he takes for granted but are a minefield to the blind. The canine author must acquire an awareness of the pitfalls and stumbling blocks on which the upright-walking readers are liable to chafe their shins or bump their essentials. The reading customer must be guided painlessly, not over, not under, but *around* the obstacle.

Better still, the accomplished Alsatian bitch, far from guiding the blind, restores the eyesight the engrossed reader had thought was lacking. It can be done!

Fearlessness of, but respect for words and sounds are essential ingredients in the success of the outpourings emanating from the pen. Above all else, one must not be in awe of the reader. From the outset one must show who is boss. Let me reverse the dog simile. The canine reader will sense your anxieties and with vigour make straight for your buttocks at the first manifestation of

82

nervousness and apprehension. Once in motion, the expounding narrator hasn't got a chance in hell of outrunning the intellectual and analytical terrier.

I have been writing since I was twenty years old but never put pen to paper. Until one day, around the age of sixty, I bought a pencil sharpener and an India rubber and began to write in earnest on the backs of envelopes and on the insides of breakfast cereal boxes. I had caught the bug. There was no turning back.

What is it that actuates the perpetrators of the memorial and the anecdotal, or indeed the fictional? What possible reason is there for sitting day after day on an old swivel chair hammering tentatively and attentively at the electronic keyboard? What benefits can be derived from the pursuit? What promises does the effort hold? Not many reasons have been propounded in the endeavour to explain the compulsive chronicling of events. There are those who say it all stems from the narrator's urge to come to terms with the circumstances and happenings surrounding her or his life. Others talk of a desire to indulge in introspective self-praise or flagellation.

Whatever happened to straightforward vanity, plain exhibitionism? What about the desire to assert oneself, to project one's neglected self, to bellow downwind, 'Listen I'm no idiot, I only look the part.' And what about the prospect of bags of dollars, resulting from the effort? How's that for motivation and drive?

I am a sculptor, moving around the forming narrative; now looking at its left profile, now, from its flat feet projecting an imaginary line to its balding apex. I must at times step back and monitor from a distance and at other times, close in with a magnifying glass.

I don't pretend to be an historian. I am not conversant with all the facts as they affected my environment

83

and my progress through the years, directly or indirectly. All I am able to convey is a subjective account of the ups and downs, the pain and the laughter, the anger and the joy I witnessed and experienced, the inevitable flow of events, and the prevailing feelings and flavours.

I have been hanging around this planet for seventy-nine years. Gravity is getting me down. My confusion is flourishing, my ignorance is expanding and my inability to comprehend is increasing. But the realization that it does not matter is steadily growing. I don't know what it is all about and I suspect that those who do, don't know what they are talking about. It seems that with advanced ability to control and manipulate nature, our perceptions are becoming more and more impaired.

I am having difficulty in comprehending that which motivates the purveyors of symbols, respectability and decorum; gangsters in Baroque costumes, practitioners of the superficial, the ceremonial; dignity on high heels. What are they trying to prove? Grown-up poodles, displaying, parading, cavorting, pirouetting; festooned in feathers, garlands and gold brocades; sporting tassels, bronze plaquettes, castanets, bunting, chains, sashes, garters and gaiters. What are they telling me?

They prance about with straight faces in the scorching sun, exchanging brass and silver discs, hung from colour-coded bands and pinned to the ever decreasing space on their chests. They strut along rows of people who stand rigid, having surrendered their inheritance and their birthright; Guards of Honour, equally kitted in brocades and bunting, cock's feathers, tassels, sashes and galloons; whose honour are they guarding? Who is impressed? Who are these people? Where do they come from? What are they trying to prove?

What are they trying to convey?

Why is it that my ability to enjoy and appreciate such innocent pursuit is impaired? Why? It is my firm conviction that there are people out there who take seriously and relish such rococine buffoonery; such performance, such antics. There must be those who are roused by that sort of thing.

Still, it is opinions I am expressing when I am not reminiscing: my opinions, my hang-ups, my frustrations with the scheme of things, my disappointment with history, my vexation with the effects of reality and gravity and the suffocating confines of three-dimensional space. I have been wrong more often than I have eaten Victoria plums; I have been tricked and deceived by my senses and perceptions a thousand times; I have been dumbfounded on many occasions. It is not for me to condemn or justify or explain. It is not my province to draw conclusions, I can only make observations. So, this is a biased recording of happenings, and my interpretation and expressed opinion arising from the sum of my experiences. I am thinking aloud while groping in the dark, and may the devil take the hindmost.

Lao's Dilemma
When the keeper of the pass – or douanier as they liked to be known in central China of the seventh century BC – admitted the old man into his home for the night, he followed a custom that had been honoured by many generations of douaniers. It was to give assistance to the wanderer who passes by their homestead. His father and grandfather had practised it and many fathers of fathers before. It was a douanier's prerogative.

But sitting at the table that evening with the stranger munching chicken breast, the keeper, or customs official, detected the spark of wisdom in the old man's eyes.

The next morning, after a sleepless night, he decided to make the old man pay. For our douanier, or customs official, was corrupt and innovative.

'Repay me,' he demanded. 'Compensate me and the world. Show your gratitude for all offerings of bed and breakfast, heretofore bestowed on countless generations of tramps, as is now bestowed on you.'

'I have no money,' interjected the old man, with embarrassment and dignity.

'I have no money,' aped our valiant official in his picturesque way. 'I don't want your money, I want your story for pestiriority.'

Reader! You must forgive the official for his quirky vernacular. He was a semi-educated man; a mere peasant, but hungry and thirsty for knowledge and willing to learn.

'I have nothing to say.' argued the old man, making use of one of his many paradoxes.

'Then commit it to the scroll,' countered the douanier with urgency, tying the sage to the bench, leaving his right hand free to wield the brush. And since our douanier had to tend his terraces, he assigned his grandson to cater for the old man's needs; to supply him with fresh almonds, matured eggs and apple juice; to scratch the old man's back, and to empty the bucket periodically.

So, Lao Tzu had little option but to comply. He wrote his life story, leaving out all that was personal. And he built into it his great contradictions, namely that wisdom is silent and in order to overcome one must yield.

In the weeks he wrote, he was fed and watered, his shirts deloused and mended, his ox shoed and his shoes cobbled. Now and again he was given time off to sit in the sun and stare into the pond. And ponder.

Injustice of history! The reluctant writer's name has been chronicled, whereas that of the instigator, the keeper of the pass, the man without whose guile the fragments of the Tao te Ching would have been lost to us, he has barely survived in the mist of speculative legend.

But then, does he deserve any credit? Does he deserve praise? Has he not committed the unforgivable? Has he not interfered with the great paradox?

However that may be, our quick-witted douanier could henceforth enjoy sound sleep. Never again would world literature and recorded philosophy be making demands on him, gnawing at his slumber.

It is at this point that the author, clearing his throat, decides to pause and gratefully acknowledge his indebtedness to numerous personages. The time has come to give thanks for inspiration and discouragement, help and harsh words, cheers and frowns to: Herbert Aichinger, Béla Bartók, Bill Bennet, Peter Bowering, Helen English, Piero della Francesca, George Gamow, David Gilmore, George Gombos, Julie and Paul Haines, Julian Hall, Barbara Kenyon, Rod Kedward, Omar Khayyám, Sheila McHenry, Tinch Minter, Alan Mounteney, Friedrich Nietzsche, Belinda Parham, Jean, Amy and Peter Plisner, Helen Polin, John Richardson, Peter Roget, Rowena Skelton-Wallace, K.V. Junior, Wallace Stevens, Yussif Yossarian and many many others; as indeed to all humanity and living beings on the face of this earth and below the waters, the organic and the inorganic, and all that fits into neither of these categories. Thanks to the concrete and the sublime. They have all, all of them, contributed to this assemblage of regimented black symbols on recycled paper. From far beyond the stillness of the ragged edges of the universe, dynamic lines of power converge on the centre of this page which is the epicentre of this bombastic edifice.

Thank you, thank you, thank you. Hurrah and thank you.

The term 'apropos', at this very moment, forces itself on to the scribe's mind.

Apropos what, pray tell?

Apropos dedications of course. Yes, while I'm here, let me add a few homilies on the practice of dedicating a written piece, a practice which started in the seventeenth century, as an exercise in grovelling. Something on these lines:

TO
SIR EDMUND CRADOCK HARTOPP BART,
THE FOLLOWING
HUMBLE EFFUSION
IS BY PERMISSION DEDICATED
BY HIS GRATEFUL, AND OBLIGED SERVANT,
H.H.H.

The above pales to insignificance in the light of such gems as: 'to the right noble . . . the most excellent, virtuous and exalted . . . sentiments of the most profound humility . . . may your Lordship accept . . .' And so on comma deeper and deeper into the mire. In anticipation of the treat to come, the author begged a person of substance to 'accept my prostration at your most noble feet while offering your grace these very feeble attempts.'

For goodness sake, someone open the window.

The benefactor, his boots freshly licked, would then deign to support the volume thusly dedicated and, through his good offices and pulling of strings, benefit the author. Since those days, however, dedications limp on, as smooth repetitious ritual and sentimental void, to appease spouses and secretaries or give pride to offspring, supporters and friends.

This heroic volume, esteemed reader, the one you are cradling in your precious hands, is dedicated to no one. No one, you hear! If I am to play games, I will set my own rules, thank you very much.

Had I been thuswise inclined however, I ask myself

whom I might have chosen to dedicate this work to. Maybe the publishing house which has had the foresight of securing the rights to this story of epic proportions, or the multitude of my devoted readers who I am indebted to. On reflection, and I must repeat that it is not my intention to dedicate this narrative, who might I have devoted this volume to? The mind boggles! But then, try as I might, could I have picked a better crowd than that heroic band of people who gave up their comforts and for months and years exposed themselves to ridicule and official harassment and foul weather, standing guard over the conscience of the world? It would have to go to those dauntless, determined, defiant and most distinguished ladies of Greenham Common and their sisters around the world.

Cheers!

At an early age my fervent patriotism gave way to indifference where symbols and rituals are concerned, and today no tunes or colours will accelerate my heartbeat. After shedding my Judeo-Austro-German loyalties, I never again saw myself as part of any national, racial or religious group.

Patriotism, or love and loyalty to one's country, one's town, one's street corner or one's water-polo team, have passed me by. In this respect I am underdeveloped. When it comes to group fidelity and clan allegiance, I am deficient. Loyalty is a term I dislike and shun as much as I dislike and shun old English pewter or Marc Chagall's paintings. Loyalty calls for the abdication of thinking, of appraising, of forming judgements. It demands unquestioning, blanket support of whatever or whoever one has been brought up to be loyal to. It urges one to lie and cheat in the pursuit of ideals and visions and in support of rogues who think likewise and bolster one's interests.

MY COUNTRY, RIGHT OR WRONG!

All those walking on their hind legs are my tribe regardless of . . .

But that includes the gibbon, for Pete's sake!

Gibbon . . ?

Yea the gibbon, the gibbon!

Welcome aboard . . .

. . . where was I? . . . ah yes . . . those walking on their hind legs are my tribe regardless of the depth of their tan or lack of it (some of my best buddies happen to be albinos), whether they are hazel-eyed or slit-eyed, whether they come from this or the other side of the river or railroad track or mountain or man-made border, it does not matter. It matters little, whether they share my lifestyle, my beliefs and opinions or not, but admittedly it helps if they do. Anyone who admires me is my friend.

Good fortune has accompanied me throughout. Today, I have all the material comforts and no reason to fear the future. I lack nothing; the house is paid, the bed is made, food is in the larder. The ruthless socio-political system of the 1990s is favouring me. My children have slotted into positions of promising continuance.

Material sufficiency. Material saturation. Opulence even.

But the spirit, that is something else. Spiritual wealth is lacking. Spiritual well-being has passed me by, because of my stubborn refusal to engage in a little innocent self-deception. How inflexible can you get? What is wrong with a little autosuggestion washed down, if need be, with a tumbler full of applejack? I am living in destitution where the soul is concerned. I have searched and have failed to find. I have pounded on many doors. Those I have managed to prise open, have jammed solid, revealing at best a limited and highly distorted view of the world. The will and the desire have always been with me and hope of a measure of enlightenment has not entirely vanished.

History has been good to me. I know, I have said so myself. But look, see how she is treating millions of others. Open your eyes. How can anyone be satisfied? How can I sit here and count my blessings? And thank my guardian angel? How? For no apparent reason, I have been spared. Why me?

How can I sit here and thank a demanding deity or a caring divinity or creative force, or providence if you like, for bestowing upon me long life and material abundance while others went under and many many more, at this very moment, are suffering and being born to suffer. . .

STOP THE WAILING, FREDDI,
SENILITY IS CLOSING IN.
SHE IS POUNDING AT THE GATE.

Paris

Je suis Françoys dont ce me poise
Né de Paris emprès Pontoise
Qui d'une corde d'une toise,
Sçaura mon col que mon cul poise.

Paris, for no fault of her own, was bugging me.

Boredom was chewing up my spirit, and my self-respect was severely mauled by enforced inactivity.

The refugee committee had placed me in a shelter for Jewish down-and-outs in the rue Lamarck by the side of the Church of the Holy Heart on the Mount of Martyrs.

With monotonous regularity we, the residents, brushed down our rags and went out between meals. Artificially unemployed, we were carrying the indignity that goes with not being needed in an opulent city. We were feeling sorry for ourselves and accepted our fate with bitterness and a complete lack of initiative.

One of the inmates of the shelter, a Pole who emigrated to France many years ago, having been recruited to work in the steel mills of Lorraine, was forever voicing his hopes for war. Why he had ever left his secure job at the mills, nobody knew. But the life of idleness among refugees in Paris seemed to suit him.

War would make us rich as had been the case in 1914, he maintained, and furthermore there would be masses of women on the loose, wealthy and big-breasted women to be had for the asking.

During the Munich crisis, he was given the nickname of 'Gare du Nord', on account of spending every day

92

between meals at the major rail terminal nearby. On his return he would describe in glowing terms, between mouthfuls of potato stew, the ever-increasing number of soldiers being shipped east and north.

To his great disappointment and ours – most of us refugees felt like him – after jovial negotiations between France and Britain on the one hand, and Germany and Italy on the other, Neville Chamberlain returned to Croydon Airport with his umbrella in one hand and a piece of paper raised above his head in the other.

That piece of paper, fluttering in the autumn wind of South London, represented the capitulation – well nearly – of Herr Hitler who had been pressured into proclaiming that he had no further territorial aspirations after Czechoslovakia.

Czechoslovakia, ' . . . a far-away country of which we know nothing', was not consulted. She was the cause of all the trouble. She was the only democracy left in Central Europe with the strongest army on the eastern borders of Germany, 200 kilometres from Berlin as the crow flies. But the crow didn't fly and she had to be sacrificed for peace.

'Peace in our time!' said Neville Chamberlain.

Duff Cooper, Winston Churchill, Gare Du Nord and us, the guys at the rue Lamarck hospice, were left to sulk for another year.

Out of this rut there were few avenues and what avenues there were held little attraction. A small number went to Paraguay and British or French Guiana. Some emigrated to the International Settlement in Shanghai, where there was a supportive Jewish community. The Japanese, who had been in occupation of Shanghai since 1936 I believe, didn't challenge the foreign enclaves until December 1941 and turned down repeated German requests to extradite the Jews within Japan's jurisdiction.

I met a man who knew how to get to England. He told me of a London-based carrier with two boats plying between Tilbury and Boulogne. They were sailing every two days in opposite directions. If I remember correctly, their names were *Kingfisher* and *London Pride*. He offered me the plan, giving timetables and a layout of Tilbury harbour in exchange for my Waterman fountain pen and the promise that I send him a postcard showing Buckingham Palace.

It was December 1938 when my friend Marder and I set out for Boulogne. After several days of dithering and hesitation we finally plucked up enough courage and with the help of a few measures of Armagnac everything went well on that freezing afternoon, until we got kicked off the boat while noisily removing the weights that held down the tarpaulin over the trap door.

Having failed, we put Plan B into operation. Plan B was to cut into Belgium. Anything to break the monotony. We had been told that we could get the assistance of the French gendarmerie in crossing over. Apparently the ministry of the interior encouraged this, provided they weren't told about it. The obliging Belgians helped refugees, going the other way, to avoid French and Dutch border-guards.

Marder went to Belgium and I turned around and walked back to Paris.

Several weeks earlier, Mother, together with her parents, her sister Margarete with her son Felix, plus three friends, a highly conspicuous and cumbersome group, had travelled to Karlsruhe to probe the border. After spending interminable and arduous days and nights in the open country, they finally penetrated into France

94

near Lauterbach. They were promptly caught by agents of the Commissariat Special (Wissenbourg) of the Sûreté Nationale. Their passports were stamped with a *refoulement* and they were warned not to show their faces on French soil again.

Or else!

Before returning to Vienna they went to Basle to reconnoiter the German railway station situated ex-territorially inside the town. There my cousin Felix, who was only fourteen years old, managed to slip past the frontier-guards on platform six and escape through a hole in the fence into Switzerland. Apart from a three-year stay in France, he has remained there ever since.

Promptly, Mother returned to the border region and crossed into France on her own. Once again she was caught, but this time they couldn't send her back, because this time she had violated the law. Breaking the law had saved her life.

She was sentenced to one month's imprisonment and fined 100 francs for infringing article 8 of the decree of 2 May 1938. Further, it was noted that 'the presence of the above-mentioned on French territory, is of a nature as to constitute a hazard to public safety – *à compromettre la sûreté publique.*' Signed by André Viguie of the 4th division of the *Deuxieme Bureau*.

After completing her sentence she was 'enjoined to depart from French soil forthwith.' She was given a *refus de séjour*, a pass for the outward journey to a border of her choice to be crossed within three days. She promptly took the train to Paris and much to the credit of the French authorities, that refusal was continually deferred. There was stability!

In 1939, those that managed to avoid the border police and reach Paris were issued with a *refus de séjour*. This was renewed at the whim of the officer with the rubber

95

stamp at the prefecture. Sometimes they would give you three days, sometimes as much as three weeks. There, at the Ile-de-Paris, the familiar Viennese queues had been resurrected and were being re-enacted with the original Viennese cast. Almost every day, the last of those in line couldn't be processed before closure. They were given a priority number for the next morning. But that didn't give them legality. If they were caught with their identification paper not up to date in one of those frequent checks, they could spent the next four weeks at the *Santé*. The *Santé* was the local nick. It was neither healthy nor was it sanitary.

Very few people had the initiative or the foresight or the astuteness to take up residence in places where there were few or no refugees. Everyone crowded into Paris. Everyone had an uncle in Paris.

Klaus Leinhof, who spent a couple of nights at the Jewish shelter and whom I was to meet again in Brive, was a political refugee from Berlin. In 1938, he had jumped out of the back window when the storm-troopers rang his doorbell in order to escort him to Dachau. He didn't stop running till he reached Cherbourg. There he took up residence and had no problems with the police nor was he prohibited from working. He was probably the only refugee on the peninsula.

France has frequently been criticized for not treating the refugees as heroes. The term 'shabby' could be heard. What people are forgetting is that the French authorities were landed with about seventy thousand people no other country wanted. France may have displayed indifference but was far from inhumane.

In the spring of 1939, I put my name down for a training scheme which was being planned for young immigrants. After weeks of agonizing delay and uncertainty, I was given a train ticket and told to report to an address at the nearby town of Argenteuil. There, an old factory was being fitted out to provide living quarters and engineering workshops for about forty to fifty youngsters from Germany and Austria. It was run with military efficiency by a retired French naval officer. It was he who conceived the layout of the workshops and the dormitories as well as the construction of the wooden bunks and individual storage arrangements. In spite of our inexperience in woodwork, the task at hand progressed speedily and, thanks to his simple design, attained a professional touch. Being of the warrior caste, he was a right-wing conservative. But he grew fond of us, regardless of where our varied political sympathies lay, and we established a good working relationship with him. Broadly speaking, our group mirrored the political configuration of displaced mid-European opponents to fascism from the far left to the centre-right, and our discussions were fierce and continuous.

As it had proved again and again in years to come, my apprenticeship stood me in good stead. Here in Argenteuil it gave me status both with my contemporaries and with the management. I didn't attend craft classes but worked mostly in the forge, producing necessary components and jigs. On the whole, the training centre at Argenteuil was a holiday camp. There were sports facilities and a good library. The food was tasty and wholesome.

Alas, it lasted only four glorious summer months. On the 3rd of September 1939, on a sunny Sunday morning, two days after Germany's attack on Poland, we were sitting around the wireless receiver that was buzzing with fateful news. We heard Chamberlain announce that since he had not heard from Herr Hitler, England was regretfully and halfheartedly at war with the German Imperial Government, from eleven o'clock that morning.

France was to join after vespers.

On September 1st 1939, Germany had invaded Poland. Britain and France, who had underwritten Poland's independence, had dragged their feet for two days, before reluctantly declaring war. Or rather they noted that 'a state of war existed' after their ultimatum calling for Germany to withdraw expired. Following that effort, they dragged their feet some more. Having noted that World War number two had started, the British donned their gas-masks and their tin hats and went back to bed hoping it would all go away. And in Paris, slogans were pasted on hoardings extolling the ethics of the coming battle. '*Nous vainquerons parce que nous sommes les plus forts.*' Army officers were requisitioning private cars in order to conduct, more efficiently, the serious business of requisitioning apartments and private cars. France had made provision for a defensive strategy, a war of attrition. *Guerre d'usure.* A war of wearing down the enemy. 'We are the stronger,' and 'Time is on our side.'

But the Germans saw it differently.

One would think, would one not, that the French civil service, being far better prepared than the military who were leaving the German army unmolested while Poland was being cut up, had drawn up plans well in advance, to tap the evidently valuable resources of anti-Hitler refugees who had more reason to fight the Nazis than anyone else in the land.

One would indeed think so, and one would be wrong.

Far from harnessing the anti-fascist forces who had emanated from Germany and the occupied territories, plans had been drawn up to intern the lot. Even those Saarlanders who had fled for their lives, having campaigned against Germany for a French Saarland in the plebiscite of 1935, were now enemy aliens. Back in 1919, at Versailles, it had been decreed that the population of the Saar, a coal-rich territory, was to choose whether to remain a League of Nations trusteeship, join France, or rejoin Germany. In the event, those opting for Nazi Germany got a thumping 90 per cent in a secret ballot.

September 4th. We in Argenteuil assembled in the yard where *le capitaine* addressed us and reminded us of our duty. He shook each hand in turn and we marched off to the station cheered on by the locals who, seeing a group of young men in formation with packs and valises, assumed that they were off to the battlefield to save *l'honneur de la France* and its women, from the Boche.

We and all the enemy aliens in the department of Seine et Oise had been directed to assemble at the racecourse of Maisons-Laffitte where we were duly deprived of our *liberté*, never having experienced *fraternité*, let alone *egalité* in the host country.

I must repeat, it is all too easy to criticize France for its ungenerous treatment of us refugees. But what did Britain do for us, or the – give me your huddled masses – United States? France provided a haven, albeit without enthusiasm, for the bulk of those who had nowhere else to go.

One day I am going to find out what they had done with the horses, the former inhabitants of the race-course which had been cleared to accommodate us. Maybe they had been sent to the Camargue where their wild cousins roamed. But no, that would have been racially unacceptable.

Within the next few days, the *Deuxieme Bureau* moved in and we were screened and given the oppor-tunity to declare our desire to serve in the war effort. At the time my political orientation was such that I would have opened my umbrella had I been told it was raining in Moscow. And since the USSR was not a participant in the war, the conflict was deemed imperialist by the likes of me. In the logic of the

Stalin-dominated days, any conflict among the capitalist countries was one of defending or expanding their imperialist interests. Only when the Soviet Union became involved, as was to happen in less than two years, was the war to be called: the struggle of the freedom-loving peoples against oppression and fascist dictatorship.

I shared a stable with a German diplomat and a travelling salesman from Breslau, who somehow hadn't managed to get out in time. We were thrown in together because I, along with a few communists, had refused to sign the declaration of loyalty as had the Germans.

What I did not find notable at the time was the total absence of animosity between Jews and Germans in the camp. Neither in Maisons-Laffitte, where the Jews outnumbered the Germans ten to one, nor in Athis/Orne, to where we were soon to be transferred, and where there was parity, was there any racially motivated friction.

The only deep-seated antagonism continually in evidence on numerous occasions, was that between the German and Austrian Jews. What the Austrians, who were largely easy-going, complained of was the alleged conformism of the Germans and their pandering to authority.

Meanwhile, at the front, the Poles were fighting back with heroic gestures watched and applauded by their allies who supported them with propaganda and advice. While Hitler's boys had mechanized their forces, the Poles had built up the most powerful cavalry in Europe and the newspapers carried photographs of the hussars in their dashing outfit armed with lances and sabres as they charged the German tanks. Heroic sacrifices were made, but none of the generals and army commanders perished in the suicidal attacks.

Athis

' . . . Athis, Athis?' agonized Dr Altmann, addressing
the composer and the historian. 'When? What?
Where?' The surgeon, dishevelled from twirling the
remnants of his hair in desperation, got up and began
pacing. 'How? Why? I mean . . . what?'

'Nothing ever seems to have happened here . . .' said
the historian whose opinion had been sought. 'Sit
down, you're making me nervous. You will just have
to try another approach,' he added, returning once
more to his bishop who was being threatened by a
powerfully situated pawn. Before long, the writing of
the anthem for Camp Neuf at Athis sur Orne, the small
town in the Suisse Normande, was successfully concluded. Time was on our side.

The previous week, we had been turned out of the
racecourse and dragged into this chilly old mill-
house, away from our regulated existence in the
stables. In Athis no supper had been provided after
the long train journey and routemarch, and what had
been designated as dormitory was dirty and damp. On
that raw night, we snapped at each other before being
overcome by sleep on the straw-covered floor. The
black coffee in the morning did its best to compensate

for an uncomfortable night. Someone with initiative and outside connections had got hold of a shipment of fresh croissants and they were selling like the legendary hot cakes. After the inevitable *rassemblement* – the one permanent and unchanging feature – lining up for the head-count, followed by the allocation of boring jobs such as scrubbing cauldrons, peeling carrots, chopping wood and carrying water – we called a meeting.

Although we originated from divers backgrounds, our immediate interests were identical and a great deal of enthusiasm was generated on that first morning. We were determined to get things moving, and moving our way, making the best of a bad job. As is the rule, a group of sharp talkers got themselves elected to represent us *vis-à-vis* the French, and we proceeded to discuss requirements and priorities. All decisions were taken by show of hands and a microcosmic social entity was in the making, buzzing with activity. During the next few days the entire camp population were busy redesigning and rebuilding the interior, constructing two-tier bunks, and shoring up parts of the building. It was a barn on two levels that had once stored grain and flour and it provided ample space for two hundred and fifty internees. The ground floor was to become the dining and meeting hall, and the one above was to serve as dormitory.

The pragmatic approach and far-sightedness of the committee in conjunction with our rapidly evolving think-tank, was evident at the initial meeting. The second most important item on the agenda dealt with the stairs leading up to the dormitory. The staircase, it was found, was inadequate and in anticipation of an emergency, fire escapes would have to be provided. It was decided that fixed ladders were to be constructed, one to each window. An appointed group was to supervise these, test them periodically, keep them in good order and report at regular intervals to the assembly. The alarm system was to consist of appointed fire officers who in the event of fire breaking out, were to shout 'Fire!' and 'Feu!', as well as 'Fuego!' for the benefit of Pavlo, a middle-aged Castilian who, inexplicably, had got thrown in with us although he had never been anywhere near Germany. He provided a headache for the pen-pushers and the paperclip wallahs.

However, the most urgent and pressing need was the siting and building of the latrine. The task was completed in record time in the first week and incorporated the biggest flushing system in the world. The seating arrangements, with a capacity of twenty-two, had been cantilevered over the edge of the river that formed one side of the camp perimeter. A communal lavatory, it provided a meeting place where discussions were held, friendships and enmities forged and where the local bore found a captive audience.

Here, among the internees, there was a rich variety of talents. Engel, the well-known jazz pianist, had played in the prestigious Jockey Club in Berlin. We clubbed together, and acquired an upright piano for him to entertain us. There was a young Viennese who drew poster-size caricatures in seconds. There were doctors and architects and academics, and intellectuals of every hue. And there were artisans and technicians and engineers along with a sprinkling of inexperienced youngsters.

Budzislawski had been the editor of the left wing weekly *Die Weltbühne*, and it was natural that he would be called upon to report and comment on the week's events. Every Friday night a chair was placed on one of the tables in the dining hall. There he sat swaying, like a Jewish scholar reciting interpretations of commentaries on the Law, as he gave his views on current affairs. Commenting on developments was not easy in the days of the 'phoney war', when happenings were few and far between. He complained bitterly about the French for not making use of his potential in the war effort. What he had completely misread, as indeed almost everybody had, were the signals emanating from the military and a powerful section of the political landscape, showing reluctance to fight an opponent who had so skilfully destroyed the trade unions and had ended the democratic process.

Presently, a living and lively community with its essential components came into being. Behind the scenes, jostling for position and canvassing for votes was taking place. The outcome was a democratically elected oligarchy – the very same people who had been provisionally appointed on the first day – which benefited all, and raised the standard of comfort of the whole community. The camp inmates benefited greatly from the disproportionate medical and academic capacity which our mixed group was endowed with. A clinic was installed, providing an efficient health service. Courses and discussion groups sprang up, covering a wide variety of topics and interests.

For organizational and supervisory purposes, the inmates were arranged into twelve sections of twenty-four men, section eleven being reserved for the upper crust among the internees which included the elected management. Within section seven, there was what had loosely become known as *la clique communiste*. This consisted of Kautschke who had been a delegate at the Reichstag, three Jewish Stalinists and, apart from myself and a few hopefuls, several followers of opposition factions which had been expelled from the German Communist Party. Liebermann was such a one. One year older than I, he had a brilliant mind and a black soul. He was an anti-Stalinist communist of the Brandler/Thalheimer variety. But unlike most adherents of these groups, he was no intellectual in that he failed to use the great mental potential he undoubtedly possessed. He was a fanatic and a climber and showed contempt for everybody. He would have manipulated himself into a commanding position in any hierarchy.

The communist dissidents who had found it too hard to follow the Stalinist line due to their inability to desist from observing, thinking and reasoning were, by and large, well-meaning people, aware of their own shortcomings and prepared to see things from various points of view. They ran rings around the doctrinaire, conservative and conventionalist commies. On one occasion, Shapiro the leading Stalinist, in an acrid discussion with Opel, a follower of the Berliner Opposition, flicked through a work of Lenin which he carried at all times, found the passage he had been looking for and read it in support of the point he was making. Another BO supporter sitting within earshot polishing his boots, butted in and said, 'If you turn to page 233, you will find that the passage you have quoted is qualified to apply solely in circumstances which in this particular case clearly don't apply.' At times like these, all that was left for the conformists to do was to resort to invective, calling their opponents capitalist lackeys, and agents of Mussolini or Franco or even Trotsky. Occasionally, in times of stress, the Stalinists would resort to fisticuffs, always provided they found themselves numerically superior to their adversaries.

Kautschke, poor old Kautschke. He was no fanatic but continued to conform in the vague hope that his leaders, Thälman and Stalin might, in the end, prove to be right, that there was a hidden logic in the many distasteful facts staring him in the face, and that the doubts that surfaced in his mind from time to time were the result of his conscience playing tricks on him. In his heart of hearts he knew that the revolution had gone sour. All the historical arguments he had put forward against Christianity, the direction it had taken over the centuries, could now be applied to communism. Like delayed boomerangs those arguments now returned, striking when least expected. And yet, how could he admit to himself the momentous truth which would put into question his life's work?

He must have been getting on for sixty, a kind, soft-spoken man who had been in the merchant marine in his earlier years, and would tell me interesting and amusing stories about his travels around the world. No doubt, he had been a diligent and dedicated party official and had finally made it to the Reichstag. However, that was nothing much to crow about, he told me. The group of representatives of any given party would contain only two or three bigwigs who would make the speeches and decisions, and the likes of him were there to raise their hands when given the cue, and be thankful for a cushy job.

This was the Calvados region and the spirit to get high on was Calvados. The wealthy among the internees, however, got stoned on whisky and slivovitz. Had they, by some quirk of fate, been interned in the Scottish Highlands, they would have found ways of getting tiddled on Calvados and Cognac. That's the way it goes.

There in Athis one late night, a group of Viennese and German Jews sat retrospecting over events. On that occasion, there took place an exploration of sorts, of the possible causes of the Jewish predicament, *la condition juive*, as Otto Schreiber put it. The question as to whether there could conceivably have been a contributory element of wrong-doing or provocation on behalf of the Jews, surfaced in this session.

It started with a light-hearted survey of the various attributes given to the Jews over the years. The rich employer Jew exploiting Gentiles, the banker Jew sucking the blood of the country's economy, the left-wing Jew leading the workers astray, the Jew lazy, making demands on the social services, the Jew over-industrious, raising the stakes, the wandering Jew, devoid of loyalty to the host country. The calculator, the manipulator, the schemer, the raper of Germanic maidens. To the anti-Semites the Jew was the evil communist and the wicked capitalist, the murderer of the Redeemer – to whose Jewish origin nobody ever gave headline treatment.

'. . . anything they have been saying about us can be easily refuted. I tell you . . . the lazy Jew, the over-industrious Jew, the swarthy Jew, the ritual murders, the ahhm . . . the aim at world domination . . . the . . .' Lipshitz paused and drew on his cigarette. 'Listen . . . I mean . . . yes, the absurdity is blatant, yes. But are we entirely blameless? Have we not contributed in some way to all this? Have we ever sat back . . . and . . . and looked at ourselves?'

'I don't know . . . the real issues, listen . . . listen, have the real issues . . . did anybody ever look at . . . ahhm the real issues?' Spivak too was groping for words. He was regarded with awe for he had money. Back in Frankfurt he had been an investment consultant, something at the *Börse*. Gossip, however, had it that his wealth derived from arms supplies to numerous private armies in Sinkiang who were fighting each other and the central government. He delighted in the air of mystery and flamboyance that rumour bestowed on him. 'Are we entirely without . . . errh blame?'

Poldi Schönberg was reluctant to concede. Under normal circumstances he would not have tolerated the implications coming from Spivak's outrageous question. But tonight was not normal. Tonight Poldi was deep in thought and not his usual self. Reproachful, yes. Resentful, no.

'So the anti-Semites are right?' There was silence.

'If we hadn't existed they would have found somebody else to persecute.'

'In some countries nobody is persecuted,' said Krein.

'But us, they were always beating. For two thousand years, everybody thinks the Jews a . . . a punch bag. What . . .'

'Come on, we only remember . . . I mean, we have always been told of the bad times . . . the pogroms, the persecution, nobody ever talks of the periods of peace and prosperity, the intervals in history when Jews took an active part in the life . . . you know, in many countries. Why doesn't anyone ever talk about that?'

'That's right! Jews were invited . . . yes *invited* to take part in the founding of the Polish Kingdom . . . I mean when it was first founded. We played a leading role sometimes in history. Sometimes in history we were respected.'

'Yea and today they are the greatest anti-Semites, the Poles . . . and the Lithuanians.' General murmur of approval.

'And the Romanians,' added the tailor.

'Tell me, would we have acted different from them if we had been the majority, and they . . . ahm . . . it's . . . it's human nature.' Lipshitz was pacing up and down. His son and widowed daughter and his three grandchildren were stuck in Magdeburg and all he was able to do was pray to God for a miracle.

'. . . and the worst are the Tshelyuks, I know, I was in Russia . . . I . . .'

Poldi didn't finish. Old wounds were being reopened. On that night there didn't appear to be the excitement, so prevalent in debates among people deprived of their liberty, regardless of the subject. The isolation of the Jews within the host nation was looked at. How much of it was self-inflicted? Egon Krein who now spoke was a research biologist. He had fought in Spain in 1938 and when the International Brigade was disbanded, he had come to France and found a position with a pharmaceutical laboratory somewhere near Pontoise.

'Where was . . . I mean can anybody tell me why . . . why did we always have to remain aloof . . . always we have been isolated from the host country everywhere we went . . a foreign body, we've been . . . I know we've made contributions to many cultures.' He raised his hand to show Poldi that he hadn't finished; at the same time, his eyes shut, he shook his head vigorously to indicate that he knew exactly what the nature of Poldi's interjection would have been.

'Sure, Jews had been restricted to the ghettos in the Middle Ages,' he conceded. 'Yes that's correct but with emancipation in the eighteenth century, full rights were given. Jews could follow any occupation.'

Poldi who had been in the fur trade in Vienna, knew my father and my uncles. With his flat hand, he was sweeping crumbs into a pile.

'Is it not a fact that for many of us . . . for many of our forefathers, you see . . . these new freedoms, how shall I say . . . they spelt the end of security? Suddenly the continuance of the race was at risk. You know, with the opening of the ghetto gates, many became assimilated. We were exposed to the outside world. I tell you . . . I mean, basically, we probably lost more people from the exposure to the new freedom than in all the pogroms. Right? It's like when you go out into the cold from a warm room, you can catch pneumonia. It can kill you. No?'

The probing continued.

'Why did we have to assert our special position? Would you rejoice, when the other guy keeps telling you that he has been chosen, that he is privileged in the eyes of God? I mean, how would you like it?'

'Yes, but "chosen" has been grossly exaggerated . . . or . . . or rather distorted.'

'Who distorted it? We distorted it. You are telling me . . . chosen, it sounds like . . . don't you think it is a little bit arrogant? We should have dropped it long ago, together with a great deal of other ah . . . ah . . . anachronisms.'

'Yes? And what is left? Is it not our special position in the world . . . I mean how . . . I mean without it, how would we have survived as a nation? How *can* we survive? Answer me that.'

'How can we, how can anybody expect to be treated as an equal and yet . . . and at the same time remain an outsider. You can't . . . you want your cake and . . . I know Poldi, yes . . . listen, how can you insist on remaining an outsider and expect to . . . to benefit as a member of the club. I mean . . . tell me, go on tell me how can you make claims to equal rights? How? Is there an answer? So tell me.'

Poldi continued piling up crumbs.

'So that is a reason . . . a . . . a justification to kill Jews like in the pogroms?' Spivac interjected.

Krein turned to me, who had crept along the bench slowly, trying to get the gist of the debate, and with his right hand shovelling air he beckoned, patting the seat beside him.

'So what's the answer, what's the solution?'

'There is no answer . . . a Greek drama it is.' Lipshitz was shaking with emotion. 'A Greek drama, a tragedy . . .' he mumbled.

The session went on: self-recriminating, exploring, justifying, masochistically enjoying the painful issue. Krein told an anecdote which I remembered from my childhood. My mother used to tell it with relish. It went like this:

A Russian peasant in need of a loan goes to the local Jew and takes along his fur coat as security. The Jew first asks for one rouble by way of application fee. He then takes the coat and advances the peasant five roubles from which he deducts three roubles representing the interest and two roubles by way of storage fee. On returning home, the perplexed peasant utters the punch line, a Russian tongue-twister, the gist of which is: 'I haven't got a loan, I'm one rouble the poorer. I'm five roubles in debt and I'm freezing without my coat.'

Some recognized the story.

'Anti-Semitic propaganda,' someone mumbled.

'But that's just it,' Krein said with ardour. 'This story . . . and many others like it . . . it was told among Jews . . . it was a big joke . . . a big joke it was.'

'It's not a . . . a believable story.'

'Excuse me, but that is not the point . . . it's obvious it never happened . . . the point is this, it was told as a joke . . . with contempt . . . with derision . . . do you know what I am saying . . .' Krein was momentarily losing his scientific cool. He was an atheist, or rather an agnostic who was constantly being badgered by people who demanded of him to prove the non-existence of God, as if he owed them thirty dollars or something.

'How can we expect them to respect us? I mean mutuality . . . reciprocity . . . do you know . . . I mean . . . ?'

I have forgotten the name of this man who was having difficulty articulating, trying to compensate by nodding vigorously, desperate to make himself understood. He was the tailor. In Vienna he had barely scratched a living. Now he was earning money, forever sewing something or other for the camp inmates. His needle had been swinging while he had been listening. By candle light.

'And yet . . .' he had put his sewing down and his right arm was stretched out on the table, palm upwards, 'to be sure, there has been a disproportionate number of Jewish medical practitioners and lawyers and we were prevalent in many . . .'

'Yes, why are there no Jewish taxi-drivers and welders and bricklayers and . . . and . . .' Kutschera, aloof and reticent, was probing for further categories. With the back of his hand he was sweeping crumbs into Poldi's pile. He belonged to a band of erudites who were playfully called the 'Hegelarium'. They walked around, tomes under their arms, heads in the clouds and never knew what time of day it was. It was he who had kindled in me a love for pure mathematics. He got up, raised his head and spread his arms. Everything went quiet. Slowly he inhaled and after a moment of intense concentration, delivered an exploding sneeze. He managed to extract his handkerchief just in time to catch a long rubbery drip. A murmur of *'gesundheit'* and *'wohlsein'* emanated from the group. Spivak wiped the side of his face.

Poldi yawned and looked at his watch.

'Ach, du lieber Himmel! do you know what time it is, Freddi? Almost half past one!' He got up, yawned once more, stretched and scratched and made for the stairs. Spivak got up. He stretched and he yawned and he waved as he went. One by one, we followed, stretching and yawning and scratching.

The tailor wetted his forefinger and thumb, extinguished the two candles with a sizzle and put them into his pocket.

The Athis episode came to an end after no more than five months. No doubt the Town Council had put in a reclamation form for the now renovated buildings and site. We were shipped to Mesley du Maine, situated between Laval and Le Mans in Britanny. Uncle Walter was there, but he was soon transferred elsewhere.

Mesley was a far bigger camp of about eight hundred souls. The routine was uneventful and, although there were sports facilities, football, tennis, boxing, a bridge club and a variety of intellectual activities, the place lacked the community spirit of Athis. Here we had the best football team in the area. One day, and that sticks in my mind, our camp was visited by a team of Spaniards who worked nearby. They were brilliant individualists but, as a team, no match for our boys. It got to the stage, when our side was leading nine to nil, that we began to feel mean and our sympathies shifted to the guests. So, at half time, a group of spectators called on our captain pleading to let the Spaniards score. He demurred and at their next attack our boys went into pretending mode, trying their hardest to allow the opposition to score. But their acting wasn't too good. It was a rare sight to see the Spanish centre forward dribble his way past our burly defenders. But then he twigged, and finding himself confronted with a soulless goalkeeper, he kicked the ball out of the field, refusing to accept the favour.

Brive-la-Gaillarde

Today it can be revealed. The French, in their infinite wisdom, had planned the conduct of the war in the minutest detail. They were to play it by ear.

And as if on cue, on the seventh of May 1940, I together with a group of eighty fellow Mesley internees, were given our papers and sent on our way to report to the 94th Infantry Depot at Angoulême. On cue, because three days later the war really started.

Blitzkrieg!

In Angoulême our group was kitted out and sent to Brive where we were to work in a new armament factory, in part still under construction. I was now a *prestataire* in the 30th Company of foreign workers. The term *'prestataire'* had, in the past, been used to describe those who, for lack of cash, paid their local taxes by making themselves available for work in the general upkeep of the parish.

'Have you heard?' I said to Poldi, the ex-Viennese fur dealer who was operating the power press.

'Heard what?' he muttered without taking his eyes off the thudding machine. He was very methodical. His

*pieces, stacked in military fashion, were neatly arranged in
piles of twenty and no edges were allowed to protrude.*

'I've just been to the foundry; Max told me.'

Max Blumenfeld was Poldi's buddy. He had owned the
biggest candle factory in Vienna. What he didn't know
about candles wasn't worth looking at. He could talk a
whole company of prestataires to sleep, just by expounding
the pros and cons of beeswax, stearin and additives. Unlike
many of his contemporaries, he had salted away the bulk of
his money out of reach of the Nazis and consequently had
everyone in his pocket, including the sergeant who had the
ear of the camp commandant. On arrival in Brive, Max had
bribed his way into the fonderie having rashly associated
it with the German term Fonds, suggestive of financial
activity.

'Max told you what . . . what? Why are you always
grinning?' Poldi replaced the component which I had picked
up and examined.

'Hasn't anyone told you? Switzerland has declared war
on Japan.' I paused and let it sink in. Poldi's face length-
ened, though he didn't laugh. So I left him to his thoughts
and went back to my bench and to the monotony of filing
and scraping.

Poldi's machine was thumping monotonously and I had
completed one more of those wretched ejector toggles. Scraping and filing and polishing another component, I observed
Poldi from afar as he stopped the press, wiped his hands and
turned up moments later.

'But Freddi,' he looked pulverized, 'how are they going to
get there?' He raised one of my ejector toggles to eye level,
to give our chat an air of authenticity, deceiving the over-
seers in the elevated glass cage into believing that we were
discussing the intricacies of production.

'How is who going to get where?'

'The Swiss, the Swiss . . . to Japan.'

'How do I know? Nobody tells me nothing.' I shrugged.
'They say that the Shah of Persia will let the Swiss troops

through . . . I mean he has given transit approval, on condition that . . . if the Swiss agreed to build him an opera house or . . . or a railway station. When . . .'

'Iran, Iran, it's not called Persia anymore. They've changed their name, don't you know nothing?'

Having got that off his chest, Poldi shook his head and curved his lips.

'No Freddi, the way I see it, they fly their soldiers to Russia in aeroplanes. OK? And in Moscow, they catch the train to Manchuria . . . the Trans-Siberian. I know . . . I've been to Russia. I was a prisoner of war . . . I . . . I played chess with Astrakhov when he was a nobody.' Excitedly he pointed at the component, looking past it towards the glass cage.

'Yea . . . the Trans-Siberian to . . . I tell you . . . the Trans-Siberian, all the way to . . . to Vladivostok and from there to Japan is just a stone's throw, ein Katzensprung. You don't know Astrakhov?'

'First you ask me, now you're telling me.' I was getting bored, and from the cage I was getting bad vibes which I pointed out to Poldi.

'You don't know Astrakhov?' said Poldi as he was leaving, 'He . . . he's a big shot in the communist party. He's the top man in . . . in Voronezh.' Mumbling to himself Poldi walked off.

' . . . he doesn't know Astrakhov.'

I watched him as he stopped at Schleimberg's capstan lathe and from the look on that man's face I deduced that the news had been unloaded. Schleimberg could now be seen huddling with his fellow-operators.

Now three from the capstan group left their machines to pass on their knowledge to their respective cronies.

As I continued scraping and filing and polishing yet another one of those tiresome cartridge-ejector toggles, I watched with amazement and witnessed how, with ever-increasing speed, the rumour was spreading. The place was humming with excitement. People were coming alive. The habitually sleepy faces were sparking. From where I was placed I could observe the fanning out of the story. It had become an entity with its own momentum and centrifugality, spreading surreptitiously across the factory floor, feeding its hundred workers in less time than it takes to file, scrape and polish one of those despicable toggles, no doubt moving across to other departments with the speed of sound. It had the proliferating potential of an epidemic and, as had been the case with Pandora, I would have been unable to put it back into its bag, had I wanted to. It had to be left to run its full course.

The story was now making inroads among the French workers who constituted the upper echelons of the workforce in the hall, the group leaders, the aspiring lance-corporals.

Juan Calderon, one of the Spanish construction workers, was assembling a steel pier for another hall in the course of erection. He was singing at the top of his voice: 'Oh yes, we have no bananas . . .' as he was approached by Otto, eager in his role of bearer of the latest disclosures. But there was little excitement or interest shown by Juan as he clamped yet another piece of angle iron into the jig ready for drilling and riveting. Facing Otto, he roared, ' . . . negro negrito mi corazón,' and turning once again to his ironwork he continued drilling. He didn't give a damn. Switzerland, Japan, Germany, war, peace – what did he care? What mattered to him was to get through the day and to feed his family.

He came from a small village in Murcia where he had grown up in a hovel, where the Middle Ages were still in their infancy, where the landlord could beat up his father at will, or lay his sister. And as far ahead as he had been able to see into the future there was no way out of that existence. Halfheartedly, he had fought in the Republican Army when he was drafted. But he was a peasant and as such could never warm to the idea that any government would have his interests at heart. Now, as a refugee, he lived a life of luxury beyond his wildest dreams. He and his family rented a small room sharing the kitchen and the toilet with two other families. He had never had it so good. Everybody liked him because he was stupid, or so they thought. It was an impression he encouraged. It suited the role he was playing. Without degrading himself, he made people laugh in a self-deprecating sort of way.

Calderon had married a French girl of Polish-Jewish descent and they had two children. They were his religion. He visualized for his two little girls a future far better than the one he would have taken for granted only a few years ago.

I was to meet him again, briefly, in September 1942 in Pau. He had just returned from the mountains where he had expedited his wife and children into Spain. Although his young wife was French, she and the children were not immune from being deported to Germany, but in Franco's Spain they were safe. He was heartbroken at not being able to join them. At the same time he was relieved at knowing them to be in relative safety. In the scheme of things and in its contemporary logic, they had a better chance of survival in countries other than those they were born in.

The guys in the glass cage were getting restless and sent Claude down to investigate.

'Mais qu'est ce qu'il passe?' You could read the words in his face at that distance. He had tackled the foreman in charge of the milling machines who was waving his arms in explanation.

'Merde!'

Claude, the certified pen-pusher, could be seen returning to the cage taking two steps at a time. One could almost hear him draw la grande conclusion; it would mean the Germans would have to redeploy troops and equipment from the north of France to speed to the aid of their Japanese allies.

By this time, near permeation had taken place among the hundred or so workers. The big news was about to reach me.

It was approaching in the shape of Otto who, not having got any joy from the Spaniard, had withdrawn empty-handed so to speak.

Otto had owned a photographic studio in Vienna and was now operating a cutter grinder. It was he who in a rash moment had vowed never to utter another German word until the Nazis had been wiped out. Here, he was telling me in picturesque French, how a group of militant Swiss missionaries had overrun a Japanese garrison in Tsingtao. They were waiting for a ferry to take them across to the Korean peninsula where they intended to surprise the Imperial Japanese positions in the rear.

'Unbelievable,' I exclaimed. 'My God . . . the Swiss . . . it means war . . . this is . . . I mean, how are they going to get there?'

He was getting excited and in order to illustrate his account he put down the component he had brought along, and with his fountain pen drew a map on the palm of his hand showing the Yellow Sea and Pusan where the surprise attack was going to take place.

My astonishment knew no bounds.

'How do you know . . . I mean, where did you get . . . how did you obtain all the details?'

Otto smiled, and with his index finger tapped the side of his nose.

'Keep it under your hat,' he said departing. 'Some people can't help shooting their mouths off.'

Meanwhile, one of the electricians had approached Klaus Leinhof, the trade unionist from Berlin who had spent two nights in Paris when he had fled in 1938, on his way to Cherbourg where there were no refugees, which saved him a lot of bile and hassle with the French authorities.

Slowly, as Klaus listened, I saw him shaking and then, unable to contain himself, throw his head back and burst into laughter, much to the electrician's indignation.

Now, as the rumour had reached near saturation, Klaus's laughter set off a similar pattern in the way it spread among

*the less gullible, who had second thoughts as they became
infected with the Berliner's uncontrollable, and disrespect-
ful, giggling.*

Our arrival on the 10th of May had coincided with the
invasion of neutral Holland and Belgium. It was the
first major turning point of the war. It marked the end
of the phoney period. Poland had been carved up,
Denmark had been occupied, and Norway, after a brief
fight, had been forced to surrender. But now the big
push had begun and the Germans poured through the
Low Countries and Belgium into northern France by-
passing the impregnable Maginot fortifications.

By the time General Hering handed Paris to the
Germans, we had conveyed our fears to our commanding officer. Lieutenant Berger, a well-intentioned man,
receptive to our forebodings, promised that he would
do all he could to evacuate the company to the south.

Throughout the ensuing days the feasibility of obtaining transport for evacuation receded. Finally, on
the 21st, we were issued with our army book and a
paper stating that we had been employed by the Ministry of Armaments and had performed magnificently
pour la France, and that we had been authorized to
make our way *vers la frontière*. Except, that was, for a
group of about twenty, who had been singled out the
previous day to be transferred under guard. Nobody
knew by what criterion they had been picked, nor
where they were going. The rumour was that their
destination was a camp near Bordeaux. The scene, as
they were assembled, had an ominous air. I never
found out what happened to them, but the disorder in
those days was such that hardly any scheme embarked
on was brought to a conclusion. They may have run out
of petrol halfway to their destination. Who knows?
Their guards may have deserted them one night, or

again there may have been a quite innocent explanation. Perhaps someone needed twenty men to dig trenches to bury sewer pipes.

Who knows?

There was a little ceremony around the flagpole as our commandant took leave of his troops. He emphasized how the country would remember our contribution. Alas . . .

He then raised the cashbox above his head.

'These are your wages,' he said shaking the padlocked steel container. There had been no time to do the paperwork. The company would reunite in the south and there we would be remunerated.

'*Vive la France*,' he concluded and he pressed everyone's hand in turn.

'*Dépêchez-vous mes petits*,' he called as he got into his requisitioned, chauffeur-driven Studebaker, with Max Blumenfeld in the back seat. Two hours earlier the German panzers had reached the outskirts of Tulle, thirty-five kilometres up the road.

A few weeks before, I had encountered evidence of what I had heard on numerous occasions but could never quite believe. As I was helping unload a new lathe and manhandle it into position, I glanced at its brass plate depicting the maker's name and year of manufacture.

It read as follows:

EUGEN WEISSER & CO.
HEILBRONN.
Baujahr : 1940.

It confirmed that this machine had been built in 1940 and that countries at war do not necessarily cease trading, and that money is mightier than patriotic precepts.

Our stay in Brive was distinguished by its brevity. It lasted a month and a half. We got up at six, left our quarters half an hour later to march in formation and arrive at the *ateliers* at seven. There we worked twelve hours with one hour dinner break. That got us back to base at half past eight to a wholesome and plentiful meal. Fourteen hours on the trot. Only once did we get the Sunday afternoon off and were shepherded to the river for recreation. In the end it was the *Wehrmacht* that liberated us and got us out of that deadly rut. Or rather its impending arrival.

Friday, 21st June 1940. After 292 days of deprivation of liberty, I took my first tottering step into the outside world; a free man, chasing the next meal and in pursuit of a sheltered mattress at night.

Living by your wits didn't ensure eternal life. It helped. But you had to live beyond your capacities and even then it was essential that you had, crammed into your kitbag, a huge portion of pure and unadulterated luck.

L'Exode

For months, the slogan 'We will win because we are the stronger' gave people a sense of security. Anything other than outright victory was inconceivable. But people had seen Poland being cut up and no action from the French or the English; no action at a time when Germany was at its most vulnerable in the west. People were bewildered but never worried. Germany was not so much a hate object as a nuisance. She had forced France's lethargic hand and France was annoyed.

France and Britain had declared war halfheartedly and with no intention of attacking Germany. It was to be a defensive war. A war of leaflets. A war of sitting it out behind fortified positions.

Guerre d'usure!

But to a powerful group, it seems to me, this was a good one to lose. The working class had got too big for its boots and a military victory over the Fascists might enhance their political prospects in the foreseeable future. Just as in 1870 when France's defeat by the Prussians checked the advance of the liberal-progressive forces, so this time defeat would assure the survival of privilege. That, at any rate, is the way I think the reasoning went among those in France who were calling the shots.

The shock of the last few weeks left little room for despair and despondency. Refugees were clogging the roads, walking in a daze. They didn't know what had hit them and they didn't know what to expect. Not far from Cahors, I came upon a rest place established alongside a fountain in the central square of a small town. I put my pack down and sank to the ground. A woman resting nearby sent her little boy over to offer me a beaker of water. People tried to be kind to each other, but in the ever-changing situation there was an unfathomable and potentially explosive undercurrent which was worryingly unpredictable, in particular to the likes of me.

'*Merci infiniment*,' I called across to that smiling heroine.

If for no other reason, her gesture was necessary to confirm – or rather persuade herself – that something akin to normality still existed.

How did families like hers manage? The little boy was about four years old and would have had to be carried most of the way, and there was a heavy pack of absolute necessities. And if your shoes didn't stand up to the strain, what then?

At the end of a day's march they might encounter a reception centre. She and her husband would most likely be separated. She would spend the night with a group of women in some schoolhouse while the men might be lodged in a barn of lesser comfort. In the morning they would reunite smiling and kissing and get on with the business of increasing the distance between them and their ever-receding past.

They were market gardeners from Melun. They and their neighbours had fled two days before Paris surrendered. A municipal van carrying a loudspeaker had been racing up and down the streets shouting '*Sauve qui peut!*' There had been no comforting words nor advice. It seems that the last act of that decamping municipal executive was the administration of panic.

Run for your lives!

Just past Orléans they had been machine-gunned by Stukas and had dived under a cart. But the horses had bolted, leaving them lying exposed in the field. They laughed at the memory. But people had been killed that morning.

Their cabbages would be ruined, that was certain. Where were they going? They had no idea. The enormity of their situation hadn't sunk in. For the moment the shock of it all seemed to cushion them from utter despair. They were following the crowd.

The scene was peaceful. People were arriving. Others were getting up and continuing. It was ideal weather for trekking. There were blistered feet and sunburn and stomach upsets and toothaches, and little relief. And it was all taken with dignity and resignation.

Who were these people? They had left everything behind. Some had come from Holland, Belgium, and the north of France. Had they all felt threatened? Did those who had stayed behind feel secure or were they too lethargic to face up to the issues? What had moved those who had left their homestead? Apart from the mid-European refugees, there were many who had fled as a result of rumours spread by the Germans and those in the French administration who, for reasons of their own, had caused alarm and panic.

Taking all this into account, there still lingers the suspicion that for many people the flight from the Germans was an adventurous opportunity, an escape into the unknown, away from the humdrum future they had seen marked out ahead of them. Might they have regarded this unfamiliar situation as an opportunity for renewal?

As always, in circumstances such as these, rumours abounded. The passing on of information by

125

word of mouth can be a creative and imaginative form of communication.

Two middle-aged Spaniards passed with enormous packs on their backs. They walked fast and with purpose. Four soldiers nearby were playing cards, quarrelling noisily. Two Air Force trucks stopped and the drivers alighted to fill their canteens. They didn't stay long, particularly since there were infantry men around. The soldiers resented the airmen, blaming them for their absence in battle. Now, anybody wearing the air-force uniform had to take the blame for the incompetence or worse of the high command. The air-force men were mystified at the hostility. How could they be blamed? Remaining grounded had not been their choice. But go tell that to the mob.

An elderly lady was offered some bread and meat ration – *du singe* – by a Chasseur Alpine, recognizable by his enormous floppy beret. She thanked him profusely and went into a tirade about 'our brave boys' having been betrayed by the British who hadn't shown their faces in battle and had scarpered off home when things had got tough. He protested and went on to tell her how the British had retaken Arras. It had been one of the few reversals the Germans had suffered in the campaign. He fell asleep having barely finished his *casse-croûte*.

'We have been betrayed', the universal stock phrase of the defeated soldier, was on everyone's lips. *Trahi et vendu*. Betrayed and sold down the river. The analysing and pinpointing had not yet begun, the hows, the whys and the wherefores were still to be explored and covered up. Scapegoats had yet to be created. In the meantime, Anglophobia – *perfide Albion* – presented itself as a natural and spontaneous choice, with xenophobia a close second.

*

A small, tracked vehicle caught my eye as it approached in a cloud of dust and I said *adieu* to little Pierre and his friendly and disorientated mother and father and sidled up to the new arrival. He was well-groomed and had a neatly trimmed beard.

When the front broke he had rushed supplies to Chalon. There, they had cursed him for turning up with the wrong ammo. How could they blame him? He was only driving the bloody vehicle, *sacré bleu*. When he got back to Troyes the depot had been evacuated and his unit had gone. Where to? Go south, they told him. Make for Cahors, they told him, '*demerde-toi*,' they had said. In Cahors, nobody knew from nothing. Try Toulouse or Tarbes or Montpellier.

No, he couldn't give me a lift. 'See for yourself', there was one seat in his tiny armoured vehicle and the rest was chock-a-block with ammunition and land mines. '*Très dangereux!*'

Two cyclists, shouting and gesticulating, were now catching everyone's attention as they raced past us.

'They are right behind,' they called without slowing down. '*Ils sont derriére.*'

That was the signal for a lot of people to come out from under the shade and move on, unhurriedly. I stopped further down the road, waiting for the driver of one of those air-force vans, of which there were a disproportionate number about, hoping for a lift.

While I was waiting, not knowing when he was going to return, an exited lady emerged from her shop and, taking me for the driver, berated me for the mess *I* was making, pointing out how oil and petrol were dripping from the engine. Why did I have to park in front of her establishment? And while she was complaining and I was denying responsibility, a column of

127

military ambulances was passing through, presumably on the lookout for hospital space.

Waiting has never been my forte and so I moved on, leaving the oil-polluted lady to her seemingly most pressing problem.

As I reached the open country, an elderly man detached himself from a group and without preamble told me that he knew my grandfather. He had lived across the road in the Glockengasse and had seen me often.

'How did you get out of Vienna?' I asked, just to make conversation. That, he couldn't divulge until after the war, he was pledged to secrecy. What he did divulge, however, was the information that this line of refugees stretched all the way to Gibraltar, where the British fleet was taking us to safe havens in Palestine, British Honduras and Paraguay.

How people fed themselves, where they slept, I cannot remember. There were reception centres of varying degrees of efficacy along the way. I don't recall going hungry during those days on the road, nor did I sleep rough. But mine were different and untypical circumstances. I have always been a loner, not by choice but rather by nature, more as a result of my unfortunate talent for antagonizing people with my arrogance, and out of a streak of self-destructiveness which would trip me up all too frequently. Back in Brive, people had paired up or left in packs of fives and sixes and I was stuck on my own. On top of that, while the bulk of refugees were going south to Toulouse or south-east to the Mediterranean, I drifted in a south-westerly direction, seeking minor roads.

On the first evening out of Brive I stopped at a farmhouse and asked if I might be allowed to settle in the hayloft for the night. The lady smiled and said the memorable words: '*Vous êtes arrivé comme le roi.*' I was bang on time for supper and the table was laid. That lady, her husband and their daughter overwhelmed me with their friendliness and hospitality. Receptions of such exceptional warmth were not the rule and the degree of hospitality varied from one house to the next. The night before I reached Pau, I asked for shelter at a watermill. The penurious miller was clearly reluctant but after an internal struggle mumbled to himself, '*Il faut partager.*' He made room for me at the table where his large family were having their evening meal. Another bowl was brought out of the cupboard and later a bed was made up.

In the woods of Compiègne the Germans were busy, dusting the old railway carriage for the signing of the surrender terms by the French when the shickled groover was to perform his Tyrolean jig for the newsreel cameras. It was the carriage that had been retained by the French as a historic reminder of the signing of the armistice in 1918, when it was the Germans who had run out of steam.

On the 23rd of June then, there in the forest, with a mere flick of the wrist and a stroke of the pen, the French negotiators stopped the Wehrmacht dead in its tracks.

Who said the pen wasn't mightier than the sword?

Pau

I made straight for Pau, the capital of the ancient province of Béarn, tucked away in the south-west corner of France; Pau, the home of Henry IV, the first Bourbon monarch, the socially conscious sixteenth-century king whose ambition it was that every French peasant should afford a chicken in their Sunday pot.

The previous month, when the Germans had crossed into France, Mother, now a potential fifth columnist, had been sent to the notorious Camp de Gurs near Pau which was why I had directed my steps to this unassuming part of France.

Pau was basking in the sun as if nothing had happened and presented an appearance of normality. The morning papers carried the conditions of the armistice, one of which I found particularly disturbing. It was the handing over of any foreign nationals on demand. This was worrying, but the qualification 'on demand' seemed to give the clause a moderating complexion.

I knew that man by sight. The man talking to the guard was one of those people I had seen in the passport queues in Vienna and among refugees in Zürich and Lyons. I had spotted him briefly on the road out of Agen several days before as I was passing in the back of an army truck. We had never spoken nor acknowledged each other's presence in spite of our parallel progress.

He was a smart dresser and, on the few occasions I had seen him, had always worn his coat loose over his shoulders. It was remarkable to see him today as chic and as stylish as ever, after days or possibly weeks on the road. He wore his trilby slightly cocked and, true to form, the sleeves of his overcoat were dangling by his side, as he was trying to impress the soldier with his grasp of the French language. His pronunciation was impeccable.

On that first afternoon, instead of following army instructions, I decided to lose myself among the refugees. I thought it would be safer; that I would be less conspicuous. But as has been so often the case, I was wrong.

At the reception centre, foreigners had been separated from the other refugees. We were taken to a shopping arcade which was in the final stages of construction. It was built around a central patio and we were to bed down in the shops to be, on the clean straw provided. We tried to make the best of it, tidying up and marking out our respective territories.

But when the dust had settled and I had gathered my wits it became apparent that an armed soldier was now manning the gate, the only exit from the patio to the main street. I had to move fast. Picking up my pack, I approached the guard and showed him my army book. I explained that I had got mixed up with the wrong queue back at the centre, and that I had to report to infantry HQ.

And he was buying it.

Nodding his head, he returned the document and began the laborious process of groping in his pocket that contained the key, that unfastened the padlock, that kept the chain, that retained the bar, that locked the gate, that was about to be opened.

Hoo-ray!

At this point, heroically and with no benefit to himself,

131

our fellow-refugee, the trilby-hatted dandy, addressed me. Gazing at the soldier he said:

'You can't prove that this document is yours. I mean really . . . I mean there is no photograph. You could be someone else.' He smiled. 'Don't look at me like that,' he added with a scowl, 'I'm only trying to help, you could get us all into deep trouble.'

The young peasant, dressed in soldier's garb, saw the logic in that. And anyway, he had been saved from making a decision off his own bat which was against the rules.

'Better discuss this with the adjudant when he arrives.' And he reversed the procedure that had got me to within an inch of freedom.

Tant pis.

The next morning, coffee arrived promptly and each of us received a slice of bread. The black juice, strong and sweet, revived me and raised my spirits. Two soldiers were now manning the gate, and I tried my stunt again when Trilby wasn't about, but they didn't want to know. Their job was to follow orders. Decision-making was something else.

There was a lot of coffee left over and masses of bread, and Trilby-man who had been put in charge of the cauldron and the bread-bin, waved with his ladle.

'Alfred,' he called, 'viens, 'ya du rabiot! . . . second helpings.'

Sulkingly, I accepted his invitation and wondered why more than twice the amount had been delivered. Most unusual.

It had become rather quiet in our little camp and as I wandered around exploring, I discovered behind a stack of bricks a hole in the wall leading to a side-street, and by the time dinner arrived the soldiers minding the gate were guarding a ghost camp.

Fellows-in-adversity such as our Trilby-topped specimen who would frustrate one's efforts at survival, were not uncommon. And unfailingly they would tell you that they were 'only trying to help', when, quite gratuitously and in

132

one fell swoop, they forestalled your carefully laid plans. I
had come across his kind before and was to encounter such
as him again. They are the physical extension of the legend-
ary jostler on the marketplace.
But Samarra wasn't on my agenda.

Without malice, I can see our self-styled helper talking to
the guards at the gate, smiling in the face of authority while
everybody else had scarpered. The last inhabitant of the
staging-post to God-knows-where, ladle in hand, announc-
ing in his helpful manner that everyone had vanished.
'Tout le monde est disparu.'

One story will yet have to be told, and that is the
account of the Vichy administration coping with millions of refugees from Belgium and northern France,
and masses of soldiers being demobilized. The country
had not only lost a war but also three-fifths of its
territory, containing its richest farmland and almost all
of its heavy industry and mining areas. Within days of
the Armistice, the refugees were housed. A commissariat *'pour la lutte contre le chômage'*, had been brought
into being, even before unemployment had had a
chance to raise its threatening head. Jobs were created.
Medical services were running normally and I don't
remember anybody being turned away for lack of
money.

The production of simple, centrally designed furniture was farmed out to local craftsmen. The design of
the tables and chairs and beds revealed a grasp of the
problems prevalent at the time and the brief would
have been: choice of cheap materials, function,
stackability, a modicum of comfort and above all simplicity of production. The civil service and the local
authorities had once again shown administrative com-
petence and ingenuity in the light of the gross

ineptitude displayed by the military and numerous politicians in the months leading up to the collapse. The French, having taken the heaviest defeat in their history, cut off from their richest provinces, their economy bankrupt and the people demoralized, coped with the situation better than other nations had in far less disheartening circumstances.

Liberté Égalité and *Fraternité* were out. But before you could utter *Travaille, Patrie, Famille* – the new nationalist catch-phrase – within days of the first rush of refugees, everyone was found a bed for the night. Nobody slept on park benches. It seems, and here I am speculating, that the local authorities were empowered to requisition all unoccupied space such as empty buildings, sport centres, warehouses and theatres. Reception centres (*centres d'accueil*) had sprung up and, as the refugees flooded in, their requirements were assessed and provisional accommodation was allotted.

We, the 'old' refugees, had the advantage of experience. Already, in the pre-war days, we made extensive use of the *poste restante* facilities as we rarely had a fixed address. Consequently, we went straight to the central post office at any town, as soon as we arrived, to ask for our mail. Likewise, we wrote to people at the town where they were most likely to be at any given time, care of the central post office.

Throughout the débâcle of 1940, this amenity was being used more than ever and the postal services never faltered. I managed to contact friends merely by writing to the last address I knew, which was pre-Armistice. These letters would have often followed a person through various camps and domiciles. And yet, to judge from the number of answers I received, many of them got through. I shall never know which of those unaccounted-for letters remained unanswered due to the reluctance or laziness of those I had written to.

*

' 'Ya bon soleil,' *says to me the young North African, soaking in the early morning sun and attempting to communicate his feelings of the moment. The nights are cold in Lannemezan in the foothills of the Pyrenees, and like huge amphibians we hog the south-facing brick wall.*

'Ah oui,' *I reply in a feeble attempt at being social. '* 'Ya bon . . . très bon.' *I point at the sun. '* 'Ya chaud,' *he enlarges. The conversation is slowly getting into its stride as we linger in this suntrap soaking up energy.*

Two Vietnamese return from this morning's potato-peeling fatigue. At the outset of the war some general had the bright idea of filling returning cargo vessels with young peasants from Cochin-China, to provide a reserve of cheap labour. They were now, and for years to come, stuck in transit camps, subjected to a hostile climate and a resentful population.

'Domino,' *one of them sings,* 'Domino, le printemps est en moi Dominique.' *He does not understand the words which is just as well.*

' 'Ya bon, soleil,' *the other remarks. The pidgin session is now in full swing. All the variations are being brought into play.*

' 'Ya très bon.'

' 'Ya bien chaud.'

'Et alors.'

'Fromage!'

'Me like go home!'

'Me need plenty food!'

'Me want big woman !'

These excursions into the indigenous idiom are accompanied by merriment and every statement is met with acclaim. The sun is pointed at. Home is indicated by a raised hand vaguely directing. Fingers are stuffed into mouth and 'woman' *is accompanied by violent movements from the hips and shouts of* 'Djigah djigah!'

*

This was the military camp at Lannemezan.

I had been sent there because in Pau the military didn't know what to do with me. In those days, nobody knew what to do with anybody. In those days, all the camps were transit camps. In those fateful days: June, July 1940, everybody was in transit.

The demobilized Parisians assembled on the parade ground chanting. *'Des trains, des trains, des trains . . .'* until the harassed lieutenant emerged from his office to announce the latest on the situation. Officers had lost their sparkle and were inconspicuous and conciliatory. This one pleaded in exasperation:

'When I call 'tenshun, then at least be quiet and listen. I'm trying to help you . . . *non mais sans blague!'* Any moment then he was going to burst into tears.

Although the Parisians were told that they had been demobilized by decree, they hadn't been given their papers nor had they been paid, and they were still wearing uniform. What if they were sent home and on passing the demarcation line were taken prisoners by the Germans? They weren't leaving other people to do their thinking for them. What nobody knew was that time was running out, for a few weeks later the Germans stopped all traffic across the zones.

The Parisians did, eventually, get their demobilization papers, civilian garb, and pay, and boarded the train in high spirits, not before passing the hat around for young *Alfred* whom they had taken to their hearts and treated as a mascot. They had named him *Tarduris*. The mystery of that nickname has never been resolved.

At Lannemezan, the transferables were transferred to other transfer camps to make room for newly arrived transferables.

I had ceased to be transferable because they knew not what to do with me. Having passed through various camps in the region, where no one knew what to do, they finally hit upon the idea of placing me with a

136

unit of unplaceables at the Camp de Ger, an inoperative artillery range. It was situated to the west of Tarbes which suited me fine, since it was within easy reach of Pau where mother was at the maternity hospital due to give birth to my sister Monique.

Here in Ger, there were about twenty of us manning that enormous camp. There were two Tunisians, a Pole and a small group of northerners who had either missed the train home or didn't fancy going back. We occupied the officers' quarters and left the huts to the fleas which could be observed pole-vaulting when the afternoon sun shone through the windows.

It was Sunday the fifth of January 1941 – the year of the snake – that I went on one of my regular visits to the maternity hospital. Sitting in the waiting room, I could hear Mother scream in agony. They told me that she had been in labour for the last three days. Ten minutes later, my kid sister Monique made her debut.

Four months earlier, Mother had gone to the doctor to have him look at a swelling in her abdomen. Could she be pregnant, she enquired. The doctor laughed and answered with a question. 'At your age?'

Mum was forty-six years old. Six years older than the twentieth century. She was to lose Monique two years later in Barbie country but, miraculously, they were reunited after the liberation of Lyons.

The guys at the Camp de Ger would find me tucked in bed reading by the time they returned, raucous and rhapsodic, from their alcoholic outings. I always seemed to have one book or another and there was little point in going to sleep, because it took them a while to settle down for the night.

They expressed their concern about my abstinence

137

and looked upon me as some kind of a freak. One evening, I tagged along and we became good buddies. I had made a conscious choice, acquainting myself with inebriation-induced comradeship, and hang-overs.

Riupeyrous

The Vichy ship, mutilated and badly listing due to the momentous events of the past months, was ponderously righting herself. Once again, she was cautiously braving the open sea.

The people who had installed me at Ger had been silently but inevitably beavering away at placing me in my true context. It seems to me that their difficulty had been that, although a foreigner, I was encapsulated within the army which unwittingly provided a protective mantle. Every time he saw me, the visiting *sergent chef*, to whom I was an intruder, would ask why I was still in his outfit. He eventually took me along to Tarbes, and hauled me in front of his lieutenant complaining that I would not go away. The lieutenant made a number of inconclusive telephone calls, then, turning to the sergeant, he suggested that the matter be laid to rest. It was unfair he said, to turn this valiant youngster into a tennis ball, '. . . *de jouer aux tennis avec ce brave gars.*'

It was obvious that he was no football fan.

Finally, one day towards the end of January 1941, the back-room boys had found the appropriate formula which would relieve them of the headache I was causing. I was told to report to the gendarmerie in nearby Tarbes. There I was unceremoniously turned into a protesting civilian, with apologies from the gendarmes on the night shift, 'We are only doing our job', and sympathy from the two camp-followers in attendance. The demobilization pay would reach me later. That's what they said. They didn't believe it either.

I spent the night in the cells, and the next morning was escorted to the station and put on the train to Montauban, where I was to make my way to the nearby camp. They promised to send my bicycle on a later train since the engine was puffing and whistling and it was too late to get to the guard van.

Life in the camp at Montauban was spartan. Of all the camps I had been to, this was the one with the lowest star rating. This was one I would not recommend to anybody. Of course, there were camps in unoccupied France compared to which Montauban looked like an amusement park. My poor mother had had a far worse time in Gurs, than I ever experienced. And there was even worse than Gurs. Le Vernet for instance, according to Arthur Koestler, competed in severity with the German concentration camps; the likes of Dachau, Sachsenhausen, Buchenwald.

Montauban, the camp, was poorly equipped. There were no mattresses and I couldn't get warm at nights. Food was inadequate. We didn't starve but we were hungry. But then, the French people were also beginning to feel the pinch. This was February 1941.

Here in Montauban internees spent their evenings discussing food. They recalled multi-course dinners they had enjoyed, festivals and parties were remembered and exquisite culinary terms were invoked. I reminisced about my mother's thick pea soup, which

I had disliked. How I would have loved to reverse that past rejection. An old furrier from Vienna gave me a tiny piece of chocolate, a wedge the size of my front tooth, to suck while I was sipping tea. It was a memorable event. 'When this calamity is over,' I said to myself, 'this is all the luxury I will ever want. A piece of black chocolate to suck with my tea. That and a bowl of pea soup.'

With croutons.

However, this camp, unlike those I had previously been interned in, was not guarded – not yet. For some reason, the machinery or procedure that would enable the powers in whose hands we were to turn us into fully-fledged prisoners had, so far, not been pieced together. One could get permission to go into town, even obtain a pass on compassionate grounds, as I found out when I took Mother's letter to the camp office. There, with little formality, I obtained seven days' leave.

Monique, the baby, was three weeks old but the convent sisters running Pau's maternity hospital knew that Mother had no place to go to, and were not going to discharge her until she herself was ready.

The clerk at the camp office, a fellow-internee, refused to give me my papers the day before, although I pleaded with him, pointing out that I had to catch the early bus that would take me to the station. In the morning he dragged his feet and the greater my impatience the more time he took. Eventually, my pass stamped and authorized, I had to sprint the two kilometres to the bus stop and caught the coach by a whisker. Since the journey took me through Tarbes I had planned to stop there and pay a visit to the gendarmes who had forgotten to send my bike on to the camp.

One of the friendly gendarmes greeted me like a long-lost brother. Yes of course, he remembered the bike.

'Let's go fetch it.'

He took me to the storeroom where there was no bike, so we went to see the chief in his office.

'Chief! . . . the little fellow . . . remember? . . . the bike . . .'

'*J'en sais rien,*' mumbled the chief, without looking up. He was busy sorting cobnuts from a sack into paper bags.

'*Mais chef . . . la station . . . le train . . . Montauban . . .*'

'*Moi, je n'ai pas sa bicyclette, compris? J'EN AI PAS!!!*' His reverberating outburst sent us running for cover.

I left with the satisfaction that from now on I could state truthfully that I had been robbed by the guardians of law and order.

No one can take that away from me.

On my third day in Pau, my urine was getting dark and my skin began to turn yellow. I didn't yet know that I had contracted jaundice. But I was back in familiar surroundings, and went to see the doctor. He immediately sent me to the hospital where I was put in isolation. Although my yellowness was extreme, and I was ordered to remain in bed, I didn't feel any ill effects other than being continually hungry, on account of having been put on a starvation diet – *au régime*.

Hospital was a small annexe on the outskirts of town, run by two efficient, dedicated and stern nuns who administered the place in a methodical and authoritarian way. Among the twenty to thirty patients in the men's ward were two middle-aged refugees from Germany. Whatever illness they may have suffered from had long been nullified, but the two nuns, judging that the refugees would be unable to cope with what awaited them outside, took it upon themselves to keep them on the sick list. These two humourless convent sisters wouldn't have been intimidated by a whole panzer division.

I, on the other hand, was courteously told to leave after five weeks, not because I was fit once more, but because I had broken the rules. One night Marcel, a young Breton who was recovering from a hernia operation, and I had secretly slipped out and gone into town. We knew the risks and were not surprised when the next morning Mother Superior asked us to hit the road. These dedicated, sullen nuns working all hours of the day would have kept me on indefinitely, knowing that I was in the same category as the two German refugees. But playing silly buggers; *Ça, non!* I thanked them politely and went on my way.

During my illness – my yellow period – I had sent the camp authorities in Montauban confirmation of my hospitalization and I guess they filed me away as being legitimately absent. That, I imagine, kept them from sending the bloodhounds after me. And since they didn't show the courtesy to acknowledge my letter and wish me a speedy recovery, I felt under no obligation to retain further contact with them. Had I not contracted this illness at that particular, and might I say opportune, moment the ensuing chapters would have been of a somewhat different colour. They might not have been written.

Once again I was on the loose, but I did have my demobilization papers and the hospital certificate. Marcel, my fellow-expellee, had heard through the grapevine of a scheme which offered work, board and lodging to the unemployed. We signed up and arrived in Riupeyrous, twenty kilometres north-east, the same day in time for supper. There, the 'Commissariat for the Fight Against Unemployment' had initiated a drainage project.

The *paysans* of Riupeyrous, a parish of about twenty-five homesteads, had but one vice. They insisted on being called *des agriculteurs*. It waved goodbye to the Middle Ages, so to speak. After all, they didn't thresh the corn by hand, as had their mothers and fathers, with flails. Granted, they still ploughed with a team of cows, and sowed and reaped laboriously by hand, but threshing had been mechanized. Every year, Jules from the nearby town of Lembeye made the round of the villages with his *batteuse*, a threshing machine powered by a Crossley steam engine, fuelled by the cobs kept from the preceding year's maize harvest.

The harvest itself was a back-breaking job, and while the sun shone unremittingly one was regaled with the the mirage-like view of snow on the peaks of the western Pyrenees, spread out in the summer haze like a faded piece of tapestry. The reaping of the wheat and the hay, at the peak of the summer, had to be done at a flying pace, eighteen hours a day every day, with no time to attend Sunday Mass. For hanging over it all was the threat of an imbalance in the weather. A few rainy days wrongly assigned could mean hardship for the rest of the year, and so could a dry spell at the wrong time. In the Catholic ambience of Riupeyrous, rain and sunshine were the two pagan Gods who could make or break the farmer. Both could be generous or malevolent depending on when in the season they chose to appear.

Maize and beans were additional and important crops, particularly so since they were not as sensitive to the caprices of the weather and fungal attack as wheat. They could be harvested at a less gruelling pace and at a convenient moment. They were sown in complementary pairs. The beans provided a useful supply of readily released nitrate for their companions and in return the maize would act as support for the climbing pintos.

As all farmers of the area, the Riupeyrousians were a hard-working and parochial crowd. They were wary of

outsiders, showing particular distaste for the townspeople, who travelled long distances to do their shopping
now that there was scarcity. The farmers remembered
the pre-war days when hikers and cyclists would pass
them on weekends, and taunt and ridicule them for
working in the fields at all hours and days of the high
season. Now, the townies came knocking at their door,
cap in hand, paying high prices, or bringing their valu-
ables in exchange for the odd rabbit, chicken, or skein
of wool. They even offered to come and help. The proverbial boot now found itself on the proverbial other
foot.

And it felt proverbially good.

Take note of the robust independence and stability
a community such as Riupeyrous possessed. For partly
through their virtual self-sufficiency and partly, no
doubt, because of their unchanging lifestyle and
attitudes, three years of war, defeat and occupation
had made little impact. Over many generations they
had acquired the skill and the determination to cope
with all eventualities, a quality far less prevalent in the
urban environment. They had seen it all before. Their
hang-ups were the rain or sunshine at the wrong time,
the state of their ploughs and the health of their cows.
That, and the odd dispute over hedges and boundaries.

They existed quite independently of the outside
world. Food was homegrown and they produced most
of what they needed. The wives and daughters were
proficient in the art of salting, smoking, pickling and
in the production of pâtés and sausages. They were
also proficient at spinning, which they did with the aid
of a hand-held spindle. This they twirled when driving
the cows to the pasture or sitting by the fire on winter
evenings or at any other time when their hands were
not otherwise engaged.

The services were run by the less wealthy farmers.
There was the innkeeper. There was the miller and the

tailor. In the neighbouring parish lived the woman with the loom who would weave cloth from the skeins people would bring. There was the blacksmith and the man who owned the coach, providing the Wednesday run to Morlaas and Pau. And there was the man who owned the bull that serviced the cows in this and the three surrounding villages. They were all farmers, only they maintained a sideline to supplement their earnings. But however well their business might have been doing, none of them would ever rupture the umbilical cord which was their small piece of land, a pair of cows, one or two sows and a barnyard full of poultry. Money hardly ever changed hands. Customarily the miller or the weaver would keep a percentage of the produce or settlement would consist in the transfer of a piglet or the supply of milk.

The wealth of a farmer could be gauged by the size of his herd. To have a dozen cows and a pair of oxen was the height of affluence. Here, there was a breed of small, brown, long-horned cows, who were the mainstay of the village economy. They would provide milk after a hard day in the field and would also be expected to bear calves periodically, without slackening in their daily workload. And on top of all that, their heads fitted exactly the yokes to which they would be strapped. Oxen were a luxury. They were not as cost-effective as cows, but they were less temperamental and so, better at pulling a cart or at ploughing straight furrows.

In their diligence, the commissariat combating unemployment had left no stone unturned to find useful activity for idle hands. In the past, projects that had been demanded by the communities had been given the *mañana* treatment. Now, with millions of refugees and demobilized soldiers, there was a pressing urgency. In 1940, anybody who needed a job could find employment. And any community wanting a job done didn't have a lot of shouting or wheeling and dealing to do. The work team I joined consisted of forty men who worked in ten gangs digging trenches and laying pipes to drain the water-logged fields in Riupeyrous and its neighbourhood. Sheds had been put up in the village, where we were housed and fed. Each gang had a *chef d'équipe*, a fore-man, and there was a *surveillant* supervising the foreman. The whole structure was capped by two *directeurs*, and on top of the pyramid sat *le capitaine*. Added to this was the office staff of four, plus two cooks, two gardeners, a store-keeper and last but not least *le forgeron*, the blacksmith, twenty-year-old Freddi Klausner, who alternated between the trenches and the smithy, having been assigned to sharpen the blunted pickaxes. In Vichy France of 1941–42, the France of Maréchal Pétain and Pierre Laval, I was subjected to no restrictions. For the first time since I left Vienna, I was earning wages.

'Pas de Samedi sans soleil,' *said Mme Souyéze when I noted what a nice day it was. That threw me. How could she say that?*

Never a Saturday without sun?

It was an old saying and had proved to be reliable through the ages, was her explanation.

'But what about two weeks ago when you came to the forge to have your scissors sharpened? It was cold and windy, n'est ce pas?'

'Mais oui, *I remember absolument well. I was wearing two sets of woollen stockings.'*

'Alors?'

'Eh bien, *don't you remember how the sun came out and you said the weather was turning and I said no, not for another two days?'*

'Yes, but the sun came and went in a matter of two or three minutes.'

'C'est ça, Alfred, that's what I said. No Saturday without sun.'

Go on, prove her wrong!

Monsieur Majesté-Hourné was the mayor of Riupeyrous. Like most people in the village, he was a man of few words, particularly towards us outsiders; trenchdiggers complete with hierarchy. He could never understand why so many people had to remain above ground in the pursuance of excavation, while the few in the ditches were standing around half the time resting their chins on the end of the shovel or rolling cigarettes with a mixture of tobacco and dried maize tassel. *'Pauvre France,'* he would remark sarcastically, as he passed with his team of oxen on the way to one of his fields, 'whom have you entrusted with your defence? *A qui a tu confié tes armes?'*

He was a veteran of the Great War. His generation had been promised that it would be the war to end all wars. *Le sacrifice suprême.* He had seen thousands of his contemporaries killed, but never a general or a politician. To the people of Riupeyrous, as to Central European peasants generally, betrayal and deceit had been a way of life. They took the indignity of the present condition with the resignation which had, over the centuries, become a character trait of peasants from Riupeyrous to Krasnodar.

Back in the summer of 1939 after he had slipped into Switzerland, my cousin Felix, having got bored in Basle, had boarded the train to Paris and, being a diminutive fifteen-year-old, was asked no questions at the border crossing. Being under age, he wasn't subject to internment at the outset of the war. He made his own way south, days before the fall of Paris, turning up in Pau shortly after me.

Now, March 1941, I had managed to rent a cabin from our mayor. Felix had come to work with the trench-diggers and Mother with baby Monique had joined us. Here, the four of us lived unobtrusively at the edge of the village.

Altogether, we spent about eighteen months in Riupeyrous and, compared to the situation of other Jewish refugees, ours, modest as it was, was a life of luxury. While many of them found themselves interned in camps of varying degrees of severity, and others were concentrated in conurbations to be picked off and deported from the summer of 1942 onwards, we managed to exist inconspicuously. We supplemented our rations by growing beans and carrots and by keeping a few rabbits and hens. In the late summer there were figs galore along the roadside, juicy and sweet and there for the picking, and in the autumn there was a glut of edible sweet chestnuts, adding vital carbohydrates to our diet.

It was a depressing period for us and indeed for millions throughout Europe. For at that time there was not a glimmer of hope. True, the United States had entered into the conflict in December 1941 and they certainly didn't look like losers, but we did. And while it looked as though, in the long run, Germany would be defeated, the long run was not for us. The Germans were going from victory to victory. That summer they poured into the Caucasus threatening the oil fields of Baku and on the central front they were closing in on Stalingrad. In North Africa they pushed towards Alexandria threatening the Suez Canal.

Our employment with the *chantiers ruraux*, the rural sites of the commissariat, came to an abrupt end when

Raoul the Parisian, who had finally managed to land a cushy job in the office, came to the site with a note for our *chef d'équipe*. Vichy had caught up with us. We were to take our shovels and picks to the toolshed and have our deposit returned. Then we were to collect our passes and pay and report to the nearest camp for foreign workers. As we left, shattered by this turn of events, Monsieur Tarragon, one of the *surveillants* called after us; he had followed us to the end of the field. It was he who had always shown antagonism towards us and had never said a friendly word.

We turned and solemnly he shook us by the hand. With a display of concern we had never expected, this grumpy old Norman, who liked no one and was liked by few, wished us luck.

Izeste

The work camp at Izeste was a small warehouse turned dormitory complete with offices and kitchen. It was a miserable place, beautifully set in the wooded foothills leading to the abruptly rising mountains under the Pic du Midi, thirty kilometres from the Spanish border. However, there was no barbed wire nor was the camp guarded. Around twenty-five to thirty men were housed there.

Once again, I was confronted with someone whose face was familiar from the days of the exit-visa queues and embassy crowds back in Vienna. It was the chap at reception, who was arrogant and forbidding and not at all pleased that, disregarding his wishes, Felix and I had gone to see the commandant.

The commandant was a laconic naval officer, who agreed to let us continue working and living in Riupeyrous. I had produced a note from our ever-helpful mayor, confirming that we were working in his parish as reliable and necessary casuals. We were to be *affectées speciaux*, he said. It meant that from now on we were on the roll of his group of foreign workers, on loan to whomever we were to be working for, and could be recalled at any time.

It took our fellow-in-adversity forty-eight hours to fill in and rubber stamp our identity papers for the return journey, which meant that we had to spend two miserable days at his and his two cronies' beck and call. There were no spare bunks and nobody cared. In places such as these, few people give you so much as the time of day, let alone help, and the only way a newcomer learns the ropes is by stubbing his toe or having his knuckles rapped every time he inadvertently steps out of line.

The notable exception in this set-up was a Spaniard who went out of his way to help us with our needs as best he could. He even lent us one of his blankets, a deed which in the rough climate of those painful days borders on saintliness.

In the afternoon, after having ignored repeated calls *à l'appel*, we were given to understand that '. . . there are places for people such as you!' The man who made that threat was a co-religionist from Germany.

Appel was the twice-daily ritual of raising and lowering the tricolour, accompanied by salutes and standing to attention, followed by the counting of heads. We had disregarded his calls because we didn't consider ourselves part of his outfit. The idea was abhorrent. We had only come to sort things out and be on our way. But from the moment the threat had been uttered until our departure we became model inmates. We chopped wood, swept the floors, cut the undergrowth, and arrived *à l'appel* before all others, raking the gravel beforehand.

I learned early on that you can retain a certain freedom of action by grabbing a shovel or an axe and looking busy before jobs are allocated. That way you can move around and gain a bird's-eye view of the situation with the obvious advantages that go with it. I also found that in most circumstances carrying a monkey wrench or a plumber's plunger or a plank of wood, will give access to places where entry would otherwise be challenged at the gate.

Eventually, with our papers duly stamped, Felix and I got on our bikes and couldn't be seen for dust. Two kilometres on, in Arudy, we stopped by at the gendarmerie for further endorsements. At the station a big thing was made of our well-worn documents. Since these were made of inferior paper and had to be carried at all times, they were in a pitiful state. Besides which, we weren't the tidiest of people anyway. The two guardians on duty, remarking on the state of the filthy papers, developed the theme, soon to arrive at 'filthy stinking Jews'.

Signed with commendable dispatch, we withdrew. But before Felix and I could put another dust screen up, the two gendarmes, braving the discomfort of the midday heat, came out into the glaring sunshine to inspect our bikes. They managed to book us on five counts. Each of us was in default of various legal requirements concerning bicycle regulations. In the four years of my sojourn in France, this was the only experience I had of what could be described as a manifestation of hatred towards Jews.

My mother had always derived a snobbish satisfaction from the fact that I didn't look 'Jewish'. So did I, and the question of the 'Jewish type' has been preoccupying me over the years. Go into any synagogue in Baltimore or Birmingham or Beersheba and look around you. How many of the people in the congregation look quote Jewish unquote? How many would you have recognized as being Jewish had you passed them in the street? How many? Two per cent? Five? Ten?

You can build Judeophobia upon a minority type of alien appearance. That minority then is subjected to sporadic abuse and harassment in the nordic/alpine cities of Europe. But in France, anti-Semitic hooligans have a lean time. In France or Spain or Italy, wherever the Phoenicians have dropped anchor and seed, you are forever rubbing shoulders with Gentiles sporting what could be loosely described as 'Jewish' features.

Without further incident, we pedalled home and settled back into our routine. We found a job with a Parisian entrepreneur who produced charcoal, the only fuel freely available for suitably converted cars and lorries. We felled trees and cut the timber to a manageable size, while a couple of Spaniards arranged and covered the wood in such a way as to produce a slow and incomplete combustion. It was a small-scale operation and suited us well. And since we were paid by the cubic metre, we could start and finish when we liked. We established a routine, beginning in the cool of the early morning, finishing at two in the afternoon.

Being tucked away out of sight, as we were, meant we had little knowledge of what was going on in the rest of German-occupied Europe in the summer of 1942. Accounts of deportation abounded. The drift of it was that a territory for Jews had been set aside around the Polish town of Lublin.

I was twenty-two years old and tired of running, and I had got to the stage where I didn't look unfavourably on a German-dominated Jewish region. The Lublin story didn't seem to result from wishful thinking nor did it sound alarmist. It was precisely the kind of story which tended to stand up to rational scrutiny. It carried the promise of a return to some kind of normality and stability.

But in the east systematic killing had already begun.

It seems to me that one of the factors that made possible the readiness of the victims to enter the cattle trucks was the urge for change. Any change from the tension that springs from prolonged insecurity.

There is hope in change, even in the face of further uncertainty.

Nevertheless, when the crunch came, I stopped reasoning and evaluating and got up and ran.

It was now the end of August, and the end of the easy times. That afternoon, returning from our wood-felling job, we found our mayor talking to Mother. In a sombre tone, he told us what was about to happen. The gendarmerie at Morlaas had informed him that, in accordance with procedure, they would be rousing him at four the next morning, to take them to where we lived. They had been ordered to 'pick up the boys.'

. . . *à ramasser les garçons.*

Monsieur Majesté-Hourné was a small farmer, preoccupied with his scattered fields. He was the elected mayor of Riupeyrous and enjoyed the confidence of the community. He took his office seriously, and the term *responsabilité* carried meaning with him. A patriot who had fought in the trenches in 1914-18, contributing then to the rout of the historic adversary, he had resigned himself to the predicament of the present. Times were hard and he wasn't going to exacerbate things further. We were to decide what to do in the light of his daunting disclosure. But he stuck around and helped us in a roundabout way, reviewing the situation and indirectly assisting us in our deliberations.

Suppose we had gone off to Pau and had decided to stay the night?

'Nothing unusual in that. Eh?'

Why not take some blankets and sleep in the maize in the adjoining field? The nights are warm. And we will see what happens next. Maybe it will blow over. *Qui sait?*

Duly, the officers paid to enforce the law, trained to guard and protect citizens, turned up as planned; two gendarmes accompanied by our mayor. Mother told them that the boys had gone to town and hadn't come home that night. Nothing unusual in that. They do that occasionally.

For the next few days we laid low, sleeping rough in the field hoping that inefficiency and indifference would prevail. Then, three days later, they turned up and got Felix. He had been helping Mum with the laundry while I was hoeing our cabbages across the way and out of sight. I just managed to see the three cycling past, chatting casually.

My time was up! I had to prepare to cross the Pyrenees.

The day they took Felix away, I wrote a letter to Mother and had it posted in Pau. In it I told her that by the time she received it, I would be far away, and that, with God's help, we would reunite after the war. It was a trick I must have picked up from some penny novel but it had the desired effect. When the gendarmes came back four days later, they were shown the letter. They seemed gratified, for it saved them further unnecessary journeys. Going on a sweaty hour's cycle ride wasn't their idea of spending the morning or afternoon. Much better to sit in the cool of the station playing cards or staring out of the window.

The distance to the Spanish border was about a hundred kilometres as the crow flies. But the crow didn't fly and I footslogged it most of the way following the river Gave in a southerly direction, eventually turning east to the spa town of Eaux Bonnes, thus outflanking, outmanoeuvring and outwitting the opposition who were, no doubt, waiting for me at Laruns which was the last railway station before the border. Somewhere along the way I had spotted an abandoned pitchfork which I adopted. Carrying it did not add to my comfort but it gave me confidence and an air of authenticity.

On the approaches to Eaux Bonnes one is welcomed and regaled by signs advertising afflictions and ailments. Ascending the rising road to the small town, one passes: Arthritis, Neurasthenia, Calenture, Rheumatism, Valetudinaria, Corruption, Palsy, Asthma, Canker, and many more scourges. They render lively the weary wanderer, animating his spirit, giving renewed spring to his step and a smile to his face. The peaks and the glaciers are beckoning.

Having run the gauntlet of maladies and adversities, the tired but revived traveller enters the town square with the casino to his right. He does not need to enquire the way. The mountains are there in front of him, gesticulating, inviting. The map shows how the main street emanates from the square and fizzles out into a cart track before it hits the rise.

The Pyrenees rise more abruptly than the Alps. The transition from the plain is shorter and steeper and nowhere is this more apparent than in Eaux Bonnes, the good waters. The little town comes to a sudden end at the bottom of a wooded ravine and the terrain changes from near level to a sudden one-in-one incline.

Now I entered the final lap that was to get me into the wilderness of the mountains; the last hundred metres along the High Street with its four shops, its jeweller and its restaurant. I looked at the solitary cloud ringing the tip of the Pic du Midi and felt buoyant.

The street was empty except for the jeweller and another man talking quietly. Nothing special in that you might say, other than the fact that the other man looked straight at me as I approached and said to the jeweller, 'Watch me pick up this evil little *youpin.*'

I wasn't close enough to hear the exact words, but what else could he have said? He was one of the two gendarmes from Arudy who, earlier that summer, had booked Felix and me in the midday heat. He was wearing civilian clothes.

The jig was up!

It was too late to turn around for I could already see the white of his eyes. At that point, the temptation was to skip across the narrow road and give myself up. I found the idea of capitulating appealing, and it had the added element of my taking the initiative. There was also the alluring ingredient of surprise and melodrama. The gesture would have given me the satisfaction of taking the wind out of his sail, of knowing what was demanded of me, of playing my role. How could he have treated me with less than dignity, even respect?

Thoughts of surrender and histrionic gestures might have accompanied and tempted me at that moment, but my feet kept on walking. My primal instincts took over and, looking nonchalantly straight ahead, I continued on at a steady pace and didn't stop until I found myself halfway up the mountain.

Whatever went through my mind in those long seconds, my feet kept on walking as in a trance and within minutes I reached the edge of the small town, the place where the map told me to go over the top. There was a low retaining wall which, no doubt, had been put there to impede the free movement of soil on to the path. It symbolized the demarcation between law and order, which was definitely against me, and anarchic wilderness, bearing great expectations and a feeling of security.

I had been climbing the steep incline for some minutes, slowly waking from my stupor and realizing that I had made it. I was overcome with joy and would have laughed out loud had I not been out of breath. Should the guy down below have had second thoughts and decided to come after me he would have had to dodge the loose boulders skipping towards him, for I had the advantage of height, and gravity was for once firmly on my side. I stuck the pitchfork into the gritty ground; the two-pronged hayfork with its smooth handle which could well have been the crucial factor enabling the writing of this story.

The shepherds were grazing the upper valleys around the Pic de Ger and the Lac d'Artouste when I passed that way. They bring their sheep in August when their meadows are exhausted. There they remain until the snow covers the pastures and forces them to return to their hearths and families. They were cheerful and wary of strangers and didn't ask questions. They assumed that I was off to join the Free French – and good luck to you – they were neither for nor against, they didn't wear their convictions on their sleeves.

With mistrust, sympathy and hospitality, they ushered me to the frontier, each nudging me casually in the direction of the next shepherd along the way. They guarded their sheep and their secrets jealously, sharing their shelter and food as a matter of course. They were like mountain goats negotiating the rockface effortlessly, kitted and shod in the garb they would walk around in, pursuing their daily tasks down in the villages.

The last of them took me along the final rise to the Col de Sobe, which proved to be the most difficult part. Without him I might not have succeeded. He was an old man and grumbled at my slow progress and as soon as we got to the top he bade me farewell. '*Voilà l'Espagne*,' he said, and the next moment he was gone.

I looked down and perceived a totally different landscape. This part of the Aragon is harsh, uninviting and

159

parched, contrasting sharply with the luscious green of the Béarn which I had just left. It seemed sparsely populated except for the gnarled, ageless olive trees, who utterly ignored my arrival.

Zaragoza

The two guys seemed tense as they escorted me from
the station. They hurried me along, glancing furtively
over their shoulders. *'Venga!'* and *'anda hombre'* were
the first Spanish words addressed to me, And *'por aca!'*
But as we turned the corner their tension subsided and
the younger one uttered an involuntary laugh. The
other one grinned. Their gait was now relaxed and
unhurried. The older of the two, he must have been
around sixty, turned to me and shouted.

'Jefatura . . . una hora.'

'Si,' was all I could muster in Spanish repartee.

He wasn't satisfied.

'Una hora,' repeated the rifle-bearer pointing to the
nearby clock tower. *'Una hora de andar.'* He sliced the
air vertically with a sharp upward movement from the
wrist. And then he slapped his thigh. *'Andar,'* he repeated. *'Andar.'*

Why was he telling me this? I knew they were taking
me to headquarters.

September 12th 1942. The war was at its fiercest and
approaching its major turning point. Those were the days

of Stalingrad which had fallen to the German war correspondents every day for the last two weeks. That morning, after a week of news deprivation, I had managed to catch a glimpse of the headlines. It wasn't difficult to understand the caption announcing, yet again, the imminent fall. Pockets of resistance were being 'mopped up'. For Germany's poorly equipped soldiers a second Russian winter was beckoning and Stalingrad was to become their graveyard and that of a million Soviets.

On arrival in Zaragoza an hour earlier, I had been accosted at the station by a couple of sharp-eyed dicks, who had wanted to see my papers. Having confirmed their suspicions, one of them had addressed me in French. Pointing vaguely in a northerly direction, he suggested that I had come from '*la bas*'. With an air of having done a good day's work, they handed me over to my rifle-bearing escort.

Throughout the previous days I had clambered over numerous Pyrenean passes in avoidance of the French authorities who had booked a place for me on one of their cattle trucks. The intention was to ship me to Drancy which served as the staging post to the east. For the past nine years, racial precepts had pushed me ever further south and west. From Berlin to Vienna to Zürich, Paris and Pau; and who was I to assist in the reversal of that trend?

Once again, I found myself deprived of the faculty of being in control of my own destiny. It gave me a feeling of comfort. For the time being, I was not going to be called upon to make any further decisions.

So here I was, crossing the Ebro on that bright Sunday morning with a rifle on either side of me; the Ebro, that capricious river which emanates from within shouting distance of the Bay of Biscay, but insists on going all the way across the peninsula to the Mediterranean Sea, picking up the waters cascading from the Pyrenees and the northern Meseta.

162

People were out strolling, enjoying the sun. Some were standing around watching the strollers, and there were those who discretely watched the strollers and the watchers. And I felt on top of the world, proud to be seen to be on the wrong side of the law in sunny, fascist Spain.

My two companions and I were now negotiating the incline which was the tree-lined Calle de la Independencia. Independent from whom, I wondered. The older man was now panting. He turned to me and shouted, '¿*Canzado . . . fatigado?*'

'No,' I yelled back, learning fast. '*Me no fatigado.*' I wasn't tired.

'*Pues asentar,*' he ordered in chicken Spanish. 'Then we sit.'

And without further ado the old *carabinero* dropped his corpulence on the nearby bench. He placed his rifle between his knees, pointing it directly up his nose. The younger of the two, whose name it turned out was Pedro, got me to sit and went across the road to get some tobacco. He had up till now left all the talking to the elder, Don Alban, with whom, in spite of the difference in age and temperament, he appeared to have a harmonious relationship. A mutual affection existed between the two. When Don Alban finally stopped panting, he turned to me once again and thrust his tobacco pouch at me. Then he bellowed into my ear.

'¿*Las manillas duelen? Eh?*'

I wasn't quite certain what he wanted but it now transpired that Pedro, who had returned from his foray to the tobacconist, was in command of a workable knowledge of French.

'*Les menottes,*' he rattled my handcuffs, '*elles te gêne?*'

'They don't bother me much,' I said, clumsily rolling my cigarette. But once again the old boy didn't accept my polite refusal and insisted on readjusting and loosening the steel manacles. I was moved by his genuine concern. Gradually a crowd gathered. Sympathy and more cigarettes were handed around and a shopkeeper offered bread and olives and watered down wine. The high moment came when Don Alban, with a theatrical gesture and the obvious approval of the bystanders, removed my handcuffs and encouraged me to rub my wrists. People patted me on the head attempting to comfort me. Some spoke French and expressed the hope that things might turn out all right for me after all. The commiserating and consoling had an unnerving effect on me and, as the crowd melted away and my two *carabineros* had stuffed the leftovers into my satchel, I felt apprehensive.

On approaching headquarters, the tension my companions had displayed at the station returned once again and no sooner had they signed me in than they both cantered off, without so much as an *adios* or a friendly handshake.

I was ready for the third degree.

Weeks earlier, on the other side of the mountains, while planning my crossing, I had recognized the need to assume a new identity. My name had to go, so that there would be no way for the officials to check with the Nazis or the Vichyites. It had to be, I reasoned, a similar sounding name to which my reflexes would react smartly. Furthermore, it was to have an English ring to it, as from the moment I crossed, I was to be a citizen of Great Britain. Born in Manchester and resident in Boulogne-sur-Mer since my childhood. That, I figured, would explain my fluent French and my halting English. Boulogne had been chosen for two reasons. Having spent some weeks there I obviously knew the place, and knowing that the Town Hall had been bombed, I concluded, rightly or wrongly, that verification would be difficult.

Two silent policemen whisked me upstairs and sat

me in front of a desk. They deposited a large envelope and left. I was alone. The unfamiliar smell of olive oil was the first and paramount sensation.

Soon a young man arrived and seated himself opposite. He reminded me of Buster Keaton, only he was taller and smartly dressed. Silently he removed the contents of the envelope. Twenty dollars and two thousand French francs had been taken from me during the preliminary search at the railway station. They were there on the desk together with a short handwritten note. He turned the envelope upside down in the vain hope for more, but only a solitary paperclip dropped out and landed next to the dollar bills on the antique blotting paper. Buster studied the heap like a soothsayer.

'*Papeles,*' he said quietly. He made demanding gestures, just as the official in Zürich had, opening and shutting the palm of his right hand. His eyes reflected the superiority of the ambitious young mandarin prepared and trained for officialdom through countless generations,

'*Documentos.*'

Linguistics have always held a fascination for me, and I was quite aware that, generally speaking the disparity between Latin languages was one of differing pronunciation and endings. So I said, '*Perdu en la montaña,*' simply changing the U from a French to a Spanish sound.

The interrogating official got up, leant across the desk and without the encouragement of an audience, slapped my face halfheartedly. He let out a torrent of words of which the predominant one was '*la verdad*'. He wanted *la verdad*. *Todo la verdad* and nothing but *la verdad*. So help me God. There was now a clear understanding between us.

He grabbed a pencil and prepared to scribble.

'*¿Nombre? ¿Nacionalidad? ¿Domicilio?*'

165

I was about to turn a new leaf.

'*Alfred Bresnor, Anglais* . . .' I had broken into French.

'*Alors vous parler français*.' he remarked, breathing a sigh of relief. The interrogation was to become more coherent.

'Mother's name?'

This didn't come as a surprise to me. I knew that Spaniards carried the names of both their parents, thus giving everyone a double-barrelled appellation.

'Unknown to me.' I refused to complicate matters by having too much data to remember. Three young cops had drifted in and were standing discretely in the back of the room, very much like medical students in a teaching hospital.

'Address?'

'Rue du Lion 14, Boulogne-sur-Mer, I . . .'

'How did you . . .'

'. . . I have lived in France since my childhood.'

Buster went cross-eyed.

'Profession?' he asked.

'Waiter.'

He turned to the apprentices and, with the demeanour of a good comedian who does not laugh at his own jokes, he translated.

'*Camarero*.'

They burst into laughter at his silent bidding. They didn't believe a word I was saying. It was their job not to believe a word I was saying.

Buster's handwriting was tidy and he didn't need lined paper to write straight and precise. '*Camarero*,' he mumbled again.

'Where did you cross the border? . . . When did you leave Boulogne? . . . How did you get down south? . . .' His French was good. Mine wasn't so bad either because now he paid me a compliment. My mastery of the French language was such, he remarked, that not only was I lying about being British, but I didn't hail

166

from Boulogne either. I was a Norman, he insisted, a Norman from around Le Havre.

I'll say this for him, he knew his way around.

His French was flawless, I countered, and it hadn't stopped him from being a Spaniard, had it? That warmed his cockles and he smiled and mellowed. He had studied at the Sorbonne, he explained.

And so it went on. The session had turned quite cordial. Others, presumably Buster's departmental colleagues, came and went. They added their suspicions and offered advice, coming up with a variety of scenarios. Was I a member of a Polish flight crew downed over Bordeaux a week earlier, or one of the Canadian commandos who had escaped capture after their abortive landing in Dieppe which had taken place the month before? But their efforts remained unrewarded and the interrogation came to an inconclusive end.

Alfredo Bresnor had done his homework.

I felt elated as I was taken down to the cells. The heavy door of the windowless cubicle clanked shut and for the first time ever I was confined to an area of no more than two by three metres. Soup and bread were soon produced by a smiling policeman, and a smelly blanket shortly afterwards.

Eight-thirty p.m., Sunday the 12th of September. It was the first night since the gendarmes had come to take me away three weeks ago in Riupeyrous that I was going to sleep under cover, in the luxury of a police cell on a straw mattress and with the prospect of half a litre of hot coffee and a chunk of bread in the morning.

¡Viva España!

Neither the foul-smelling slop bucket nor the noisy card game going on across the corridor, nor the harsh light, could prevent me form from hitting the sack and falling into deep sleep. It had been a hard and satisfying day.

*

167

The black-marketeer – *estraperlista* – who joined me in my cell the next morning, told me that we were being taken to the delousing station that afternoon, before being transferred to prison.

I was looking forward to a repetition of the leisurely stroll through town, which I had enjoyed the day before, but my burly co-detainee, Señor Ruiz Blanco Rodriguez, had other plans. He didn't fancy the walk and as soon as we emerged into the street he informed the two policemen that we were taking the tram, and that he was going to be at the other end of the carriage, as you couldn't expect him to be seen in our company.

'*Claro*' was the joint response of our escorting pair in the light of the fact that 'after all, people know me around here.'

Naturalmente.

Heads shaved, delousing and disinfecting behind us, our black-marketeer, Señor Ruiz, was in no mood to go by tram and anyway, he needed a drink. The riflemen didn't have long to wait for his decision. He hailed a taxi and directed the driver through the back-streets to a bar of his choice, and all five of us trooped in, to be treated to cognac and tapas. Reinforced and invigorated, we proceeded to the *prision provincial* in prodigal style.

With protest and reluctance, the two rifles accepted Blanco's generous tip before they handed us over to our new providers. One of them – he had not spoken to me throughout the trip from HQ – put his hand on my shoulder and wished me luck.

'*Buena suerte, chico,*' he said with an air of apprehension. Then he and his companion left, banging the narrow metal-clad door designed to accept prisoners of up to eight feet in height. How they could cope with the tall guys, I have no idea.

Three and a half years after order had been restored in Franco's Spain, I found myself in a cell, four paces by five with nine *muchachos*. There is no better nor quicker way of learning Spanish than being confined within a limited space with a group of intelligent young Spaniards. Señor Blanco had been placed next door.

What were they in for?

Apart from the one pickpocket, who was soon to be perceived as an informer, they were awaiting trial or sentencing for having been soldiers in the Republican army.

They had been taken prisoner in 1937 and 1938.

In the early nineteen-thirties the ruling establishment, having conceded democracy to the people, soon found that it had been a premature move. Just as in Austria, the people had abused their recently given freedom and voted for the wrong party, the party that wanted to give a slice of the cake to the poor.

That did it. The clock was set back, and the landowners could once again sleep peacefully.

There are those who say that when you're ill you mustn't eat. You don't want to feed your disease. Starve the malady and the bugs that cause it.

We lived, on average, ten to a cell in the Cárcel de Zaragoza. These were cells originally built for single occupation; no furniture, only a toilet in the corner. Sometimes we had to squeeze to accommodate fifteen while neighbouring cells were left empty. In the morning we would roll up our blankets and there was just enough space for each to sit, leaning against the wall.

One cold morning, René the Toulousian remained prostrate when everyone else had rolled up and sat waiting for coffee – one of the three high points of the day. The other two high points were the midday soup and the evening meal. René was prodded and sworn at, but to no avail. I don't feel well, I ache all over, I've got a temperature, was his case. Nobody could argue with that. Coffee came and the man wielding the ladle was told to report one of our number sick. We were swigging the black juice, when René wanted to know where his coffee was. Sastre, the pickpocket, told him that he, René, had been reported sick.

'So, where is my coffee?' René didn't connect.

'So,' explained Sastre in good French, 'tu est aux régime. You're on a diet. When you're ill, you diet. You don't eat till the doctor sees you.'

'When will that be?' asked René with misgivings.

'The doctor normally comes on the fifth day of the illness . . . well you can't expect him to see people who are ill for only one or two days. I mean . . .'

'What if I snuff it by then?'

'Then you certainly won't need the doctor, will you?'

René, who possessed a fine sense of humour and on whom the profundity of the argument hadn't been lost, was back with the living and as right as rain before the midday meal.

That's some catch that catch 22. Joseph Heller who had turned nineteen was at that very moment at college, swotting hard to attain his doctorate. The epic of Yossarian was not due for another nineteen years.

There were three categories of prisoner: short-term, long-term and those condemned to death. The bulk were political, and either awaiting trial or sentencing, or serving their sentence. They were at the disposal of a judge or military tribunal.

The number of those awaiting execution was around a hundred and twenty. They were known as the *penados* and kept incommunicado. At intervals of three or four weeks a batch would be taken out at night. In the morning their mattresses and possessions were neatly piled up outside their cells awaiting collection by their relatives.

After two weeks in quarantine I was moved to what was known as the *governativos*. It was for short-term convicts under the authority of the police who could detain anyone for up to three months without referral to the judiciary. Periodically, they would 'sweep' the streets and pick up suspects, and detain them for any unspecified felony those suspects might be about to commit.

I was to encounter a similar reasoning in educational institutions during the years in which I acted *in loco parentis*. A group of boys behaving in a way that might lead to the conclusion that they were about to act in a manner not in keeping with accepted standards, would be caned by the deputy head for what they might conceivably be about to commit. It was known as preemptive action. 'I got there just in time', or 'I don't know what they might have done had I not stepped in when I did, and prevented them from doing it.'

I had been told that, as a rule, refugees were sent to the Campo de Miranda after about two to three weeks. And here I was, with the weeks and months passing, seeing various groups of foreigners, chiefly French, come and go and no sign of transfer for me.

Exactly three months to the day after I had been incarcerated, I was to learn the reason for the delay, as I was ushered into the presence of the visiting judge who was sitting in a darkened room. He informed me that I had been on trial for criminally attempting to inject foreign currency into the Spanish economy, that I had been found guilty and sentenced to three months confinement, that I had now served my time and was free from his jurisdiction. Back in the cell, biting my fingernails, I reflected on the efficiency of the Spanish judicial system and its high-speed procedure.

Three days later I was shipped to Miranda.

Miranda

The name Miranda evoked images of coconut palms and sandy beaches. But Miranda de Ebro was in December and it was a dump. The camp was situated next to the marshalling yard of that important rail junction between Bilbao and Burgos. It was cold and muddy and for me there was no room. Upon arrival I had been issued with two clean blankets and a linen bag which, when filled with fresh straw, answered to the Castilian term of *colchon*, which generously translated means mattress or palliasse. The corporal in the straw store bombarded me with questions, having heard that I had just arrived from Zaragoza, his home town. To his great disappointment, however, I didn't know his street nor was I able to report to him the latest gossip. He escorted me to the door like someone who had sneaked in under false pretences, and when I asked him where I was to go, he made a sweeping gesture and said: 'Go, find yourself a place. *Anda.* You have compatriots in the camp? No? Everyone has compatriots. *Paisanos.*'

Miranda was a great disappointment. I had been looking forward to this place without description; the blue yonder. Now, I couldn't even find a parking space for my mattress. I wandered from hut to hut, but whosoever

I buttonholed, told me to 'sod off, we're full up.' The less abrasive ones just shrugged their shoulders and waved me on in a multitude of languages.

Each of the brick-built huts, about twenty-five of them, was divided into forty bays on two levels. Every bay was designed to take up to four men. But over the years many of the inmates of long-standing had matured into an aristocracy and had, quite under-standably, acquired a modicum of privacy, by hanging a blanket across their compartment. In some cases several bays would have been turned into whole 'apartments' inhabited by one or two people. Visitors to those residences were directed to call 'Nok nok' – as there was no point in hammering at a dusty blanket – and wait for one of the varied responses which ranged from the 'Hey, come on in, long time no see, how's your room-mate?' effusion, to a curt invitation to 'go fuck a donkey.' Some people were quite direct.

The days of 1942 were numbered and so were the days of the invaders of Stalingrad who by now had been cut off and surrounded. The passion-play season was in full swing and for poor old Alfredo, wandering around with his scant possessions, there wasn't a square metre to put down his precious straw-filled *colchon* and claim that spot as his own.

The others who had transferred from Zaragoza at the same time as I had all found accommodation. They could have helped me, but they wanted me as far away as possible. Except perhaps young Martin. But he was nowhere to be seen. I can be an awkward cuss at times, and that is putting it mildly. And at the prison I had shown little patience for my fellow-refugees when they needed my advice and help.

We had been roused at five the morning we were to leave for Miranda. While they were handcuffing us in

173

pairs, I grabbed Martin, the guy I had befriended in the last few weeks, and pushed forward in order not to be attached to somebody else.

I said, 'Come on Martin let's get manacled together or we'll get separated.' He gave me one of his perplexed looks and pulled his hand from me. There was no hurry.

'Leggo o' me,' he said frowning, 'relax willya?'

By the time our turn came, the escorting constabulary had run out of cufflinks and time was at a premium. So off we all went in pairs with our suitcases and packs through the dark and empty streets of Zaragoza, accompanied by four rifles. Like a school outing it looked, all but Martin and I holding hands.

Martin was two years younger than I and ten years my senior in maturity. He was a refugee from Worms, a city whose Jewish community was well established when the Franks arrived in the ninth century. Anyway, that's how the story goes. I am no history teacher.

Fix this in your mind; picture this five-foot-tall Alfredo Bresnor, pitiful and dishevelled, wandering about the residences of the established bourgeoisie, mattress on his back, begging to be admitted. Mind you, I might have been more successful had I just plonked myself down in one of the bays which were manifestly underpopulated. But I was unfamiliar with customs and conventions and I was dejected and miserable.

Then this guy taps me on the shoulder. This swarthy dishevelled person who had been following me for some time, bade me to follow him, uttering one short command.

'*Ven!*'

He took me to the far end of the hut where he and three of his fellow-Bulgarians lived, and arranged for me to bed down in the cul-de-sac between the end bays. On the insistence of the alarmed residents, Leon,

174

the good Samaritan, and I, gave assurance that the arrangement was for that night only. The saintly Bulgarians gave me a glass of tea, apologizing that they had run out of lemon. They also gave me half a lump of sugar through which I sipped the tea Russian-style, as I had been taught by my Galician grandfather. Furthermore, they gave me hope in that they said that they would help me find permanent residence the next day.

Now and again, in sticky and troubled situations, there emerges someone, some unreal person such as our Bulgarian, who, although indistinguishable from the unsavoury environment of the moment, shows feeling and understanding for the distress you are in and goes out of his way to help. Sometimes the kindness consists of a few words of sympathy for your predicament or useful advice offering the benefit of their experience. At other times more generosity may be shown: lending a spoon or a pencil or a piece of soap, bending over backwards to see you settled in, taking the edge off the misery of your first few days in a strange and uninviting setting. Many, however, shrug you off after having ascertained that you have no key or prop useful to their survival.

'Nobody never done nothing for me neither!'

Prospects invariably look brighter in the morning, after the issue of the inevitable black juice, and I was found a place with an Italian who worked in the kitchen. He had been interned for some years, and his room-mate had recently been freed to forced residence in Barcelona. Mario, the Italian, was now occupying a bay all to himself and needed someone to look after his 'room' while he was at work. I fitted that brief. His job was to keep the fires under the cauldrons blazing. Some months later I was to inherit that job, together with its designation *fogonero*, when Mario was freed under the auspices of the International Red

Cross, as we were eventually all going to be released to controlled residence in the autumn and winter of 1943.

Sing a song of praise to the organizers and fundraisers and the multitude of people around the world, who gave support by dipping into their frequently all-too-shallow pockets. People who barely scratched a living, diligently contributed their hard-earned pennies to keep us from being forgotten. Praise the Jewish Assistance Committee, the Red Cross and the Quakers and all their tireless workers, whose combined efforts eventually got us released from the camp enabling us to lead a dignified existence in Madrid and Barcelona. Praise the Geneva YMCA who sent me books on demand.

I for one didn't feel the gratitude I feel today. It just didn't occur to me at the time, dealing as I did with, at best, impersonal officials of various welfare bodies. I and my fellow-refugees took it all for granted. From the day I crossed into Switzerland and had my first meal and bed, probably paid for by the Swiss authorities, to the times in Zürich and Paris and Barcelona, where I picked up my weekly allowance, I was always looked after in one way or another. I was never forgotten.

And while I'm at it, thanks to those ordinary people in war-torn France, who raised my morale by showing kindness and giving help regardless of their own hardships, offering hospitality at a time when the expedient thing to do was to keep one's doors locked and windows shuttered to all comers. Those whose efforts, in the face of indifference and hostility throughout the duration of Nazi dominance, gave me and countless others the necessary edge in our struggle for survival. The penurious miller who invited me to share the evening meal and provided a bed for the

176

night when all I had asked was permission to shelter in his hayloft, treating me with the respect due, but seldom accorded, to tramps and vagrants. Without the willingness of people such as him our hardships and perils would have been so much the greater, to say the least.

Miranda was the eighth locus of confinement in my collection of loci of confinement. Maisons-Laffitte, Athis/Orne, Mesley du Maine, Brive-la-Gaillarde, Montauban, Izeste, Zaragoza prison. It wasn't the best, it wasn't the worst, but it was interesting. Compared to Athis, Miranda had an air of seniority. Over the years it had acquired the character of a town with its trades and services: tin-smiths, carpenters, tailors, cobblers, watch-repairers, barbers and prostitutes.

Prisons and detention camps are unfair to heterosexuals.

It had its rich and its poor. There were gambling joints, protection gangs, dealers in gold and currencies and confidence-tricksters. The place was bustling with moneymaking activities; one entire hut was a trading centre. Miranda was the proverbial island whose population made a living by taking in one another's washing. As the weather improved the Moroccan section turned into a flea market. They squatted outside their quarters at the edge of the camp, buying and selling anything from rusty nails to firewood.

That winter a lot of furniture went missing; so did clogs and anything combustible. If it wasn't made of concrete, it wasn't safe. The camp management clapped a permanent guard on the entertainment hut and congratulated themselves for not losing any chairs or indeed the podium. But the final preventative measure was taken by our pragmatic camp commandant. He solvedthe problem by further vigilance and, at the same time, buying firewood in town, and redistributing it at subsidized prices, thus undercutting the dealers, and wiping out their monopoly.

It was the middle of February 1943. The remnants of the Sixth German Army had surrendered in Stalingrad and the Soviet forces were pushing west. In Miranda an entertainment committee was set up and rehearsals began for a Grand Variety Evening. The committee was rigorous in allowing only performers and helpers into the hut and kept a steady eye on inventory and the good state of repair of the place. The programme was kept under wraps, to be revealed only on the opening night, the third Sunday in March, on which the camp commandant and Vee Eye Peese were to be invited.

Throughout the ensuing weeks, the place resembled a beehive. Tools, timber and paint had been elicited and props and decorations were made.

Three days before the big night, one of the soldiers on duty outside the entertainment building scratched his head. Ever since two o'clock that afternoon, he had seen people entering the hut but none were coming out. He scratched some more. In the hut it was quiet.

Now his companion began scratching.

'¿Que pasa?' he enquired. 'Lots of people go in. No one come out.' They went to investigate but the door was locked from the inside. The windows had been decorated with pictures and ornaments, heightening the anticipation and obstructing the view.

They sent for the corporal who, not being able to insert his key, improvised by opening the door with his right boot. There was nobody on the premises. It didn't take the soldiers long to discover thirty-five performers

178

and their attendants in the almost-completed tunnel under the stage.

Escape attempts occurred regularly. They were characterized by their halfheartedness in that most of them were mere exercises in panache. The would-be escapees were marched off to the *calabozo* and confined for one or two weeks. It was looked on as a big joke.

The most memorable escape was that of a young American from Lima or La Paz, who had secretly tailored a military uniform and apparently walked out of the camp one sunny day, dressed up as a lieutenant, without batting an eyelid. He was saluted at the gate and was never seen again.

The camp virtually ran itself. Whatever authority there was remained minimal and unobtrusive and found expression through the hut leaders.

The food was adequate and the housing passable as camps go. But the hygiene was lousy, and when I say lousy, I mean the place was crawling with lice and bedbugs. However, the medical services were good and there were no serious outbreaks of disease. The camp management did their best, fighting a constant battle, forever fumigating and dusting to keep pests down.

There was a shower room but no one but a few health freaks used the facility since there was no hot water. During the winter we hardly ever washed. A friend of mine, a brilliant young mathematician from the ghetto of Prague was wearing an overcoat with a safety pin that kept his collar tight around his neck. That safety pin remained untouched for the remainder of the cold season. But he removed his shoes regularly every night, before bedding down.

There is a Viennese saying: you can drown in water but dirt will never kill. That was borne out by the fact that there were no casualties as a result of slack hygienic standards.

There was camaraderie and disharmony, friendliness and violence and manifestations of generosity. There was arrogance, unassuming kindness and indifference.

I was the only 'Englishman' in the camp. But the idea of changing one's identity turned out not to have been an original one. And it also proved to have been an unnecessary precaution, for this reason: Franco's Spain turned nobody away. To the best of my knowledge, no fugitive was handed over to the Germans or to Vichy France, regardless of creed or nationality.

In the summer of 1943, the first German army deserters began trickling in. That summer the camp held approximately two thousand Frenchmen and eight hundred Poles, the two biggest contingents. The rest – about five hundred – were Belgians, Dutch, Yugoslavs, Czechs and Central European Jews. In addition, there were about fifty Americans, mainly from Argentina and Mexico, but some from Bolivia, Costa Rica and Cuba.

Many of the French, the Poles and the Belgians, had registered as Canadians. A smattering of French even with a Polish accent was sufficient reason for some people to use that ploy. For internal administrative reasons these formed six groups. Those that had declared their true identity and those that hadn't, so that a meeting might be called to discuss the interests of the *Belges-Belges* or the *Belges-Canadiens* or the *Polonais-Canadiens* or the *Français-Français*. One group that was not present at Miranda were real Canadians. *Canadiens-Canadiens*.

The Poles were part of what was known as General Anders Army, which had joined the French in order to continue fighting the Germans. They were mostly soldiers who had fled to France via Romania and Yugoslavia. They had found themselves once again on the losing side. Politically right-wing, they were greatly perturbed by the successes of the Red Army in the summer of 1943.

Most people lived within their grouping. Spanish was the lingua franca with French a close second.

Lyons

While I was frolicking in Miranda, my poor old mother was having a tough time back in France. She told me, years later, how on Felix's instigation she had left Riupeyrous and gone to Lyons. Felix had finally made it to Switzerland and had judged that the path across the border was such that she could make it with the toddler.

After Felix had been arrested he had been transferred to Rivesaltes, a camp at the Mediterranean end of the Pyrenees, French Catalonia. Both these camps had been built several years earlier for the influx of refugees spilling over the mountains as a result of the Spanish ruling establishment having decided that the people were not yet ready for democracy. (Freedom and democracy are for those who are responsible and capable of self-restraint and reliable in their voting pattern. Don't take my word for it, ask any politician.)

In mid-November Felix with his inborn agility had escaped from the camp and made his way via the Col de Balme into French-speaking Valais in Switzerland, where he was promptly caught and interned. Not too pleasant a fate even in Switzerland, but a relatively safe place to be in those days. Relative that is, with an inbuilt uncertainty factor. With the whole of France now occupied, Switzerland was completely surrounded by German and Italian forces and was making submissive noises.

On Thursday the 14th of January 1943, Mother was getting ready for bed in the little room in the rue Saint Bernard where she was spending her first nights in Lyons. 'Room' was an exaggeration. It was a space with four walls and a window looking out on an obscure air well. It had a narrow bed and a chair and just enough floor-space for her to manoeuvre into her night-clothes.

There she sat on the iron bed, dazed and dumbfounded, trying to come to terms with and adjusting to the events of the past few days and weeks. She was taking stock, trying to gather her thoughts; thoughts and images which were floating incoherently through her mind.

Felix had written, urging her to go to Lyons, intimating that he was going to help them cross into Switzerland. However, by the time she and twenty-month-old Monique had arrived, an early winter, too advanced for the attempt, had them abandon the project. So here they were, stuck in deepest Barbie country.

With what was left of her savings she obtained false papers, giving her birthplace as Strasbourg. Arrangements had to be made to place Monique so that they could get on with the business of surviving. Separated, they both stood a better chance of pulling through.

Despite the trauma of the last few months, culminating in this afternoon's events, she had to examine her options clearly and think about finding some kind of a job.

That afternoon an official of the support committee in the rue Catherine, that was placing Jewish children in safe locations, had taken away little Monique. It was a clandestine occasion which took place in the rue d'Auberge were she had been told to meet the agent. A tall lady came up to her and muttered a prearranged code. Without further ado she took the child, turned on her heels and left. Mother caught up with her near the bridge and whimpered, 'Where is she going? When can I visit her?' The woman, no doubt scared out of her wits, hissed at her to go away. Enquire with the committee in fourteen days, she added as she disappeared with the infant.

What was going to happen to Monique? How long would the separation last? Would they ever be reunited? It was the policy of the committee not to allow access nor to reveal the whereabouts of children placed, as this would not only endanger the lives of the children and the foster parents but would put the whole operation in jeopardy. All she had was the assurance that she would be informed of Monique's progress periodically. In between, she was to stay away and not bother them as their workload was overwhelming and they were operating in a dangerous climate.

Mother has never been a very religious person. At the age of twelve I asked her if she believed in God. Her reply was: '*Das werde ich dir nicht auf die Nase binden.*' It was a frivolous refusal to confide. Sitting there, on that thing that passed for a bed, she found herself *Krishma Lainen*, reciting the evening prayers. When she had finished, she quietly proposed a deal. 'Save my children,' she pleaded, 'and henceforth I will render all the worship due to you, regularly. You needn't spare me if I have proved undeserving, but please save my children.'

The conversation with the one at whom the prayers were directed would have gone something like this:

184

Mother:	*I know I have sinned. I haven't said my prayers with regularity. I fed boiled ham to my Lizzi and Fred. But pig-breeding has come a long way since the days of Sinai.*
Gott:	*That is not for you to assess. You must leave the interpretation of the law to the rabbi.*
Mother:	*Forgive me. I only ask of you one thing. Save my children. Lizzi is in England exposed to German bombing. Fred . . . I don't know where he is. He went towards the border. Has he succeeded in crossing? I don't know. Has he been caught? I don't know. Is he well? Has he got enough to eat? Is he tucked in at nights and warm? I have no way of knowing. And the baby? Will I ever see her again? Save them. I will light candles on Friday night and say my prayers morning and evening regularly, I will go to the synagogue when the opportunity returns. Punish me if you must, but save my children.*
Gott:	*How do I know you are not just saying this? You have disobeyed my commands before. How do I know I can believe you?*
Mother:	*(With urgency) Trust me!*
Gott:	*I'll see what I can do.*

Gott delivered and, true to form, Mother never went back on her word. She lived to the age of eighty-eight, seeing her children and grandchildren and great grandchildren grow and prosper. And she was thankful and she praised the Lord.

Mother went to enquire with the people in the rue Catherine three days after it had been raided by the Gestapo and missed being arrested by a whisker. Barbie's police remained for several days lying in wait for further visitors. She noticed at the last moment that the *Mezuzah* had been removed from the doorpost, leaving a blank patch. She managed to walk past the place calmly and without showing emotion. All the staff and visitors had been arrested and were never seen again.

Mother had been through very hard times in her life. But during those two years, September 1942 up to liberation in 1944, she had to cope with hardship and torment all on her own and with no shoulder to cry on.

Unassuming, petite, self-effacing . . . Mother never let on what she knew or what she was capable of. Accommodating and friendly, she presented a deceptive appearance of helplessness and simple-mindedness. She was born in the Hernals district of Vienna on the 14th of July 1894, 105 years after the people of Paris liberated the prisoners at the central gaol. Mother was proud to have been born on Bastille Day, although she never showed any political consciousness.

She, her brother and sisters had displayed pride in having been brought up in a progressive, liberal and liberated middle-class climate. Theirs was a shallow kind of 'modern' culture, barely emancipated from the Pale and its eastern mores. Her mother had come to Vienna as a young woman from her native Lemberg (Lvov), the capital of Galicia. Listening to Verdi's *Aida* on her squeaky crystal set was to my grandmother the height of cultural experience. My grandparents were denied a dignified conclusion to their few remaining years by the forces of depravity.

What saved my good mother, I don't know. If she had guile and cunning, she never showed it. She was modest and tough and stood four feet nine inches. She had endurance and she was a hard worker, never shying from the most menial of chores. But above all she could laugh. My guess is, whatever it was that gave her the edge over events, whatever cunning and instinct and intuition she possessed, she wasn't aware of it. Courage? This term has been corrupted over the years to such an extent as to render it shapeless and inadequate.

In the weeks following the liberation of France, Monique was located and reunited with Mother. It had been an untypical happy ending. In 1945 Mother, now in her fifty-second year, moved to London where she worked hard as a home help, saving enough money to buy her own home ten years later. These were the years that saw Monique through primary and secondary education and into a career in office work. She married Len, a bright young craftsman, saw her son and daughter through university and is today on the threshold of becoming a grandmother.

Haifa

Through no fault of her own, Barcelona was bugging me. There, two ex-Miranda inmates and I were passing the days walking the *ramblas* and *avenidas* in our Sunday best; gabardine neatly folded over forearm. We walked with dignified idleness, eyeing the female passers-by in critical appraisal. And we walked in measured paces so as not to hit the Plaza de Cataluña before midday. In the evening we treated ourselves to an imported film and a bag of dried figs from the street stall. Once every week we collected our quite adequate allowance as well as our sparse mail from the Hotel Bristol, where the two brothers Sequera – Portuguese businessmen – were in charge of distribution.

Round and round the *ramblas* we roamed, until one day I got dizzy and went and put my name down for a place on the steamer to Palestine. My two Miranda mates came along to see me off as I boarded the train to Cadiz.

Here in Cadiz, Spain's major port on the Atlantic coast, a few hundred mid-European refugees were waiting for the Portuguese passenger liner *Nyassa*. It had been chartered by the Red Cross for ferrying the lucky ones among the refugees to the USA and this was its first journey picking up would-be immigrants to the Holy Land.

Cadiz had been the first Phoenician post outside the Mediterranean Sea. Its history winds through the inescapable interludes of Carthaginian, Greek, Roman, Muslim and Christian dominance. After Christianity's recapture of Spain, Cadiz flourished as the supply port for Queen Isabella's expanding and unremitting genocide.

In 1936, Cadiz served as the springboard from which militant Christianity was once again reintroduced into Spain with the help of Franco's Islamic troops and Foreign Legionaires.

Our group of youngsters whiled away the days before sailing, admiring the Murillos at the local museum and, when it didn't rain, would go to the beach and gaze into the distance. In the evenings we sat around in brothels, assuming the role of men of the world.

The sun was setting in the Atlantic Ocean as we steamed into the Mediterranean Sea, and I had nobody to share the thrill of seeing for the first time, in the flesh, the familiar landmark to our left. The town at the base of the domineering rock was bathed in the last rays of sunlight, while in Algeciras on the opposite side of the bay the lights were coming on, one by one. It was an uneventful journey, some sea-sickness, two fist-fights, two robberies, two weddings. Apprehensively, on the fourth night, hugging the friendly seaboard of the Libyan desert, our boat slid past German-held Crete.

It was Sunday, January 2nd, and for the first time since 1933 I was about to enter a country through its front door, so to speak, courtesy of the occupying power. We were offered oranges as we disembarked and three hours later we found ourselves, once again, behind barbed wire. Young English soldiers had guided us to the waiting buses and taken us to the camp at Atlit, south of Haifa. It was a reception and processing centre and was swarming with recruiting agents from various kibbutzim, as well as functionaries of political parties and religious organizations. They outnumbered the officials of the Palestine government, who were mostly Jewish. We were given food, lectures and a straw mattress.

For the next three days while the paperwork was being processed and the medical examinations performed, we were addressed by rabbis and professors and representatives from all imaginable 'acceptable' Jewish political persuasions, who furnished us with historical facts and moral justifications. All possible conscientious scruples concerning our exclusive right to this land were dealt with.

Almost nineteen hundred years ago our temple had been destroyed by the soldiers of Rome. Life had been getting unbearable and with a heavy heart we had decided to depart, and join our cousins whose ancestors had left for the bright lights and settled in Alexandria and Rome, and the far corners of the Empire. By that time two-thirds of the children of Israel were living in places as far apart as Ephesus, Saloniki, Kerch, the Rhineland and beyond. There was also a large thriving community in Babylon, the descendants of those who had decided to stay on when they had been given the option to return.

The expatriates enriched their way of life and their stock with Greek, Roman and Assyrian culture and blood. They had founded thriving Jewish centres but had never forgotten their origins and never missed the annual pledge at the Passover table of, 'Next year in Jerusalem.'

The British (Brit Ish – men of the covenant) had entered the fray in 1917 when Allenby drove the Turks out of

Jerusalem. In the carve-up of the Ottoman Empire they placed Iraq and Arabia under their protective mantle, thus spreading further pink areas over the Mercator projection. And once again the Kurds had been deprived of the right to manage their own affairs in their own country.

In February 1917, the British Foreign Secretary, Balfour had written to Lord Rothschild conveying that, 'His Majesty's government view with favour the establishment in Palestine of a national home for the Jewish people . . .' But a love-hate relationship evolved with the British. On the one hand Balfour's declaration had 'legalized' the Zionist dream; on the other hand the proviso had been added, ' . . . it being clearly understood that nothing shall be done to prejudice the civil and religious rights of the existing non-Jewish communities in Palestine.' Nothing comes easy.

Then in 1922 the League of Nations appealed to Britain to use its colonial expertise and experience to adopt Palestine and Transjordan as 'mandated' territories.

White man's burden!

I was drifting once again.

I had joined the kibbutz for no other reason than having taken a liking to the guy who came to Atlit recruiting for the left-wing kibbutz movement.

It had happened before and was going to occur again. In my weakness, like a climbing vine, I would deceive myself into believing that I could expand and grow in the shade, or with the support of a 'guru'.

In Vienna I had drifted in and out of various political movements for similar reasons, even joining the Betar, the youth movement of the revisionist party. These right-wing Zionists, led by Vladimir

Jabotinsky, campaigned not only for the whole of Palestine to become the Jewish state but Transjordan as well. We sang fiery and rousing militaristic songs and wore British-style uniforms.

Austria in the mid-1930s, a totalitarian one-party state, tolerated, as did Nazi Germany, the activities of the Zionist parties. These held elections periodically and openly propagated their respective messages. The walls of Vienna, where democracy was denied to the population at large, were plastered with posters and slogans for Zionist candidates of every political hue, from left to extreme right.

As a member of Betar I had to help out at polling stations, distributing leaflets extolling right-wing Zionism. A few months later as a member of the left-wing Hashomer Hazair – The Young Guard – I pushed propaganda through Jewish letterboxes pointing out the advantages of Zionist Socialism.

The kibbutz He'amal (Labour or Effort) was affiliated to the left-wing socialist party, Mapam. In common with all Jewish political parties and splinter groups, Mapam didn't accept Palestinians as members, although its manifesto called for a dual national state with equal rights. We had ethnic separation years before the Dutch term 'apartheid' had been formulated. Even the communists who were the only party opposed to racialism and not affiliated to the Zionist Congress, were in a dilemma. They had split into two parties, on racial lines, due to some difference of application of dialectic materialism during the Arab rebellion in the 1930s.

Since no abode was available for the group when they founded the kibbutz, they squatted on council land, which had been reserved for an avenue to the beach in Kiriat Motzkin, on the Bay of Akko. There they had put up sheds for living accommodation, a laundry, kitchen and workshops. They farmed some of its people out, to the nearby brick factory, and the local bakery. Both enterprises belonged to the Histadrut, the biggest entrepreneur and employer in the country. It owned quarries, engaged in building and civil engineering and contracted projects in the Iranian oil fields in Abadan. The Histadrut is the all-embracing Jewish trade union. Non-Jews were excluded. As far as I know it was the only racially selective labour federation outside South Africa.

Shortly before I arrived, a few hundred acres had been allotted to the kibbutz at the southernmost extremity of Jewish expansion. Ruhama is situated twenty kilometres east of Gaza. A situation arose, not long after we had begun the gradual process of moving there, when we were desperately short-handed and needed people to help with the grain harvest – wheat had been sown by our advance group. What to do? The matter was placed on the agenda of an emergency meeting and after beating about the bush for a very short time the proposal was made to employ local villagers. Just this once. Zahavah the theoretician went up in flames. She tried to block the discussion by stating that the issue was not debatable because of the fundamental principles involved. How could a socialist institution . . . ? Further, how could we square it with our love for our own people at a time of widespread Jewish unemployment?

However, as so often happens in situations when restrictive idealistic scruples arise, the pragmatists carried the day. Simha, with his usual outburst of reverberating horse-sense, reminded us of the many citrus groves burned down during the period when the Arabs vented their opposition to the ever-increasing immigration of Europeans into their country. Laughing, he added: 'Give them now the opportunity to redeem themselves. That's all I'm asking. Only for this season.'

Ten days later, the socialist co-operative subscribing to the creed that he who works must reap the benefits, not only had turned exploiter, but had a strike on its hands. The Palestinians we had recruited had seen the urgency and the central part they were playing and asked for more money, as greedy workers around the world are in the habit of doing. They had us over a barrel and we had to accede to their blackmail. From then on, they worked happily through the season, having forced a rise from the original 20 per cent to nearly 35 per cent of the going rate for Jewish workers.

I am walking to Dorot along the wadi. Dorot is a neighbouring kibbutz of two years' standing. It is of another political nuance. Also socialist but more to the centre, affiliated to Ben-Gurion's party. Ben-Gurion was national first and socialist second. But then, nationalism transcends party politics.

The sun stands at midday from ten in the morning till four in the afternoon every day from April to October and it would be banal in the extreme to state that it is a hot day. A fig tree catches my attention and, as I approach in order to partake of its fruit, I notice the enemy in the shape of a young villager sitting under it, dozing. I dart sideways rather quickly, pretending not to have noticed him. After two or three urgent paces, I hear him call. He smiles and offers me a bunch of grapes, a luxury I haven't tasted for a long time.

Back home, at the dinner-table, I am told not to be fooled by appearances.

'When they are friendly, that only proves their duplicity,' says Simha, looking at me with tolerance and despair. 'Their friendliness merely reinforces our need for vigilance and

preparedness. They'll stab you when your back is turned.'
He reports cheerfully how he gave one of the youngsters
from the neighbouring village a hefty hiding with the boy's
own stick.

'Whatever for?' asks Rouga with alarm.

'That will teach the mamserim, to leave our trees alone.'

Our advance party had planted eucalyptus saplings the
previous year and now they are twelve to fifteen feet tall.
The Australian eucalyptus, the tallest of all deciduous trees,
was introduced into Palestine around the turn of the cen-
tury and has adapted well to the climate and to the sandy
soil.

Where had he cut it from . . . which tree? Rouga shows
concern. She is one of those who had nursed the trees to see
them through their initial difficulties.

Simha hasn't seen any damaged trees. At least not yet.

'You are assuming that the boy cut the stick from our tree,
yet you have no proof. Did he admit it?'

'Of course he didn't. Do they ever? Are there any trees
around here, other than ours?'

Simple justice. Proof by elimination.

Rouga was at the time still able to cope with the demands racial hostility made on her sense of justice, by
a process of self-deception and suppression. She was
to leave the kibbutz two years later, become an active
member of the Communist Party and be killed in a
skirmish in 1948 at Bab El Wad as a result of the troubles following the decision of the United Nations to
partition Palestine.

'Just because they were born in this country, doesn't
give them the right to citizenship in a future Jewish
state,' Simha would argue. 'If we treated them as
fellow-humans . . . I agree, that would be nice . . . nice
but not at all practical, because then they're bound to
like it here and they'll never go away.'

'Why should they go away?' would be the usual query. Here Simha, true to form, would reply with a question forcing the opponent into the open, and compelling that self-same opponent to commit themselves to a firm position on the spur of the moment.

'Tell me this Mr Know-all – or Mrs Know-all – aren't we already sufficiently overcrowded? What will happen if all the Jews want to come here? Hey? Will you be the one to turn them away? Your own blood? Answer me that! We will need room in years to come. Nothing to be ashamed of. We must have all of Palestine.'

'And why not Transjordan and maybe Damascus?'

'That is a long way away,' Simha would argue matter-of-factly. 'You needn't concern yourself.'

Simha was ahead of his time. He was a visionary. Long before the Jewish state came into being, he could conceive of future attitudes and requirements. The last I heard of him was that he had emigrated to the United States and was running a fashionable restaurant in downtown Baltimore.

It was now mid-November 1944. The Allies had been advancing on all fronts for most of the year. The second front had been established in the summer and had fanned out from the beaches of Normandy to northern France and Belgium. In a few weeks the Germans were going to put all their efforts into one big push. Exploiting a weakness in the configuration of the western armies in the Ardennes, they were to achieve a limited and costly success – the Battle of the Bulge. But this was the time when the war had moved irrevocably on to German soil. In the Pacific the Japanese had been forced to give up most of their conquests, island by island.

In the last two years the bulk of European Jews and Gypsies as well as millions of other European noncombatants had been systematically murdered at the hand

196

of the Nazis. And millions of innocent civilians had died and were yet to die in the bombing raids perpetrated by the US and British air forces.

I had been in the kibbutz for almost a year, and was being pressed as to why I hadn't formally applied for membership. However, the enthusiasm of these people, their purpose and motivation hadn't infected me. My inherent restlessness had not been eased. I have never been good at getting on with people and had struck up too few friendships to sustain me. I also missed the smell of steel and of cutting-oils in the machine shop. I missed the bright lights and ice-cream parlours and the solidity of asphalt under my feet. I missed the cold, impersonal and submerging embrace of the city.

After much heart-searching I left with few regrets. I moved to Jerusalem where, free of all constraints and in need of a spiritual home, I went in search of the Communist Party. Politically and ideologically, I was illiterate. I was naive and full of zeal and resentment. That was the mixture it took in Stalin's days to be able to participate in the dialectical somersaults and still retain an outward appearance of normality.

I finally found all three members of the Jerusalem section at the Café Sichel where I was promptly relieved of ten piastres by way of donation to the fund for the 'Voice of the People'. They had reverted to calling themselves the Communist Party, having preferred for some time the alliance-inspiring, appellation of Anti-fa.

I was in need of a political orientation that would satisfy my social-injustice-motivated anger. And once again it was the personalities I encountered which captivated me.

197

Jerusalem

'Beware my son, beware of those who come in peace,
bearing a mission.'

Kvadratnikoff, A.F. Pliushkin

'Shalom Baruch.'

*Deborah waves wildly and crosses King George Street to
intercept me. 'Where have you been hiding? You didn't turn
up at the trade union meeting last Wednesday.' Looking at
me reproachfully, she tilts her pretty head and declares
unsmilingly: 'You are drifting. When people don't turn up
at meetings, you know . . . they begin to lose interest and
the next thing, you know . . . they drift away . . . from the
Party . . .'*

*She is stating the obvious, gesticulating wildly. Surely,
if one's attendance declines, then one is drifting. Away or
otherwise. Inadvertently, she betrays a lack of faith in the
dogma, admitting that it needed constant ideological re-
charging and topping up. I have been retreating, gradually
losing faith in the creed, but haven't yet had the courage to
formulate the truth for myself let alone admit it to them.*

*I protest my innocence. Of course I am not drifting away.
Me drift? Whatever gives her that idea? It's just that I have
been busy studying and things.*

'You know how it is.'

*She looks at me coldly with her angelic eyes. Yes, she
knows how it is. Her mollience overwhelms me. She proffers
an open palm.*

'You owe thirty-five piastres,' she says sternly in her

capacity of treasurer. I was still on the 'periphery', a long way from 'candidature' for membership but there was no discrimination in the payment of dues.

Handing over my contribution provides relief for my guilt feelings.

'You doing anything tonight, Deborah?'

'Meeting in Tel Aviv,' she asserts curtly, advancing no alternative.

'OK. Shalom then,' I utter dejectedly, moving on.

From the other side of the road she calls, 'Ring me at the office.' The bitch! – Only because I hadn't persisted. I decide not to call. Three days later, she phones me.

'How about Thursday night?' she enquires.

Know what I mean?

I swear by the Almighty that I am not now and never have been a member of the Communist Party.

Worse!

I have always been a nonconformist, an enquirer, a rebel, questioning all structures of reference. One who scrutinizes and agonizes, one who probes, explores. One who takes nothing for granted, a sceptic and a brooder. I have gone through bouts of adherence to ideologies and political groupings but invariably it brought me out in a rash and I was eventually spat out by the movement of the hour, as unclean and as a contaminant. Nevertheless, I followed the party line for a while, feeding unexamined assumptions to people who weren't listening and to friends who were bored or amused.

But there was no room in the Communist Party for independent thinkers. Nor was objectivity tolerated.

'How can anyone afford to be objective while there is a bloody class struggle going on? Answer me that!'

These sons and daughters of the revolution had been drained of the last fluid ounce of radicalism; that radicalism and dissenting spirit which had brought them to the Party in the first place. As had been the case in my childhood, once again I was told what to believe, what or whom to worship, how to think and in what light to see and interpret events. Stalin had rid the party of radicals and idealists, not only in the Soviet Union but in every communist party around the world. And here was I, forever testing and probing. Why were Kierkegaard's and Heidegger's writings to be rejected, but not those of Sartre? Why, if cubism and surrealism were reactionary, was Picasso given the red-carpet treatment? Why? Why did Soviet diplomats dress in 'respectable' Western bourgeois grab? Why did Molotov wear a necktie? Was Stalin really a super saint? Wasn't his indulgence in inhaling nicotine a decadent bourgeois weakness? Was October 1917 the end of History?

To give credit to the communists, it was they who introduced me to what were to become my favourite writers, composers and painters. They ejaculated with venom names such as Franz Kafka and James Joyce, Béla Bartok and Alexandr Scriabin, Giorgio de Chirico, Edward Hopper, Marino Marini . . . accusing them of diverting the working classes from the revolutionary struggle. Such strictures awakened my interest. They wetted my appetite and assisted in the furtherance of my education.

My revolutionary conformism, or rather, my conformist revolutionary zeal was wearing thin. I drifted from the Party, not so much disillusioned, more uninspired and perplexed. Once again I had to painfully sever the umbilical cord. The Communist Party was not for the likes of me: radicals and rebels. Definitely no place for revolutionaries.

One element that hastened my separation was the *New Statesman and Nation*. It was edited by Kingsley Martin – the most underrated journalist of the post-war years – and practised tolerance and moderation. One day at a friend's house I had occasion to take a closer look at it and a new world opened up. For eleven years I never missed a week reading it. Through it, gradually, I became obsessively moderate.

Now and again party members and sympathizers who originated from Eastern Europe returned to their respective countries of origin behind the Iron Curtain. This was never encouraged by the Party as people were needed in Palestine where the struggle continued. Still, we gave them a hero's farewell and wished them Godspeed. They were never heard of again. What was left of them were rumours, claiming that they were alive and well and under arrest. But these things were never discussed openly.

Here in the Party there were an equal number of diehard fanatics and intellectuals. But the liberals and intellectuals felt guilty because of their academic background and made up for it by shutting their eyes and reasoning powers to the persistent reports emanating from the Soviet Union; the terror perpetrated against the people together with the personality cult of number one.

All ye who enter these premises, kindly leave your doubts and reservations on the hat rack by the door, and show your gratitude for their disposal by donating one week's wages.

Slackening fellow-travellers such as I would sometimes be singled out, taken aside and given whispered conspiratorial instructions. It was more often than not a dummy run, but it served to build up our confidence and pride. Eagerly, we retrieved the missile, dropped it at the feet of our masters and, wagging our tails, asked for more.

Sympathizers would come to our open Friday-night meetings meekly voicing their soft reservations, careful not to be too persistent. Others, sincere, level-headed searchers coming with an open mind, were less considerate and not satisfied with the tactics of our boys who constantly shifted the goalposts. They pressed their point more energetically, causing embarrassment until they were accused of being agents of the British intelligence service, Trotskyite warmongers, Truman's lackeys, saboteurs of democracy and progress. The posers of embarrassing questions were reviled from the chair and finished up being booted out of the meeting.

The practice of discrediting opponents, rather than countering their line of argument and reasoning or challenging their facts and conclusions, is not unique to Stalinists. It is universal with fanatics and extremists of all political movements and creeds.

There follows a short interval during which a list of picturesque terms used by extremists and chauvinists and all those hard of thinking, will be flashed across the screen:

Fascists, Nigger-lovers, Zionists, Lackeys of United States Imperialism, Bleeding Hearts, Liberals, Puddenheads, Jew-lovers, Anti-Semites, Intellectuals, Communist Stooges, Pacifists, Papists, Women's Libbers, Male Chauvinist Pigs, Servants of Satan, Wankers and Do-gooders.

The infatuation lasted one long summer. But throughout I had felt hemmed in. My incapacity for disciplined thinking had caught up with me and I had become subjected to wagging fingers and well-meaning arms around my shoulders. I was drawn aside and told what a good man I was and how much I could contribute, if only I would guard against outside influences.

I never graduated from the fringe area of 'peripheral supporters', and my break with the Party was gradual and painful. I was aware of having failed and having let my friends down.

Jerusalem was a magnet for prophets and visionaries and mystics. They were a familiar sight and were respected and left alone. There was the young man who spoke on street corners and emitted what to us sounded like gibberish interspersed with numbers. He carried a piece of string which was knotted in a 'significant' way. He scared the living daylights out of some people. Not me. I laughed at him. I passed him one day and as I aped and gesticulated I collided with a lamp-post that had materialized out of nowhere.

Another youngster would wave his arms, making signs reminiscent of semaphore and at times remaining motionless for minutes. One rainy day, I saw him in the middle of the road waving a bright red ping-pong bat and directing traffic into a cul-de-sac. A lot of hooting and shouting could be heard that afternoon coming from the area of the Russian church. These people were known by names that characterized their particular slant. One such was 'Kesher le Akhad'. Walking down Jaffa Street and up Ben Yehuda in her heavy German accent, distributing leaflets. She proclaimed the 'Link with the One'. Frustrated on account of the meagre response she was receiving, she readily insulted people, castigating them for their stupidity. One day during a downpour this lady, with pointed features reminiscent of Rosa Luxemburg, turned up in the entrance to an apartment block where I had sought refuge. She addressed me in German and we struck up a conversation of sorts. Why was I not getting married, she asked. How did she know?

'Oh, I keep my eyes open,' she said. She always saw me in the company of a group of diehard bachelors.

She went on to tell me about Biarritz where she had lived in her youth and about the area around Pau. Sitting on the steps that day talking to me was a different person from the one I knew. Her harsh features softened, she spoke calmly and lucidly, with none of the histrionics and fervour she was known for. Removed from the compelling demands that the urgency of her mission placed upon her, she seemed relaxed. But almost in mid-sentence she stopped chatting. The rain abated, she had to return to the fray, spreading the word. The next time our paths crossed, she refused to acknowledge my glance of recognition, and I left it at that.

During the first few days in Haifa, I had become aware of the enormous social imbalance and injustice which existed among the Palestinian population. A small boy dressed in rags protested at the inadequate remuneration handed to him for carrying a burly middle-aged man's bags to the bus stop. The urchin, tearing at the man's sleeve, was slapped across the face. Tenaciously the boy insisted; howling and deploring he followed his client on to the bus, only to be thrown off by the driver. Scenes such as this were not uncommon. But I also encountered moving gestures of compassion. A group of well-dressed young Arabs, presumably on their way home from a night out, passed one of the many homeless waifs asleep in a doorway. They stopped and commiserated and, without waking the boy, stuffed some money into the folds of his rags. Admittedly, it was a mere gesture, but it was spontaneous and genuine. 'W'Allah kharam!' was the phrase expressing their pangs of conscience. On the other hand these same people would have fought tooth and nail to retain their privileges.

I saw a man reading to a group, presumably

illiterates. They were sitting around him at lunch-times, listening attentively as he held a book in one hand and gesticulated with the other, emphasizing the high points. He was well-dressed, sporting a fez. It was an informal group and the man displayed no sign of self-importance. They, the listeners, the recipients, were country boys, *fallaheen*, hungry for knowledge. They had come to work in the city, sleeping in doorways.

Education was for the wealthy, unless you could find a place in a convent school or other voluntary institution. But even then your family had to be sufficiently 'well off' to be able to spare you from the task of helping in the struggle for survival. Most youngsters were called upon to help, tending the terraces or, if they lived in town, they would sell papers hot from the presses, work as shoeshine boys or vegetable porters. So far as girls were concerned, they didn't need an education. In many cases, a woman who displayed a minimal form of erudition, or showed interest in matters other than housework and tilling and child rearing would have been looked upon as a slut. Come to think of it, the most liberated women were the prostitutes. Unlike their sisters in France, they worked for themselves.

We looked upon this state of affairs with the satisfaction of the virtuous and righteous, observing how it was the women who tended the gardens and who, at the crack of dawn, would clamber the steep paths from the valley with huge baskets of produce on their heads. It was the women who raised the children, did the cooking and cleaning and laundering, who often were engaged in some form of craft such as spinning and weaving. Admittedly, men were also seen working in their small fields and terraces but they were also seen in the coffee establishments, out of bounds to their spouses.

The Jews came from a variety of ethnic groupings. The Ashkenazim, broadly speaking the mid- and East Europeans, constituted not only the biggest group but also the élite, the civil service and the political leadership. The Sephardim were the descendants of those who had been expelled from Spain at the end of the fifteenth century. At the bottom of the social scale were the various Asian and African groups, the Yemenites, the Kurds, the Iraqis, the Bukhara, the Persians, the Syrians, Jews from Bombay, and a sizeable North African contingent, mainly Moroccans.

All had their own language, mores and culture. They lived in segregated quarters further subdivided into regions and families. They prayed in their own synagogues and intermarriage was frowned on.

For the non-Ashkenazim there was a common epithet. They were known as Frenks or Shvartse and sometimes more kindly as Levantines or even Orientals although Casablanca is further to the west than the place of origin of the Ashkenazim.

It was these 'ethnic' Jews who provided the road-sweepers and building labourers, and the lower echelons of the police force. It was their children who were darting up and down the Jewish streets at five in the afternoon, selling the first edition of the evening papers, papers many of them would never learn to read. Illiteracy among the eastern Jews was as wide-spread as among the Arabs and their women were subjected to treatment comparable to their Arab sisters.

Mum:	*Where are you going, my son?*
Son:	*I'm going out to play.*
Mum:	*Not in the street you don't. Not with those Frenks you don't. I forbid . . .*
Son:	*Oh Mum! Why not Mum? Moshe lets me take his dog walkies, and he teaches me lots of tricks.*

Mum: Go and play with young Zalman from Manoon house. He is a well-behaved boy. He never plays in the street and his father is a highly respected shokhet.

Old City

And after Abimelech there arose to defend Israel, Tola the son of Puah, the son of Dodo.

(*Judges* 10: 1)

As a metalworker, adept with hammer and chisel, file and hacksaw, scraper and abrasives, it never took me long to find employment even in times when jobs were few and far between as they were in Palestine in the winter of 1944. The great employer of local industry, the Eighth Army, had moved ever further west and, when the Germans were finally pushed out of North Africa, Palestine as a supply and staging post had lost its importance.

When in the summer of 1942 the Germans had reached El Alamein, poised at the gates of Alexandria, and threatened the Suez Canal and the oil-soaked region beyond, there was apprehension among the Jews and business was booming and employment was abundant. As the German threat receded, however, there was rejoicing and trade stagnated and jobs were less easy to find. War, the great provider for many, had now moved to Italy where it provided hunger for the population, and prosperity for organized crime. Organized crime had assisted the US forces in the Sicilian campaign in return for concessions from which the people of the United States and Italy have yet to recover. The extending tentacles of US power have never been averse to working with corrupt elements, criminal heads of state, syndicates and abusers of human rights. Rain or shine, political expediency is mightier than the sword.

The Royal Engineers who hired me had an insatiable appetite for craftsmen of all sorts. In the Jerusalem suburb of Talpiyot they had a string of workshops where carpenters, blacksmiths, electricians and sheet-metal-workers were fruitfully employed.

The engineering workshop was well-equipped and when we were not hanging about we were busy making all kinds of articles for officers, as well as those among the lower ranks working in the office who had some clout of their own.

The machine shop produced goods ranging from ashtrays, door-knockers and ornamental brasses, to model steamboats and standard lamps. The blacksmiths would turn out individually designed wrought-iron gates, decorative fire grates, pokers and standard lamps. At the same time the carpenters and cabinet-makers were producing tasteful Edwardian furniture, fine marquetry trays, turned salad bowls as well as standard lamps. These trinkets, the officers would send home at nominal freight rates on steamers returning half empty.

The English were forever voicing their gratitude and admiration for the fine job we were doing. Unlike other employers I had come across, they made us feel important. They never gave orders when suggestions and questions would do. Instead of saying, 'You will bend this tension bar so, and weld a hook on to it here,' they would couch it in an innocent question: 'Would you mind . . . ?' Instead of yelling, 'What the hell do you think you're doing?' They would say: 'I should turn that drill around and grip it by the shank, that way you will find it more effective.'

I should . . . you might . . . would you? They were amazing.

Their indirectness was disarming and forever a source of wonder.

'I should clean up those copper ashtrays first . . . ' or 'Would you mind sharpening those chisels before lunch,' were unmistakably orders.

'It would seem . . . it would appear . . . ' It took some getting used to.

The personnel manager's name was Zahavi. *Zahav* means gold and back in Lithuania his name would have been Goldman. The ghetto names were being shed and Hebrewized. Thus the Pomerantzes became Tapoozis; the Greenbergs, Yarockys; and the Sternbergs, Kokhavis.

Zahavi was a handsome and unpleasant man who when he smiled looked as if his whole body was aching. His head was covered with a shock of hair that was borrowed from his left ear and when the wind caught him unaware it would flap incongruously from the side, like a flag crying for help. He had obtained his managerial post by being for many years a loyal member of the ruling Workers' Party, Mapai.

'Can you make cigarette lighters,' asked Zahavi, evaluating my suitability for the Royal Engineers.

'But of course,' I replied.

'And when can you start?'

'In the present time,' I answered, stretching my Hebrew.

He accompanied me to Mordochai, the timekeeper, and to the tool store. With my box full of files, hammer, centre punch, scriber, ruler and try-square, he took me to the engineering workshop. The singing and laughter stopped as soon as we entered. Zahavi allocated a workbench to me and an empty locker and scrambled off.

I said '*Shalom!*' and sullenly the guys replicated without looking up. The ancestors of some of these people had lived in Palestine since Isabella's persecutions, which had financed Columbus's voyage to India. They still conversed in Spanish four hundred and fifty years after having been expelled. They were suspicious of strangers, particularly Ashkenazim. Throughout that first day, they followed my every step with mistrust. Moshe reprimanded his cousin Raphael, the youngest in the group, for attempting to show me where the toilet was. *'Deja lo estar!'* he had ordered. I was to be left to my own devices. Throughout that first day their remarks were full of animosity, suspicion, speculation and apprehension. They had assessed me as one of *them*.

'*Them* that call us blacks! *Them* of whom the upper strata is composed! *Them* that catch the cushy jobs!'

The fact that I was an escapee from the worst calamity imaginable cut no ice with them. Hey, wait a minute! I've been here before? This was familiar territory. They cut me. They gave monosyllabic answers to my queries. My stool suddenly disappeared. The power was cut off while I was sharpening a scraper. They were looking through me, satisfaction with my discomfort showing in their faces, suspicion issuing from their every fibre.

Here I felt at home. This I had experienced back in Vienna in the geyser factory where I had been the only Jew: the cold shoulder, little things going wrong, signals in the wind, antagonism you could smell. Here, as in Vienna, I was an outsider threatening the established order. There are cushy arrangements in places such as these, where trust and familiarity are essential ingredients. I was an unknown quantity.

The next morning, not being able to stand the pressure, I played my trump card. Addressing Raphael before Moshe could pounce, I asked in Spanish where I could find *un martillo de leña*. For a moment young Raphael seemed thunderstruck. He finally managed the statement, *'El habla espagnol!'* Naturally everybody had heard, for whenever I opened my mouth everything stopped and alertness sharpened. Now they closed in on me, firing questions, giggling, patting me. The hostility had vanished. They crowded around and smothered me with their attention. Anybody who speaks Spanish, even if it wasn't their dialect, can't be all bad. I was accepted as one of them, warts and all.

There was a lot of laughter that morning and without embarrassment they appreciated the irony of my having monitored their speculations and deliberations the day before. The strain of the situation had been just as great on them as it had been on me. They had more to lose than I.

All seven were related and lived in the Old City and, as I was looking for accommodation, they insisted that I come to live with Raphael's family until a room could be found for me in their street.

'Keep your mouth shut,' said Moshe, between clenched teeth. Moshe was the self-appointed and undisputed foreman at the Royal Engineers machine shop. 'You haven't seen no donkey . . . you don't know nothing.'

'What donkey? What are you talking about?' I was in need of clarification.

'Take my advice, don't get involved.' Moshe was waving his arms. He turned to Raphael. 'What donkey, you hear that? What donkey, he wants to know.'

The outburst had been brought on by a conversation which had turned into an argument between me and the staff sergeant from the REME next door to our site. He had come to investigate how a headlight had been smashed on one of his command cars while it was being unloaded in our yard.

This is the tale of the donkey.

A moderately fat man ambles along the road when, without warning, his donkey breaks into a trot. Donkeys' ways are mysterious and unpredictable. They are individualists.

The donkey turns left as donkeys do, and makes its way through the Arch of Near Perfection, into the almost crowded souk. The portly man of middling age, out of training and slow, choking on his cigarette, quickly loses sight of his precious animal. He buttonholes a couple of water-carriers who are squatting in the shade having a break.

'You there,' he wheezes at them, '. . . donkey escaped . . . you seen it?' He points up the road. ' . . . passed this way.'

With little interest or emotion and with economy of movement they shake their heads looking through our man. That isn't good enough for the donkey-owner whose station is far above the lowly water-carriers. He looks up to heaven then grabs one of them by the shoulder. Still wheezy and out of breath he repeats the question with increased urgency.

'Piss off, willya,' replied the blind one, 'we ain't seen no donkey.'

Our man accepts their request with dignity and continues in pursuit of his costly ass, following along the Path of Half Prayer leading to the Square of Virtual Fulfilment, accosting bystanders and sightseers along the way.

'You seen a donkey?' he now asks a stallholder who is trying to reduce his stock of camels carved from olive wood.

'Donkey?' repeats the stallholder, 'Yea, I've seen a donkey . . . with a split ear . . . '

'Split ear . . . werrigo, werrigo?'

'It went that way,' says the vendor, pointing with his enormous index finger, looking uncannily like John the Baptist in Grünewald's Isenheimer altarpiece. He is indicating the right-hand turn into the almost overcrowded Lane of Partial Abundance.

'Split ear. That's the one,' repeats our donkey-driver, putting his all into the final sprint, turning into the lane which leads to the Mount of Relative Devotion.

Half an hour later he is back, storming at the fellow who is busy making a living selling trinkets, berating him, insisting that the donkey is nowhere to be found.

'Dat'sa pity,' says the stallholder, offering a picture depicting a rural scene which shows a man, a woman, a babe and a donkey, carved in the wood of the olive tree.

'Is that all you've got to say?' roars our man, snorting and wheezing and foaming at the mouth. 'WHERE IS IT?'

'Waddaya mean, where is it?' says the trinket-vendor grinning nervously.

'Waddaya mean, waddaya mean? I WANT MY DONKEY.'

'I ain't gat your donkey. Leggo of me sleeve.'

'You saw it. You admitted you saw it and now . . . now you're telling me . . .'

The spectacle turns from nasty to ugly when the resident constable happens upon the scene.

'Allow, 'allow, whart's arl the 'assle aba'?' And 'One at a time,' he calls as the two antagonists shout at him together. 'Oo is the aggrieved party?'

'Me!'

'Me!'

Having finally heard both versions, the constable rereads his notes and turns to the stallholder.

'Now you are telling us that you saw the fugitive donkey and in spite of the fact that the rightful owner wasn't seen to be riding it, you, with malice aforesaid, actively and indirectly aided and abetted said fugitive donkey in his escape? What are you? Some kind of animal liberationist?'

'I didn't know who the donkey belonged to and . . .'

'Whart else did yeouw not know?' The constable stretches his syllables; he stretches his mediocre size and thanks to his enormous calpak renders an almost formidable impression. He takes a deep breath through his dilated nostrils.

'It seems, yeouw didn't know a great deal and my patience is wearing very thin' and 'aye shall get extremely annoyed in a minute,' he adds with the studied authority which he had been taught to display six years earlier at the induction course. The policeman wetted his pencil and continued.

'When you saw the donkey, was this gentleman with it?'

'No, he arrived five minutes later.'

'So although you saw the owner five minutes later, you deliberately did nothing to prevent the escape of the donkey.'

'But I . . . I . . . how . . .'

Down at the station they shine a searchlight into the eyes of the seller of trinkets advising him to confess, to make a clean breast of it, to tell it all. Who had he sold the donkey to? How much had he got for it and what else had he stolen? Has he stopped not paying his radio licence and why not? By now the poor fool is reduced to a slobbering wreck.

'All right, I'll pay but I have only eighty kropleks on me . . .'

'That's not enough, he is asking thirty stogits. If you don't pay you stay in prison.'

'OK. I'll run off home and get the money.'

'Yeouw will not run off home, as you put it, because you don't leave here until you've paid . . . of course we trust you, that's not the point. The point is, it's the rules.'

'So I can't leave until I've paid and I can't pay until I've gone home to get the money . . . I mean . . . that is some catch.'

Khart al Yahood, the Jewish quarter, was a tightly knit community; a medieval village with its shops and trades: silversmiths, broom-makers, and cobblers, tailors, mattress-makers, metalworkers, and the inevitable barber; all living and working on the premises. Doors were seldom locked. The local burglar was part of the community and would go to the new town to pursue his trade. One was always made to feel welcome and coerced into staying for supper. The Jews, subdivided as they were into *aïdot* according to land of origin, nevertheless functioned as a coherent entity among the population of this historic site.

People were open and accessible and I made many friends in a short time. Although I was the only

'European' living within the walls and as such was marked as an outsider and intruder, I was treated like someone they had always known, one of the family. They loved me for having come to live among them.

Their children grew up speaking their own language: Spanish, Kurdish, Bukhara, Persian or North African dialects, with Hebrew the unifying speech. They also conversed in Arabic with all the non-Jewish communities around them such as the Palestinians, the Armenians, the Greeks, the Abyssinians and some Chinese traders, all of whom populated this walled-in city. There was no forced education. The lucky ones could go to the English convent school or to a number of French schools outside the wall, acquainting them with yet another language. Growing up with the means of communicating in three or four tongues was not unusual.

There were quarrels and allegiances and conflicts as one would expect in a crowded conglomeration such as this one. But the feud between the two families in Karaiim Street was many years old and as far as I know the cause of it had been forgotten. Both these Jewish-Spanish families had Roman names, Antebi and Kapeta, and lived in close proximity to each other. I was friendly with the youngsters and found the hospitality in both houses accentuated as might be expected in situations of stress.

Saturday, the sabbath, was the day of social activity when men would wander around in their pyjamas, sit in the cafés and play cards, visit and partake of each other's *hamin*. They would drink arrack and cognac, raising their voices to a pitch and losing the ability to focus as the morning progressed.

Hamin was a sabbath institution. As the Jewish creed forbids work on the seventh day, and cooking is work, the Saturday stew-pot has evolved. This had been brought down to a fine art by the inhabitants of the

Jewish quarter. On Friday afternoon the housewives filled their earthenware containers with meat, beans, potatoes, eggs, onions, dumplings, pearl barely, spices and water. This was taken to the local baker who placed the pots into the still-hot oven after the bread for the weekend had been taken out. Throughout the night, the meal is cooked at a low heat.

Hamin, or *tsholent*, is served from eleven when the men return from prayers or poker games, until well into the afternoon. Youngsters drift from house to house eating a boiled egg in one place and taking a swig of arrack in another, still munching as they arrive at their next location. There they are greeted enthusiastically, brought up to date and drawn into the conversation.

In the afternoon the open space near the Zion Gate would become the local corso.

The corso, this open-air theatre, battlefield of the sexes, the Grand Canyon to the observer and student of social unfolding, was where the cognizant spectator would guess at, and anticipate, developments. Here the keen onlooker would return, week after week to his regular place for the next instalment. This took place prior to the advent of the sterile, prepacked, preheated, predigested and heavily sledge-hammered, electronically transmitted spectacle. Prior to the days of the piped image, people would walk the streets of their neighbourhood after supper or stand on street corners or at their windows, all of them participants and spectators at the same time.

Oh where are the snows of yesteryear?

The boys would parade in groups, prospecting. The girls would come merely to exchange giggling messages pretending that the male gender didn't exist.

The corso was a living garden. All phases of growth were represented through the various stages of relationship and attachment. Gradually, as the season

217

progressed, the older ones would pair up and drift out of the scene, returning as engaged or newly married couples with the beginnings of furrows on their foreheads.

The coffee-house was the grandstand where the men, engaged in their noisy card games and backgammon, kept a wily eye on their daughters and sisters. The women sat on the low wall the other side of the open space, chuckling and wailing. They complained to and commiserated with each other, over the lifelessness and the exigent demands of their respective spouses.

On one such day, a Kapeta boy detached himself from his group and began chatting to one of the Antebi girls of which there were two, still unattached.

No eyebrows were raised in either of the feuding families as the friendship grew into commitment and, unlike their Veronese counterparts, the pair were welcome in both houses. In preparation for the wedding a truce evolved between the feuding families. The hostility lost its momentum, and was never again rekindled.

Sarafant

Sarafant was a dump. Sarafant was a huge ammunition dump that had served the Eighth Army in its push west, expelling the Germans from North Africa – El Alamein, Tobruk, Tripoli, Tunis – and was now ticking over, retaining its importance because of its central position and proximity to the Empire's fuel supply. It had twenty-five miles of Tarmac roads, and segregated toilets for Palestinians and Europeans. Managed by the Royal Engineers, guarded by a Northern Rhodesian regiment, it employed a hundred and fifty civilians for its maintenance and building projects as well as those manning its workshops. I got myself a job there in January 1945. There was a lot of money sloshing around and, where there was room for two people, one was deemed insufficient. We, the mechanics, electricians and plumbers, were sitting around in our office drinking tea, reading, playing chess, staring into the void and humming or just staring. We were on call in case something came up. Most of my workload at the time consisted of taking the Royal Enfield from the motor pool next door, riding to one of the building sites and starting the concrete mixer, returning at lunch-time to operate the lever that stopped the flow of fuel, bringing the engine to a halt. The cycle was repeated in the afternoon.

In order to mystify the unskilled labourers, we would act like shamans pretending to esoteric knowledge. Simple tasks such as starting and stopping the engine, replacing a filter or adjusting the coupling were presented and performed as highly sophisticated and elaborate operations, requiring a sequence of precisely timed manipulations, the loosening and tightening of bolts, and various unrelated manoeuvres creatively invented on the spur of the moment. What I had to do could be learned by the average twelve-year-old in ten minutes. Making a simple task look like an occult pursuit is a device used by professionals and experts in all walks of life.

The menial labourers were brought in by the truck-load from the surrounding villages. They had little and earned meagre wages and were regularly cheated by the pay clerk. But their hospitality was natural and a matter of course. You had only to walk past where they were squatting during their lunch break and they would beckon.

'T'faddal,' they called, insisting that you came and shared. And it was more than just a formal gesture. T'faddal! No matter who you were, friend or enemy. Some of them would not hide their animosity reserved for an intruder like myself, but when I came within sight of where they were eating, or happened to walk past their modest abodes in the evening, they insisted that I accept their hospitality. T'faddal was more than a mere word to the original inhabitants of this country. Those fallaheen were paying rent to their landlords who sat in Damascus or Paris or Rio de Janeiro, and who were not averse to selling land to the Jews over the heads of their villagers. Those landowners knew full well that the first thing the new occupants, in most cases left-wing socialists, were going to do was to evict the tenants.

> Wild companions blown in the wind,
> Princes in rags and in tatters . . .

I was reminded of these lines from a German *Wanderlied*, as I watched a group of labourers, clothed in rags, huddling in the cement store on a wet and blustery day. They were sipping coffee out of tiny cups and conversing or singing quietly, squatting around a small fire. Their job was to unload and stack the incoming bags of Portland cement or to load the dusty merchandise on to trucks to be distributed to other army establishments with stops en route to drop consignments at the sites of Arab and Jewish entrepreneurs with whom there was an arrangement. The bags showed clearly the War Department logo, but the cement itself was untraceable in the foundations of a building or in the lintels of a doorway.

Dead men tell no tales!

With the proceeds the officers would buy presents of Arab and Jewish trinkets, or furniture and standard lamps from those in charge of the carpentry shop.

On that day, an itinerant work gang had arrived to be transferred to a neighbouring army camp where, no doubt, some trenches needed digging or filling in. As they were waiting in the drizzle, one of the cement-loaders went to investigate and invited them in out of the rain. There ensued a ritual in which the spokesman of each group introduced the members of his gang in a formal manner. The individuals of the incumbent group got up, bringing the palm of their hand to the chest in reverence after each handshake, as is the custom, and the arrivals were invited to sit and were offered coffee. The poetic beauty of that scene did not register with me for many years.

Respectability goes with appearance. That is why I entered into my mental diary, the words: 'If ever I was to become respectable, I will have lost all my self-respect.'

There was dancing in the streets of Jerusalem, as in most cities of Europe and North America on the day the war in Europe finally came to an end. Meanwhile in Germany, ten minutes after the howitzers and katyushas had fallen silent, the women of Berlin and Hamburg, Frankfurt, Dresden and Mannheim, dragged themselves out of the shelters, rolled up their sleeves, put on their headscarves and aprons and proceeded to pick up the pieces. The pieces and bricks and roof tiles and rafters. Now that the men had finished their job, it was the turn of the women to get to work. They cleared the roads and sorted the rubble and scraped the mortar off the bricks and building blocks, so that their town could be put together and, once again, turned into a living organism.

And in Nuremberg, preparations were made for the war criminals on the losing side to be put on trial by those on the victorious side. And while the judiciary investigated, and teams of special agents searched the German countryside to uncover candidates for retribution, other specially trained teams were silently scouring the country for suitable former Nazis to serve on the side of the United States in the next stage of the conflict: the crusade against communism. An escape route was organized and murderers were given a new identity.

A friend of a friend had moved up-market to Beth Ha-Kerem and let me have his room in town at a reasonable rent. I was now living smack in the centre of

Jerusalem. My neighbour was a prostitute who plied her trade with little fuss. She was friendly and she kept the stairs and passage clean. We shared the toilet and washbasin and little else. Why had I left the Old City? I don't know; that's the truth. I was twenty-seven years old and did not know where I was going. My new abode was around the corner from Zion Square and five minutes' walk to my new job in the Rehov Hanevi'im, the Street of the Prophets. I had left the Royal Engineers and obtained a job with the Palestine Public Works Department as a mechanic, servicing and overhauling stationary diesel engines. That was two months before the troubles started.

Strictly speaking, the troubles had started in 1897 when the first Zionist Congress was held. There, it had been decided that the time had come for the Jewish people to reclaim Palestine which at the time was part of the Ottoman Empire. But that is another story.

In 1947 the British government had decided to relinquish the mandate it had held over Palestine, and drop the matter of its future into the lap of the United Nations. The current unrest I am referring to was the explosive anger displayed by the Palestinians at the decision of the United Nations General Assembly to take from them more than half of their country. In the early stages of United Nations involvement the representatives of the Jews had been invited, as were the neighbouring Arab governments, to appoint liaison officers to accompany the fact-finding commission, the third in ten years. This one was known as the United Nations Special Committee on Palestine, UNSCOP. Its eleven members consisted of nine Europeans and Euro-Americans as well as two Asians. It was an all-male commission.

The Palestinians were not asked. Officially, they did not exist. Years earlier, the slogan had been coined, 'Palestine, a country without people, for a people without a country'. UNSCOP instead approached the Arab League offering it the opportunity to assign two of their people to represent the non-Zionist side. The Arab League, brainchild of Anthony Eden, declined, recognizing that nobody but the Zionists stood to gain from the inquiry. Had the Palestinians been invited, they too would have had to decline for who, with history staring them in the face, could sit in and participate in the fragmentation of their country and the uprooting of their own people? I ask you.

To accompany the UNSCOP boys in their travels, and to influence them favourably to the Zionist cause, the Jewish agency appointed David Horowitz, an economist and up-and-coming young Abba Eban, Cambridge-educated oriental scholar and a future foreign minister in the Jewish Labour Government. On several occasions in his writings Abba Eban boasts of the astuteness and of the skilful strategies of the Zionist negotiators.

On 29 November 1947, the General Assembly of the United Nations voted in favour of the plan proposed by UNSCOP. Having obtained the necessary majority, the Jews were jubilant. The final outcome was that 52 per cent of the territory of Palestine was to go to the Jews, an area surrounding Jerusalem and Bethlehem (about 1 per cent) was to be administered by an international commission, and the rest of the country was to remain at the disposal of its original inhabitants.

The Palestinians were thunderstruck. It looked as though they were destined to have to pay the price for the catastrophe which had befallen millions of European Jews.

At work the next day, they were standing around in dejected groups, discussing the implications. They were to lose Haifa, Jaffa, the Negev, half the Galilee, but above all Jerusalem and Bethlehem. They were to be left with hundreds of thousands of their people stranded under Jewish domination. In the event the Palestinians were to lose all their lands.

Jewish youngsters were lining both sides of Jaffa Road near the Barclays Bank and Colonial, waiting for the Arab bus which had to come through here to get to the Nablus Gate of the Old City. As they hurled missiles at the accelerating vehicle, those rocks and bottles aimed too high or cast too late would invariably hit the brick-throwers as well as innocent passers-by on the opposite side of the road. No doubt hooligans recipro-cating in the Palestinian part of the town were filling the casualty wards in the same way. It is a sobering thought how thugs and delinquents in opposing camps always raise the temperature and set the pace. It is not in defence of their own side that they are doing it; these people are nowhere to be seen when a situation arises which would put their mettle to the test.

I have a dream. One day, we may achieve the un-achievable: to get all the thugs, the colonels, the big-mouth extremists, and the big-prick machos on to an uninhabited island, supply them with Kalashnikovs and hand-grenades and enough food to keep them alive, and let them abreact their patriotic and manly emotions.

No, no, no! It can't be done. It would be unfair to the flora and fauna. Maybe the north pole. Or how about the moon. Those left behind would be smiling in their sleep.

WHAT? AND LEAVE THE PLANET IN THE HANDS OF THE PACIFISTS AND DO-GOODERS? NEVER! YOU HEAR, NEVER!

Making peace is very often a lengthy and cumber-some process. Starting a fight needs only a few squint-eyed miscreants. It only requires one single safety match to burn down a forest.

It didn't take long for the skirmishes to turn into full-scale hostilities with the British army and police force standing on the sidelines. The Jewish army took over the workshops the day of the withdrawal of the British and we carried on working under the new management as before. We had been formally dismissed by the Government of Palestine as of 14th May 1948, for reasons of 'Termination of Mandate'.

It was the night the Jews had taken Katamon, a Palestinian suburb of Jerusalem. That night I was off duty but couldn't sleep on account of the shooting, which was incessant. I went on to the verandah and watched the fireworks. Phosphor streaks formed momentary designs against the black sky, producing random patterns such as those made by a three-year-old when let loose with crayons on a blackboard. The war was being fought with tracer bullets. Now and again shells were impacting and a shower of sparks would illuminate the target. One projectile hit the tower of the German Church of Dormition. In the brief flash I could discern the clock which stood at five past two.

There was a blaze seemingly coming from our workshops in the Street of the Prophets. I got up and scurried across Zion Square up Ravcook Street where the fire station was and told them that the Public Works Department was on fire.

'What's that?' shouted one of the two firebugs on duty.

He couldn't hear me on account of the noise. I went over and turned down the wireless which had been blaring Rimsky-Korsakov's 'Capriccio Espagnol.'

'Aren't you going to do something about it?' I asked, naive as ever.

He moved his pawn to QB6 threatening the black rook.

'My wife thinks I should bring home some water for washing the children and you talk of fire extinguishing.'

' . . . and petrol?' said the other guy, waving his rook,

punctuating petrol. He was wearing his British tin hat.
'We're immobile. You got petrol?'

I could have asked him what they were doing at the station if they were inoperative, but I knew what his answer would have been. It was their turn for night duty he would have replied, moving his rook to a position safe from the harassment of the white pawns which were relentlessly migrating north in their quest for the big prize.

No damage was noticeable when, in the morning, I looked across to the tower of German Dormition. The clock was about two minutes slow by my reckoning. Last night's impact showed itself in a large inkblot-like mark against the pink stone. It reminded me of the one on the wall of Martin Luther's study in Wittenberg. That one had come about when the short-tempered reformist threw an inkwell at Satan who had been annoying him. But Satan ducked, causing the famous tourist attraction.

At the Public Works Department the building housing the power station had burned down and so had the bus terminal in nearby Jaffa Street.

From the positions of the Arab Legion, the army of Trans Jordan, in the Old City, mortars were being pitched at us. They came down at irregular intervals in bursts of two-minutes' duration, three or for times a day. Some people admired me for my stupidity at not running for cover. They thought it was sang-froid.

A young USArian stopped me, wanting to know what was happening.

'Hey buddy,' he called with alarm, 'are those shells or mortars?'

'Mortars,' I replied, 'it's the Arab Legion, they . . . '

'I prefer shelling,' he cried excitedly as he rushed on, his briefcase covering his head.

At about this time Mao Tse-tung had taken Mukden and was on his way south to Nanking, the capital, freshly equipped with US Army ordnance, bought from Chiang Kai-shek's boys. They had been selling at bargain-basement prices to all comers including the commies, enlarging their accounts in Zürich and Lausanne, courtesy of the United States taxpayer. Throughout the war, Chiang Kai-shek's US-backed nationalists, and Mao Tse-tung's Red Army, had fought the common enemy side by side. With the Japanese surrender in August 1945, they were once more fighting each other. By the end of 1949, Chiang's government was evacuated to the island of Taiwan whose original inhabitants have been suffering foreign occupation by various powers, but mainly by the Chinese, since the sixteenth century. They have been living under renewed Chinese repression since their island was evacuated by the Japanese. Nobody gives a damn. It happens all the time.

Abdullah al Tal has never been elevated to the rank of Righteous Gentile. Righteous Gentile is the title given to those non-Jews who have saved Jewish lives. On the day the Jewish quarter of the Old City surrendered to the Arab Legion he saved the lives of sixteen young Jewish fighters.

The Jewish population of the Old City, maybe two thousand, had been assembled on the open ground inside the Zion Gate. The women and children were to be passed to the UN Peace Mission and the men of fighting age were to be taken into captivity in Amman. While the sorting was going on, some hooligans from the souk, who probably hadn't been anywhere near the fighting, singled out a group of young prisoners and, winking at the guards, were about to march them off. This kind of thing had happened before on both sides. It happens in wars and conflicts and is termed 'regrettable' with a shrug of the shoulders by diplomats and politicians.

Abdullah was one of those unsung heroes in a position of power. He was the general in command of the Arab Legion's operation in Jerusalem. He was to be a member of the armistice commission negotiating with the Jews, and Count Bernadotte, the United Nations representative, who was later assassinated by members of the Irgun in Jerusalem.

On that morning Abdullah al Tal saw what was about to happen. He intervened and gave strict orders for all the captives to be treated in accordance with accepted conventions. None of the Jewish prisoners were harmed, and those who were marched off into captivity were returned safe and sound several months later.

Diesel Mechanic

Our sergeant, a recent arrival from Romania, had been sent on an induction course on how to put veterans of the 1948 war through their paces. Bent forward, his forearms dangling like demented pendulums barely touching the ground, he strode up and down performing his role with contempt, arrogant expertise and venom.

The fighting ended, I had been enlisted in the reserve army, to serve one month in every year, and found myself playing silly buggers on the parade ground.

'I have two hands,' exclaimed the aspiring field marshal, with an expressionless expression. He stopped pacing and showed us the palms of his hands. 'A right one and a left one.' Each hand was raised in turn. 'I can be good and I can be wicked.' He pulled out his handkerchief, wiped his mouth and resumed cavorting. 'I can be your best friend and I can be your worst enemy. The decision lies with you.'

Out of his top pocket he extracted his watch and held it up for all to see.

'It took you rabble three minutes to line up.' He had by now abandoned his John Wayne drawl and was into

James Cagney. 'Three and a half minutes.' His watch raised above his head, he was stabbing it with his right index finger.

'You – call – your – selves SOLJAS?'

And so he went on. The issue of weekend passes was entirely his prerogative and we were to fix this firmly into our thick skulls. He could be gentle and he could be tough.

The only time I ever saw that man smile was the time he had an infected wisdom tooth and his jaw was badly swollen. For some days then that sergeant smiled continuously.

They had taught him elocution. Stock phrases flowed freely from his wet lips.

'Let's be clear about this.'

'Make no mistake . . . '

'Just you try and see what will happen.'

'The outcome is entirely up to you.'

'I can make you and I can break you.'

These were delivered with studied intonation followed by a heavy hissing intake of air through dilated nostrils. When he had finally burnt himself out, our sergeant left it to his aspiring lance-corporals to sort us into groups.

'Car mechanics over here,' one of them called, pointing to his corner of the assembly area. 'Carpenters this way,' sounded another call. Sheetmetal-workers, drivers, electricians, all were accommodated and found a position on the parade ground. After the dust had settled, troublesome Klausner hadn't moved from his original place. He had not been promoted into one of the groups. On the game board he had not advanced one single metaphorical square.

Menacingly, the corporal in charge approached, firing questions which sadly lacked sparkle. What the hell was I doing standing there? Why wasn't I with my group?

'What group . . . '

'What do you do . . . I mean work . . . what's your trade?'

'Diesel mechanic.'

'Diesel mechanic?'

'Diesel mechanic.'

'Wait here,' he articulated as he went off in search of enlightenment. Just before he reached the hut he turned.

'Wait there,' he shouted excitedly, pointing at where I was standing. He was rising to the occasion.

I grabbed a shovel so as not to look conspicuous and wandered around the camp monitoring progress as the various groupings began busying themselves with their assignments. The truck-drivers had been given the task of pulling up grass and roots, and generally clearing and raking the ground around the main hut, housing headquarters. The carpenters had been entrusted with the task of moving a pile of rocks from the perimeter; rocks which, undoubtedly, had been put there by a previous group, and which would have to be shifted some place else by succeeding generations of reservist carpenters. The car mechanics were peeling potatoes and scrubbing cauldrons, and the electricians were planting eucalyptus saplings.

Once again they didn't know what to do with Klausner.

In the afternoon, the corporal finally caught up with me.

'Where have you been?' he demanded to know. 'I have been searching for you, high and low. I thought I told you . . . '

'I replaced the . . . '

'Never mind, come with me.'

He marched me into the office and into the presence of the lieutenant where he pointed to a spot on the floor and impressed upon me to stand 'over here'. The three of us now formed an isosceles triangle with the lieutenant sitting at its apex.

'Does he know anything about cars or trucks?' asked our valiant officer hopefully. That way he could have farmed me out to kitchen fatigue with all the other car mechanics. The corporal conveyed the question to me.

'Only stationary diesels,' I replied. 'I can dismantle and reassemble a Bosch pump blindfolded.'

'Only stationary diesels,' said the corporal. 'He can dis . . .'

'I heard,' said the lieutenant, chewing on a matchstick. The pain of deep thought shone through his sour expression.

'Where does he work?'

'Where do you work?'

'I run the generator unit at Satav.'

'He runs . . .'

'OK. Tell him to wait outside.'

Once again I went off with my shovel, inspecting progress, taking messages from one group to another and handing out unsolicited advice.

The next morning I was doing my shovel stint again, only this time I carried a plank of wood. But today they were quick at locating me.

'Are you Baruch Klosanar?' A lance-corporal clutching a note had crept up on me.

'No!' I countered, and tempering his disappointment I added, 'The name is Klausner. Kuf, Lamed, Aleph, Vav, Samekh, Nun, Resh. Number 107146.'

'Pack your bags. You are going to Akko.'

I was to report to captain David Yazdah at the naval unit in Haifa. He needed some work done on a marine diesel situated outside Akko, the harbour and fortress held for many years by the crusaders. Did I know anything about Paxman-Ricardos? Did I know . . . my God, Paxman! What a question. Paxman-Ricardo, the one with the turbulence chamber in the head. Diesel engines with pre-combustion turbulence chambers were my passion.

233

What happens is this: the air drawn into the cylinder is compressed into the spherical chamber, to one-sixteenth of its original volume. This raises the temperature to above that of the flashpoint of the fuel which is at that moment injected tangentially, thus creating a whirl which aids and accelerates the fuel-air mix, thereby achieving efficient combustion and giving thrust to the power stroke.

Fascinating, isn't it?

Our unit was stationed south of Beersheba, and Akko was about the furthest they could have removed me to. Ten miles on, and I would have hit the Lebanese border. I was given a wad of vouchers for travelling, eating and accommodation, then they dropped me at the bus depot and sped off without looking back.

I was on my way.

I arrived late in Haifa and booked straight into a boarding house to get a good night's sleep. One doesn't want to keep a Paxman-Ricardo waiting, does one? In the morning – I was in a dormitory of four – one of the blokes on getting dressed found that his new boots had gone and an old pair had been left in their place.

I had lived in hostels and tramp refuges, populated by the here-today-and-gone-tomorrow tribe, and had always taken the precaution of setting the legs of my bed into my boots even though, more often than not, they were not worth stealing. I had learned this ploy from reading Egon Erwin Kisch's accounts of his extensive travels, and as is my duty, I am passing it on to all members of the hobo fraternity who may be listening.

Kisch was a communist intellectual from Prague, who called himself *der rasende Reporter*, an apt description, since *rasen* means to rage, to rave and to rush. He doesn't rate an entry in the *Encyclopaedia Britannica* but that is just as well. After all, the *Britannica* demonstrates its brain-brawn ratio by allotting one page to the game of

234

chess and ten pages to baseball. Kisch is all but forgotten today, but like his contemporary Karl Kraus, the polemicist, poet and editor, he will no doubt experience a revival.

It took me all morning to find the captain. Nobody seemed to know him. Eventually, I was advised to seek the help of the barber across the road in Kingsway, who directed me to the cabin of a disused crane at the far end of the harbour. That was the captain's office. It gave him a magnificent view of the commercial harbour and his own flotilla berthed to one side. Where had I been, he wanted to know. Why had I not reported to him yesterday? He was a friendly guy with a face that was always smiling, the kind of person who never gets rattled. I took an immediate liking to him as, indeed, I imagine, everyone else did. He would have made an excellent con-man. We got into his jeep and drove along the bay past Kiriat Motzkin where I had spent time in the kibbutz, seven or eight years earlier. Not far from Akko we stopped at a lonely jetty which accommodated two boats. There he dropped me off and, without stopping the engine, he nodded at the larger of the two. Captain Yazdah was in a hurry to get back.

'You'll be seen to, presently,' he shouted as he sped away.

I was alone with my Paxman-Ricardo.

'Howdy,' I said.

'Paxman of Colchester', said the brass plate on the cylinder-head cover and it listed all its patents. Worldwide.

David's concubine arrived half an hour later and wanted to know what I was doing on the boat. There was an immediate rapport between us; one of dislike and aversion. I could see how she hated me by the way her fingers were spread out by her side as she talked. She was the opposite of him in temperament. Why had I taken the head off, she moaned. I had removed one of the cylinder heads in order to catch a glimpse of the turbulence chamber but I couldn't tell her that. Anyway what did she know about it.

'I thought the duct might be obstructed,' I asserted.

'How can you assume that . . . you only have to look at the nozzle . . . look at it . . . clean as a whistle . . .' She was waving the injector in front of my face trembling with rage. 'The rocker arms . . . the rocker arms . . .' she was lost for words.

I'll say this for the major, he liked his tarts hot.

'David said someone will come to tell me what needs doing,' I said apologetically.

'So . . .?'

'I thought . . .'

'Why was David in such a rush. Why? . . . tell me . . . how . . . how am I to . . .' She was blaming me for the major's neglect. 'Why didn't he stop and tell me he was here?'

I began to understand her problems.

'Put the head back on,' she ordered, 'and make sure the gasket . . . soak it before you put it back . . . and make sure you put it back the right way round . . . with the folds face down . . . you know . . . the bits folded over . . . errh . . . face down. The rocker arms need new bushes, that's what you got to do and the injection pressure needs looking at.'

She picked up her mini-poodle and left. From the far end of the jetty she called. She was calmer now.

'You will need to . . . what's your name? . . . you will need to adjust the injection pressure . . . one of the push rods . . . I've got all the necessary data in the house. Have you eaten?' I hadn't. 'In that case, I'll fix some lunch. Wash your hands and come to number three.' She pointed to some houses, 'After, I'll take you to the garage at Kiriat Motzkin where you can avail yourself of their test pump . . . oh, and one of the anti-dribble valves needs replacing, I think.'

Things are never as bad as they might appear in the first place.

Eight days later, stretching it to the limit, the Paxman restored, I was reunited with my unit. It had been the highlight of an otherwise uneventful month.

On Fridays they had us assemble on the parade ground and made the handing out of weekend passes into a ceremony, as if they were handing out decorations. After some pirouetting and gambolling, each of us had to stand to attention when his name was called, smartly march up to the sergeant, salute, take the proffered piece of paper which legalized our absence from the unit, salute again, about turn smartly, and march back to our place in the formation. This took about three quarters of an hour. Another Quickstep and one more *paso doble* and we were released to make our way home.

On one of his inspection bouts, the lieutenant espied a blotch of oil on the workshop floor. Without fuss or investigation, he shopped five of us and we were to stew in the camp throughout the coming weekend.

No furlough!

At the Friday afternoon ritual, however, we were handed our passes without explanation. We didn't ask questions and went off that day as if nothing had happened. On our return we were summoned into the office. We had disobeyed orders in spite of the fact that the passes had been signed and handled by the same person who had decided to make us stay behind. We were reviled, referred to as 'these people'. Them who sit on their big fat arses leaving all the hard work to the careerists. We were referred to as scum, treated as subhuman. The hierarchy was pressurizing them, and their only satisfaction in life was to pass the hassle on down the line. The frustration at not being able to do better than soldiering was written into the furrows of their brows. Nor was the typist going to be outclassed in acidic abuse. Never addressing us directly, she contributed constructively to the harangue, pausing now and again to continue with her manicure. Glowing hatred, the indispensable lubricant without which no standing army can function, animated these people.

Hey wait a minute. This was familiar territory. How does this differ from anti-Semitism? Mid-European officials could have learned one or two tricks from these guys who were working hard trying to turn a rabble of Haganah veterans into a streamlined unit of performing monkeys.

Career soldiers are, like teachers and policemen, incapable of holding down a job other than one which falls within their narrow frame of ability, and consequently must show contempt for people outside their sphere of comprehension. And this applies equally to racists and other fomenters of resentment and strife. The kinship manifest among these groups can be a revelation.

It was time to move!

In August 1953, nearly thirty-four years old, I packed my bags and left behind the performing sergeant whom I had had to endure periodically; and left behind the fanatics and the national socialists and the Moscow-orientated socialists; and left behind the ten years I had spent in this country; and put it all down to experience.

I had failed as I had failed in Barcelona. At the age of thirty-three I hadn't even started. I didn't know where I was going, nor what I was striving for. In the focus of my confused vision were petit-bourgeois images of 'settling down', holding a responsible, well-paid position in accordance with my potential, raising a family, cultivating my garden.

In Jerusalem I had been an outsider. Nationalism hadn't set my spirit ablaze. It had departed long ago when I was fourteen years old and had made no comeback. In this country, mere nationalism was moderation. If you were not a chauvinist you were a liberal.

'Objectivity? How can we be objective in the light of what has happened, tell me. It is the Palestinians who are the intruders. Isn't it they who are refusing to go from our land? Where can we go? Answer me that! They have Lebanon, Syria, Iraq, Saudi Arabia, Egypt. Want me to go on? Libya, Morocco . . .'

'What about Jordan, you forgot Jordan.'

'Jordan is different. We shall need to expand in years to come. There won't be enough space for all our brethren. Besides, look at the Bible and you will find that the Kingdom stretched across both sides of the river Jordan.'

Austria

By the time Metternich arrives on the scene, Vienna has out-Louis-quatorzed, Louis XIV himself.
Knowledge for the industrious Classes, A. F. Pliushkin

With bitterness in my heart I returned to the place of my childhood, the place where my friends and relations had either fled or perished. After an absence of fifteen years I had come back. Back to the place where, once again, I was not going to make it.

The landmarks of my childhood and adolescence were all there. The Nepomuk church in the Praterstrasse where, without our parents' knowledge, Marie had taken us toddlers, Lizzi and me, to Sunday Mass. The Carl Theater, which was now closed, glowering resentfully at the cinema, the Nestroy Kino across the road. It was at the Nestroy Kino, where I had seen my first piano-accompanied silent flicks; tobacco smoke swirling in the stroboscopic light.

The landmarks were all there, but another soul inhabited the body. In this part of the second district, where before 1938 about 70 per cent of the population had been Jews, where almost every shop had been Jewish, where the characteristics of a small town had been manifest with its peculiar smells and noises and faces, an eerie silence prevailed. I had reappeared in Vienna, the place of my childhood, in familiar surroundings, but I knew nobody. I was walking the streets I had grown up in and nobody knew me. It was

as sad as that. I was embittered and filled with resentment and felt that the world owed me. Who were these
people who had occupied the vacated spaces, who
looked upon me as a stranger? Whoever they were and
whatever criticism one might level against some of
them, they were just about now – 1953 – beginning to
get their act together and cope with the trauma of the
past twenty years. The people of Vienna were still
under occupation by four foreign powers, and were
carrying identification papers duplicated in Russian,
French and English.

Whatever outward changes Vienna had undergone
since my departure in 1938 were due more to decay
than to the battles in the last stages of the war. Being
consumed with ill-feelings, I gloated at the damage
and the visible decline, and dissociated myself from
'them' and 'their' problems. I resented the casualness
of their reaction to my having been persecuted and
their pretence that it hadn't anything to do with them,
that they too had been victims. I resented the absence
of compassion towards me. I resented the fact that they
didn't treat me with special consideration, that they
didn't wear their guilt-feelings on their sleeves.

Technically I was a foreign citizen when I reappeared in the town of my nativity. That was brought
home to me when my application to enrol in the public
library was turned down. But I came out of that library
not so much smarting – more contented and rather
glad of the confirmation that 'they' had rejected me. I
was glad because I had found further sustenance for
my bitterness and hatred. My grudge and my rancour
were all part of an exercise in masochistic flagellation.
I revelled in it.

I have, in the past, reacted to mishap and tribula-
tions with ill-feeling and animosity. Understandable
maybe, but unwise. Not at all a formula for survival
even in times of relative safety, because surviving

means living and you're not living when you're consumed with hatred and anger. I should have known better, having spent two years in the land of the English whose slogans such as: 'Make the best of a bad job', 'Grin and bear it', 'Try again', 'Look on the bright side', were dispensed liberally.

This I have learnt. Hatred is an infectious and consumptive disease, feeding on its own waste and thriving on reciprocity. Like all emotions, hatred denies reason. It is instilled in the young and presented as a virtue. It differs from physical disorders in that it is not recognized by the carrier and the contaminated. Anti-Semitism – a misnomer – is one of many virulent branches of the condition. And so is the detestation of communism and capitalism. And so is racial and religious exclusivity. And so is every form of xenophobia and bigotry. And so is the arrogance and the resentment that go with our hierarchical erection.

With advanced age, I have managed to discard the need for antagonism and frustration and resentment. I have recognized the futility of it; the futility of these negative passions.

Or passionate negations.

Hate screws your mind; hate and pride. Hate is the fire that consumes the torch-bearer. It blinds the issue. It hurts them who lug it around. Hate serves no purpose. As the Savoyard said, when asked if he wanted revenge for his brother killed by the Gestapo, 'A quoi bon?'

A quoi bon?

I don't hate the Germans for killing millions of Europeans. Neither do I hate the inhabitants of the USA for their contribution to oppression and destruction and disrespect for human rights. It is pointless! I don't hate the French for their excesses in North Africa, Indo-China, Madagascar . . . nor do I bear hatred towards the British for allowing the genocide of the population of the island named Tasmania, and the forceful pushing of hard drugs into China, destroying the lives of millions by turning them into junkies. I bear no animosity towards the Belgians for the holocaust in the Congo. What good does it do?

A quoi bon?

What is the use of simmering hatred, passionate vengeance . . . and who needs pride? What's the matter with you people?

I don't hate the Spaniards and the Portuguese for their part in the history of wanton killing and destruction. I don't hate the Nazis, past present and future. Or rather, I must control my emotions so as not to descend to their level and in order not to fail in my duty, which is to pitch my combative powers against the condition; the aberration which plagues us all.

This I have learned. There are far more efficient ways of saving a drowning person than extolling the virtues of living on dry land and calling for a display of contempt towards water. There are more efficient and cheaper ways of fighting fire than using flame-throwers. When I helped out in the fire service, we fought fire without excitement or passion. I learnt that pride, hatred, loyalty, allegiance would not quench flames. We used water and foam to good effect. Fire must be fought, and fought efficiently. Animosity towards fire makes no contribution in the rescue of lives and property. None whatsoever! On top of which the good fire-fighter does her or his best to make fire-fighting obsolete.

Patriotism can build cemeteries for young men, but it won't replace the pumps, it won't solve problems. Nor is a desire for revenge an adequate substitute for a turntable ladder, nor is flag-waving helpful; quite the contrary, it actually fans the flames. Nationalists are the maggots who boast, they are the descendants of the noble horse whose carcass they are feeding off. That's who they are.

This I have learned. Hatred is a boomerang. It hits him who launches it. And when they tell me that we must never forget, I agree and I want to take them at their word. Let us never forget Auschwitz and Cambodia and the genocide that has been going on on the continents named America and Australia for the last four hundred years, and let no one group or nation monopolize – as some do – the term cataclysm or calamity or indeed conflagration, using it for their own political ends.

Let us never forget!

Let us never forget the millions who don't have a memorial and whose victims or descendants receive no compensation, not even a comforting word, as in the case of the Incas, the Kurds, the Armenians, the Apache, the Maori, the Aztecs, the Mayas, the Gypsies, the Irish, the Algerians, the Sioux, the Diego Garcia islanders . . . do you want me to go on . . .? the Palestinians, the Iroquois, the Hawaiians, the Eritreans, the Timor people, the Tibetans, the Nagas, the Navahos, the peoples of the Amazon Basin . . . the list is endless.

Let us never forget!

In 1876 the last inhabitant of the island which the Europeans had named Tasmania, died in Hobart. Within her lifetime all the inhabitants had been exterminated by the immigrants and their missionaries. The name of the island has been forgotten or maybe it never had a name because to the inhabitants it was vast enough to represent their universe. Of the various tribes that made up the indigenous people, only a vague memory has lingered on. Nothing has remained of their language, their culture or their history. Nothing is left but a few artefacts and bleached bones.

Let us never forget!

But how can we forget? It is happening all the time; every day, at this very moment. At this very moment, all over the world, well-paid gunmen are roaming the countryside terrorizing landless farmers. At this very moment, in the cities of the Third World, homeless children are being killed by the forces of Law and Order. At this very moment. Mayan peasants are being dragged from their homes, never to return. All over the world people pay with their lives for being suspected of dissatisfaction with their poverty. Nothing has changed. Nothing has changed.

No, let us never forget and while we are at it let us be there when human rights are violated. This planet is soaked with the blood of the innocent, and plagued with the indifference of the unaffected. And while we are at it, let us put an end to the concept that human-rights violations are an internal matter of those who perpetrate them. Abolish non-interference where state crimes are concerned. Why can't we have an agency that represents the will of the human community; an agency with the power to guard and protect the freedom and dignity of the individual, ensuring their rightful stake in the wealth of this world?

YOU ARE BEING SOMEWHAT NAIVE, FREDDI, BUT DO CONTINUE. DO CARRY ON.

The landmarks were all there.

The bench in the Augarten where I had sat with Jenny Drimmer. The fist-fight that had taken place behind the Karmeliter Church. The basement in the Kleine Pfarrgasse where we had congregated, singing rousing Zionist songs. Kalafatti was no more; the six-metre-tall Chinaman, with his drooping moustache and enormous pigtail, who had formed the central shaft to the most memorable merry-go-round at the Prater fun-fair. His head touching the roof, his arms dangling by his side, his enormous index fingers pointing at his polished black shoes, he would revolve to the tune of Smetena's 'Bartered Bride'. How did this Mandarin get his Italian name? With awesome benevolence, he gazed down at his clientele, subdued infants, as they sat through six revolutions on the rudimentary benches on the turntable. To the thumping of the cymbals accompanying the mechanical organ, generations of solemn Viennese infants learned that departure and arrival take place in the same plane.

Vienna was falling apart. Vienna was decaying. And yet, to the outside observer, the splendour remained. The imperial grandeur and the Catholic mystique have always outshone the shoddiness. In Vienna shoddiness and grandeur went forever hand in hand.

Still, the historical magnificence passed me by. For me things hadn't worked out. I had come back full of unspecified expectations and spurious visions. Austria had not given me the red-carpet treatment and I wasn't making it with the other sex. My psyche was giving me a hard time and my irrationality was given free rein. It was a period of tantrums and weird behaviour giving rise among my few friends and acquaintances to the belief that I had blown my fuse.

No answer had arrived from senator Joe McCarthy who, together with his handmaidens Cohn and Shine, was good for another year, setting standards of political and conscientious morality and expediency. I had written to the senator complaining about a book by Lancelot Hogben.

Back in 1950, while Harry (the buck stops here) Truman was the incumbent at the White House, the senator had gone to Wheeling, West Virginia, and delivered a speech to an assembly of more than 275 middle-aged ladies and members of the press. He revealed that '. . . I have here in my hand a list of 205 . . . a list of names that were made known to the Secretary of State as being members of the Communist party and

246

who nevertheless are still working and shaping policy in the State Department.' The State Department is what would be known elsewhere as the Ministry for External or Foreign Affairs.

After the United States' 'loss' of China to Mao Tse-tung's communists in 1949, the search was on for a goat to do the scaping. *By Gard*, somebody was going to have to pay. Mind you, China hadn't belonged to the United States in the first place, it has always belonged to the Chinese. But go tell that to the mob.

Chiang Kai-shek, yesterday's man, however corrupt, had been 'our man', whereas Mao, whatever his merits, was his own man and that was bad for business; business and trade the United States had a God-given entitlement to.

Investigations into 'Un-American activities' became the order of the day and you had to proclaim your allegiance to the flag at all times. If you needed to buy a railroad ticket to get from say, Kirksville, Missouri to say, Winona, Minnesota, if you wanted to order a meal in a restaurant, if you intended to book a room at a hotel, it was required that you signed a declaration of loyalty to the Ku-Klux-Klan and sang 'My country 'tis of thee . . .' while waving the Stars and Stripes, a pocket-sized model of which you would carry around at all times. Those were the days in the United States when, if you wanted to keep your job, you had to appear before the House Committee on Un-American Activities and declare that, 'I swear to almighty Gard that I am not now and never have been a member of the Communist Party.' In those days you had to sing for your breakfast and forever protest your innocence if you wanted to be assured of your next meal. Everybody in those days had to be innocent of one thing or another. Those were the days!

However, for the sake of geographical accuracy, let us remind ourselves that since this mental state did not apply to Valparaiso or Vera Cruz or Vancouver, the term 'American' is wrongly applied. Thus for 'un-American activities' read 'un-United States activities.'

That's better!

In the letter to the senator, I had complained about a book by Lancelot Hogben, a writer on scientific subjects. In his *Mathematics for the Million*, he had used the distance from London to Moscow as an example for a calculation. This book was available on loan from the United States Information Service which had branches all over Austria, indeed all over the world. The gist of my letter was that a man who can mention Moscow without batting an eyelid, without denouncing communism, without washing his mouth and gargling, so to speak, was not a man fit to have his books openly displayed, exposing my children to doctrines of an undesirable nature. I demanded that the author be removed from the shelves and those responsible for putting him there severely investigated.

By 1954 the senator was beginning to lose his grip while his accomplice, Milhous (I am not a crook) Nixon, was to enjoy six more years as Eisenhower's vice-president. He subsequently won republican nomination for the presidential election in 1960 losing to J. F. Kennedy by a whisker. When, in 1962, he stood for and lost the governorship of California, he told reporters that from now on, 'you won't have Nixon to kick around anymore'. He went into the wilderness and opened a private law firm and that was the end of him.

No it was not!

Richard Milhous (I am not a quitter) Nixon, was to resurface in 1968, becoming the first President of the United States of America whose lies wouldn't stick. He had got entangled in miles of magnetic tape over a petty felony and resigned from office five minutes before being impeached, thus salvaging for himself the salary accorded for life to all ex-presidents. He was pardoned and purged of all crimes by his successor, who had never been elected but appointed vice-president. That successor had been picked by Nixon following the resignation of vice-president Spiro T. (No contest) Agnew, who had chosen to resign to avoid having to answer corruption charges.

Vienna's doors were closed. No blame. I found it difficult to knock and I found it hard to acclimatize. What *Gemütlichkeit* there was – and that applies equally to the *gentillesse* of the French and the bonhomie of the British – was largely alcohol-based and therefore confined to the ghettos of induced joviality.

I consider myself lucky inasmuch as alcohol leaves me stone cold. I enjoy an occasional drink of beer or wine to accompany and complement a good meal, but I do not *need* it. And if tomorrow all supplies of inebriating fluids were to be discontinued, I would not join the mass demonstrations, I wouldn't be grief-stricken. I mean, I would not fall apart. Nor would it upset me if no more cannabis or coke should reach these shores. Who needs it?

The same applies to nicotine.

Nicotine? Somebody once claimed he could bring people to ruin their health and pay hard-earned money for it in the bargain. Bets were taken and he won hands down. That's how it started.

What started?

Nicotine-addiction started.

He became a millionaire by making people pay for paper tubes filled with noxious weeds which they set light to, the fumes of which they inhale, depositing sticky black glue on the walls of the air-intake passages, so inviting lung cancer and bronchitis into their lives. They are paying hard-earned money for the privilege of destroying their health. Do you know what I'm saying?

I myself was once a supporter of the tobacco industry. I should know.

Meanwhile in South-East Asia, the French army who had bolted, fleeing the Japanese in 1941, returned as victors in 1945. After a long struggle they had now, 1954, been expelled by the Vietnamese. But no sooner had they been shown off than forces from the Far East, from beyond the Pacific Ocean, began infiltrating into Vietnam, eventually raising their number to half a million fighting men backed by tanks, artillery and planes which were to bomb the indigenous people 'back into the Stone Age'. It was to take the people of Vietnam twenty hard years to expel them.

Just as I had reached a particularly low ebb, Aunt Paula came to Vienna on one of her business and shopping trips. It didn't take her long to assess my situation and, on the third day, without preamble she said to me, 'Pack your bags, you are coming to Vöcklabruck!' It was a timely rescue and enabled me once again to run away from whatever it was I was forever running away from.

My happiest childhood memories relate to the times I spent in Vöcklabruck, this magic town with its streams and rivulets, its watermill, its steaming cowsheds, its marketplace with its dominant medieval watch-towers, its proximity to lakes and mountains and dense forests, its abundance of nasturtiums, bilberries and wild strawberries, as well as *Eierschwammerln* and other edible fungi.

Aunt Paula, my mother's sister, was the outcast of the family because she had married out of the faith. On a skiing holiday she had fallen in love with a good-look-ing *goyishe* guy from Vöcklabruck, 250 kilometres from Vienna: Joseph Weiss, the handsome *goy* had a shop on the market square which specialized in winter-sports equipment and *Lederhosen* as well as orthopaedic appli-ances. He was killed when his motorbike crashed into a speeding train at an unmanned crossing in 1932. Aunt Paula, without prior experience, had to manage the shop and bring up her teenage daughter. She had no one to help and comfort her. But it turned out that she had a hitherto undiscovered gift for business and made a success of it. She was never a great cook or a spick-and-span housewife, but when she worked the cash register you could observe a pro on the prowl.

In 1939 the Nazis took her possessions and kicked her out of town. Destitute, she returned to Vienna where she joined her sister, Aunt Margarete, Felix's mother, whose husband Tino had been dragged to Dachau following the *Reichskristallnacht*. Paula sur-vived the hard times, returned to Vöcklabruck, retrieved her property and flourished. She tended the shop every day until her death at the age of ninety. Uncle Tino got out of Dachau in 1939 on the strength of his visa to Bolivia. There he spent the war years. Aunt Margarete was deported in 1942 and perished in the great conflagration.

I obtained a job with an engineering firm in nearby Attang-Puchheim and, having little else to do after work, followed the invitation on a notice displayed at the railway station, exhorting the uninitiated and unenlightened to join the Esperanto Federation and learn the international language. The language that was to bring peace to the world. The language of hope.

An elderly lady and her fat pug answered the door at the address I had noted down.

'Yes?' she enquired.

'Esperanto,' I said.

'Es-pe-ranto!' she exclaimed 'Ah Esperanto. Yes! Vi paroli Esperanto?' No, I didn't paroli, I had read the notice at the station.

'Everybody should learn Esperanto. It's such an important language. Listen, come to our meeting . . . we have a club in Vöcklabruck . . . we have regular meetings you know.'

'When?'

'Let me see . . . how about tomorrow evening?'

'Where?'

'Here.'

'Here?'

'Yes here, at my apartment.'

'I'll be along.'

'Eight o'clock. Bring pencil and paper.'

I turned up fifteen minutes late. All three were there, Leonora Unterhofer, the host, Fräeulein Fritzi, a lady of middling age, and the pug. It couldn't really be called a pug; it resembled nothing. All one could say for sure was that it was a fat vertebrate that lay on the rug and farted when it didn't snore or wheeze.

Fritzi was full of fervour, diving straight into Esperanto, embarrassing me with her ebullience. The catchphrase, 'Whatever happened to the others?' was exclaimed several times that evening. It was sometimes exchanged for, 'Whatever happened to Hedwig?' The two ladies fired questions at me in Esperanto and translated them. Then they translated my answers which I had to repeat. Within a short time they knew about me, all there was to know.

'Why didn't Hedwig turn up tonight?' said Fritzi for the fifteenth time.

'She assured me she was coming.' replied Leonora. 'I paroled with her this morning at the shop . . . I saw her at the shop.'

'Hedwig works in her father's shop, you know,' Fritzi enlarged. 'They sell kitchen utensils,' she added in her shrill voice, '. . . the shop near the library next to the passage.' Every time Hedwig was mentioned, meaningful glances were exchanged.

The meeting ended with the singing of the Esperanto Himnio. A sheet was pressed into my hand and I had to follow the chorus amid prompting and encouragement.

'Our next meeting is on Thursday,' they told me. That was three days on. I couldn't make it, I lied. 'So we will hold it on Friday. No sweat.'

They had plans!

Hedwig was a nice young lady, beautifully endowed. Had she shown indifference or had she been hesitant, I would have gone through agony and sleepless nights. However, she responded to my timid advances with affection and warmth. But a girl that could be attracted to a guy like me wasn't my kind of a girl. On numerous occasions we went out and sat in the park. And when she suggested I come round to the house and meet her parents, I hurled my belongings into my suitcase and caught the first train to Lugano.

Lugano was where my cousin Felix had set up house and from there, two weeks later, I hopped on the midnight train that got me to Victoria Station in time for breakfast.

Good for Hedwig. She deserved better.

UK

It had turned January when I arrived in England.

January of 1955.

It was the year that was to mark the end of the Churchill era. Winston Spencer Churchill was now eighty-one and hanging on to the job. He fell asleep once too often and, when he awoke in April, he found he had been eased out of his prime-ministerial position and placed on the back benches.

1955 was the year when Anthony Eden, Churchill's successor, sounded the alarm about Britain's most pressing problem: inflation. It stood at a staggering 1.5 per cent and something had to be done. Promptly the bank rate was increased from 3 to 4.5 per cent.

It didn't help, but it helped.

Eden called a general election in which his party obtained 38 per cent of the votes of the electorate, which gave them a 55 per cent representation in parliament. Comparable percentages are the rule in England, and the technique was going to be brought to a fine art in later years when a party would obtain a landslide majority of 60 per cent of the seats in the House on a 30 per cent share of the electoral number without batting an eyelid. There were, believe it or not, no less than six women among the 630 members.

In Algeria the people faced seven more tragic years before regaining their freedom. It was here that the hand-cranked magneto was used for the first time to get suspects to tell their French captors what they wanted to hear. The previous year the French had been defeated in Vietnam by the indigenous people and sent on their way.

In Britain, Teddy Boys resurrected Edwardian culture, Bostik was the cure-all for domestic breakages, Mondrian was being dusted off and elevated to saint by the architectural establishment and plain-clothes detectives were working overtime in public lavatories in their quest to quell quirky sexual nonconformity. The Festival of Britain euphoria had abated and was forgotten but for the indestructible concrete debris left behind on the South Bank.

People were waltzing to the tune,

> 'Ow much is that daw
> Guee in the window?
> Window!
> The one with the wagon-lit tail.
> Boum boum . . .

In the absence of substantial news, flying saucers lodged themselves firmly in the minds of those men and women who had plenty of room to spare.

'Hey, did you see that flying saucer last night?'
'I didn't. I didn't know saucers could fly.'
'No, UFOs, UFOs. I mean UFOs.'
'Whatsa Yoofos?'
'An unidentified flying object.'
'I didn't see no Yoofos.'
'I sawrrit. I tell you, I sawrrit. It was shaped like a cigar.
– You don't believe me.'

'I do.'

'You don't believe me, I can see it in your eyes.'

'Believe what?'

'That I saw a flying saucer.'

'I do believe that you saw a flying saucer . . . or . . . or a cigar.'

'Did you ever see a flying saucer then?'

'Nope, I never seen no flying saucer.'

'There you are. What's the use of telling you anything? YOORRA SKEP TICK!'

1955 in the league table of eventful years, is not to be found in the top ten. However, the one occurrence that stands out and which puts 1955 on the map was an event that marked the beginning of the end of an era. Admittedly, all events that 'mark a new era' are no more than parts of an ongoing process; each event forming a perceptible evolutionary nodule embedded in the unending sausage of history.

This particular event, the event I am talking about, was so momentous that it ranks among the top events of the decade.

In angry defiance, on a downtown bus, on a chilly day in December, a lady refused to relinquish her seat to a man.

'So what? Whoever heard of a more preposterous request,' I can hear the tortured reader of this ponderous narrative mumble. And justifiably so.

'Not so fast,' I would plead with her – or him – 'bear with me, for the denouement is about to be presented.'

This is it.

The lady was black, the man was pale, and the town was Montgomery, Alabama.

And there was no going back!

The event was momentous and classical in its initial simplicity. Rosa Parks is the name of the heroine. Her refusal to acquiesce in the continuance of pink-skin dominance led to the black bus boycott and brought about the beginning of the end to segregation in the USA. Before 1955 was out, an enormous dent had been made into albinoid supremacy and pride.

Arriving at Victoria Station on that blustery day marked for me a new beginning such as no previous arrival had done. Cliché or no cliché, that is how I felt at the time and that is how I feel today. It was as if I had finally come to roost. I was back where I had left off in my childhood. I was back with the people I admired – rightly or wrongly – for their pragmatism, their cool, their modesty, and above all, their trust. Unless you had proved to be a liar, unless you had let them down, unless you had taken advantage of their trust, they would believe you and believe in you. It took me little time to appreciate the expression '. . . the benefit of the doubt.'

SUCH CRUDE GENERALIZATION, COMING FROM YOU, FREDERICO; IT'S IRONICAL. IT LEAVES US BREATHLESS.

Yes I know. But this *is* 1955.

A taxi-driver, emerging from the toilet, whom I asked for a light – I only wanted to make contact, get the feel of the place – grudgingly held his glimmering cigarette to mine. At the same time he politely indicated where I might buy a box of matches. I went straight into the tobacconist and bought the current copy of the *New Statesman and Nation*, and a bag of mints. The London air was rendering me reckless.

I had been starved of the *New Statesman* ever since I left Jerusalem. It had weaned me off my hard-left position through its sober and fair assessment of current affairs and its moderate and open-minded outlook.

Kingsley Martin, the editor, was the personification of that spirit in the post-war years, a spirit of tolerance and of trying to come to terms with the intolerable; a spirit of introspection and self-criticism. It has been favourably instrumental in the formation of my post-communist make-up. It has made me receptive to a humanitarian-liberal outlook and has sharpened my perception to lines of reasoning from whatever quarter. Through its personal column a whole new world was opened to me. I joined ongoing groups and attended meetings organized by political and social circles and fringe movements.

ENGLISH UNDERSTATEMENT.

The residence of the prime minister of Britain from where the most powerful Empire in the history of mankind was ruled, is situated, not in some huge extravagant mansion, in a thoroughfare appropriately called Excelsior Avenue, or Boulevard of Naval Supremacy or on some grandiloquent New Imperial Square, but in a sober terraced house in a cul-de-sac named Downing Street, obscured by the foreign office, for all it's worth, forever blocking out the sunlight.

Sir George Downing, after whom the blind alley is named, one of Cromwell's cronies, was an opportunist diplomat, greatly admired and respected for his skilful duplicity and treachery.

Ever since my return to these shores, luck had turned in my favour. Fortuna herself was smiling at me.

Personally!

In my second week on this island I was knocked down by a black Humber whose learner driver had mounted the pavement. I was taken to Hackney Hospital where my leg was packed in plaster. The insurance company settled out of court and I was £250 the richer. I found a job with Terson's the builders, servicing and overhauling their concrete-mixers and hoists.

Thirty-five, young in maturity, the good times were beckoning. My mastery of English was modest, but there were no communication problems. Alas, to this day, I can conceal my foreign origin only as long as I keep my mouth firmly shut. My alien accent has remained my faithful companion.

With gusto and enthusiasm I immersed myself in the language. The language of Vladimir Nabokov, William Saroyan, Joseph Conrad, Arthur Koestler and the Authorized Version. With diligence I plunged into the idiom. I was now thinking English, breathing English and dreaming English. I was *eating* English. I took to turning my fork around, balancing mouthfuls of food on the wrong side. I even disciplined myself to eating ham sandwiches, made with gooey, manufactured bread. An English dictionary was used at all times and no words were looked up in translation. I can't say this has been the most brilliant idea to emerge from my scheming mind. It inhibited all comparative insight and sadly estranged me from my mother-tongue, thus arresting all further development, so much so that I am forever groping for words when called upon to converse in German, forever slipping into English modes of expression.

Among the Europeans the English are the most forgiving towards foreigners and within the next few months I made more friends than I had made in my home country in years. John was one of them. I had answered his advert inviting people dabbling in prose and poetry to come along to the group he had recently brought into being. The meetings took place at the home of Mrs Webb in Highgate. Mrs Webb herself was writing under the pen name of Stella Gibbons. Her daughter was John's future ex-wife. And John's sister was the young lady mentioned in the first chapter.

Talk of coincidences.

Sometime in July that year, John sent a note inviting me to his party. 'It would', it said, 'start roughly around eight o'clock, and end even more roughly.'

'Come and meet my sister,' said John, refilling my glass.

I had been nursing my first drink, looking around, and while everyone else was imbibing alcoholic potion she was sipping fizzy lemonade. She sat quietly by herself and struck me as having, in addition to her good looks, an inner beauty and happiness quite different from the others. I had looked in her direction several times but she had shown no interest. Ten months later we were married.

Mother:	*Where are you going my son?*
Son:	*I am orf to be married, mother dear.*
Mother:	*Not to one of Them, I hope. Not that girl you are having fun with. Not while I'm alive. Not . . . and she's no virgin . . .*
Son:	*Neither am I, Mum, However, she . . .*
Mother:	*That's different, yourra man.*
Son:	*. . . she makes excellent pancakes and she is pregnant.*
Mother:	*She should have been more careful, shouldn't she? But They never are. Are They? No one in your family ever married one of Them. Never! Why don't you take a girl like Karolla Weintraub from number twenty-nine. Her father is a highly successful entrepreneur and she doesn't need to make pancakes. . .*

The house at Tollington Park – another one of those misnomers – had been a windfall. It was the result of a series of lucky breaks, the two-litre Humber being one of them.

I put a deposit on this property the day I lost my job with Terson's. I lost my job at Terson's because the price of petrol had gone up. The price of petrol was increased because Gamal Abdel Nasser had blocked the Suez Canal. He blocked the Suez Canal because Egypt had been attacked by the joint forces of Israel, France and Britain. They had attacked him because . . . anyway, that's history. And while the headlines were screaming SUEZ, the Soviets, having just pulled out of Hungary, returned and savagely suppressed the people's desire to run their own affairs.

In those days, the bad old days, a modest house could be bought for a sum the average mechanic would take two and a half years to earn. Today, in the last decade of the twentieth century, a comparable freehold property would cost the equivalent of ten to twelve years slog by the self-same mechanic's mechanical grandson. At Terson's I had been earning about £600 per year and the freehold for the house in Tollington Park was up for £1,200. Jean and I scraped together £500 deposit and borrowed £700 from the building society on a ten-year mortgage, at $4\frac{1}{2}$ per cent interest.

Tollington Park is not a park. Regent's Park is a park. Finsbury Park is a park. But not Tollington Park. Tollington Park is a road. And so, by the way, is Cranley Gardens. A road, that is.

The day the news broke that the first artificial satellite had been launched, bleeping Russian signals back to Earth, I was scratching around in the front garden, not knowing precisely what I was doing nor what I was going to do. I was annoyed because my meal wasn't ready as I could have expected coming home from a hard day's work. Jean, my wife of six months, had turned out to be a rebellious creature and was in no way prepared to accept me as the master of the household. Her creed was equality of the sexes, would you believe.

I was in the front garden trying to make some sense out of the growth of undesired plants displacing the ones that I had introduced to lend respectability, when I was startled by a sound I had never heard before. A kind of suppressed scream coming from the road. She was only clearing her throat. Haaa-khuck.

Some throat.

She, was a plumpish woman approaching middling age, the remnants of her good looks maturing into matronly allure. In fact, she was born at the same hour of the same day in the same year as I – How do I know? I don't know. I just know. – She gave me the eye without turning her head and grinned triumphantly at having made me glance at her.

What I am about to say, may sound melodramatic. So be it.

She had been sent to harm me.

She didn't look the way people imagine witches would look. Of course, as everyone knows, real witches don't look like real witches. That, after all, is the essence of witchery.

Three weeks later I was standing on a ledge, painting the outside of the first-floor window, concentrating on the job in hand, and precariously balancing on that narrow projection formed by the top of the portal. Suddenly there was this report again, this high-pitched crack. Haaa-khuck, the cough-clear-throat. It caught me unawares and I nearly lost my grip as I compulsively spun around. Instead, the paint-pot took a dive and there on the front steps remained the evidence; a constant reminder and a warning. It was the splashed paint, which had formed a pattern, that has since kept her at bay. She had goofed. No doubt, she was to be hauled over the coals for it by her superiors. I never saw her again.

Just for the record; it was in both these encounters that I was facing north, while she had been proceeding west.

262

Man on Luna

'*I believe that this nation should commit itself to achieving the goal, before this decade is out . . .*'

The goal of what? Achieving social justice? No . . .? Ah, ending corruption in high places.

No!

Fight organized crime? Provide health services for all? Democracy . . .? Human rights throughout the hemisphere . . .? No?

No!

I know! This nation should commit itself, before this decade is out, to abolish malnutrition throughout . . .

No, no, no! Nothing as banal as that. Think historically.

I give up.

So shut up and let the man finish.

'*. . . before this decade is out, of landing a man on the Moon and returning him safely to Earth.*'

You're kidding, surely. . .

Would I joke about a thing like that? It's on record, J.F.K. to Congress: May 25 1961.

What our man Kennedy had committed himself to, in addition to the above, and in addition to numerous dramatic artists of soft contours, was intensified interference in the affairs of smaller nations, leading to the invasion and eventual destruction of Vietnam, Laos and Cambodia.

Three Ars

It is the task of the teacher to assist young people in acquiring the skills of thinking for themselves, in accordance with accepted standards.

A. Barbés-Rochechouart

As far back as I can remember I have admired the teaching profession for its enlightened working hours and its magnanimous holidays. In the late 1950s, young Aussies began appearing in increasing numbers in the streets of London in pursuance of their grand tour of Europe. They stopped over at Earls Court between forays into the mysterious continent. Some worked the petrol pumps while others went in for a 'spot of teaching'.

Ever since the Suez Crisis, when I got the push at Terson's, I had become restless and during the following year and a half I had changed jobs five times. So much so that one day in January 1959 I picked up the phone in the booth outside the Geffrye Museum in Shoreditch and dialled the education department of the LCC – the London County Council.

'Education,' reported the voice at the other end.

I pressed the button and irrevocably the penny dropped.

'Ahem . . . ah . . . ah . . . I would like to know . . . ah . . . could I speak to somebody . . . could you put me through to someone who . . . who can give me information about teaching metalwork?'

'It is him you are speaking to,' came the Bengali voice from County Hall.

'I . . . I . . . ahem my friend told me . . . he teaches English and he told me that you're short of metalwork teachers.'

My friend Peter Bowering, having attained his English degree at Birkbeck, had left his job as an industrial chemist and had gone in for 'a spot of teaching', in the East End of London.

'You must talk to the inspector. Can you come to-morrow morning at ten?' I certainly could, and it took me two hours to get over the shock of not having been turned down outright.

Promptly the next morning I turned up at the office of the handicraft inspector. I was wearing a shabby overcoat, and a grubby scarf was hiding my dirty shirt.

The inspector, an unsmiling yet friendly man, put me at my ease and placed a sheet of lined foolscap on his immaculate desk. Having sharpened his pencil he proceeded to set out in neat characters my name and address.

'Nationality?' he asked.

'Austrian.'

'Age?'

'Thirty-nine.'

'Pfffffhhh . . .'

Mr Moore, the handicraft inspector, looked at me reproachfully. He bounced his pencil several times catching it on the rebound. I felt he was sympathetic and was trying to help me. At the same time he was desperately trying to help himself for, as I found out later, there were thirty-eight schools in North London with fully equipped workshops and no teachers to man them.

'What are your qualifications?'

'I finished my apprenticeship in Austria.'

'You have never taught in this country?' I hadn't

The pencil, poised to chronicle my academic and educational accomplishments, dropped on the desk where it took up an incongruous position. The inspector leant back, spread his arms and faced me.

'You have nothing to offer,' he declared with finality.

'Mr Foulmere! Just how on earth do you expect the children to show respect for you, when you don't show the slightest regard and consideration for me? Wouldn't it be nice . . .'

Young Foulmere, the new music teacher, had crossed the playground and found himself pinned against the rural science department by Mr Spoondekker the headmaster, or Guardian as he loved to be called. Foulmere was stupefied.

' . . . I mean, wouldn't it be nice,' Spoondekker continued, outstaring Foulmere, ' . . . wouldn't it be much more appropriate if you kept your hands out of your pockets, dear boy? Wouldn't that set a good example? And could your necktie not be straightened?' Spoondekker smiled angrily. 'You might like to get a copy of our code of conduct from Mr Gantry and study it.'

After a few well-aimed questions, an open-ended suggestion.

Before Foulmere could catch his breath, Spoondekker had breezed on, his black cloak billowing and flapping in the fresh autumn flurry. He had discharged one of his periodical forays onto the playground, when he would sally forth, clip a few ear-holes, censure young members of staff and move on.

Hit and run!

I entered the education circuit at the beginning of the Easter term on a temporary basis at an hourly rate, on condition I produced a Full Technological Certificate within three years. I passed the finals after twenty months and overnight my salary doubled.

*

Contrary to popular belief, teachers are not infallible. But they are close. And they are the first to admit to gaps within the bounds of their extensive sphere of erudition. And nobody can tell me they lack the faculty for self-criticism. Just because you haven't seen them exercise it, doesn't mean they haven't got it. Good God, if they can sit in the staffroom and slate the headmaster and all others who happen to be out of earshot, then you can't tell me that they are incapable of looking at themselves analytically.

Where is your logic?

If you listen carefully, you may hear a teacher admit, she – or indeed he – has been wrong and with breath-taking frankness, confess to their limited wisdom. Why, only the other day the head of the science department said to me, 'Fred,' she said, shaking her pretty head, 'Fred, I don't know what this world is coming to. I really don't.' She nearly cried.

There you are, she admitted to her own ignorance. Well, they don't come more honest and introspective than that, do they?

Her bewilderment had been prompted by the realization that the price of air fares had gone up without warning, and before she had had the chance to book her holidays.

Hammer the poor teacher, that's all you know.

We are a hard-working crowd, slogging relentlessly from half past nine in the morning till a quarter past twelve with only fifteen minutes' break, most of the time on our feet. And back for more from two to four in the afternoon. We hand out books, we wipe the blackboard, we clap our hands. One moment we explain the intricacies of carbon chains, or point out the industrial potential of the Republic of Mali, and the next moment we must list the names of the wives of Henry VIII for the umpteenth time, or acquaint our charges with the life and times of Barbés-Rochechouart.

Throughout, we do our best to give those unreceptive and ungrateful brats an education in the most trying and tiring circumstances. Morning and afternoon. Day in and day out. Five grinding hours every day, five unremitting days every week, with barely six to eight free periods, three quarters of every year of our working lives.

And all that, with precious little acknowledgement from the community at large. No wonder only the strong ones survive that pace. Many are those who succumb to nervous breakdowns and have to take sabbaticals.

You should try it. See how you fare.

The fact that education is confrontational is entirely due to the refusal of children to co-operate. They are inordinately mistrustful of their teachers and contemptuous of what we are trying to do for them. At best they are uninspired and lazy. It is a sign of the times that children are treated like Vee Eye Pease in their family environment, expecting everything to come to them easy.

The catch phrase goes, 'You can take the mare to the water, but you can't make her drink.' If a more sensible approach were to be adopted, one with a realistic set of choices and consequences, one that would find expression in a slogan such as, for example, 'Drink or drown', then we would be contravening the law which protects the pupils far more than us. Why, even the slipper or the bamboo cane are now being challenged. And that in the name of human rights by an outlandish court, with the proceedings being conducted somewhere in Central Europe in a foreign language.

Now, we have philanthropists even in this country, who pay lip service to those alien ideas of soft pedalling and child psychology. Would they ever have attained a position such as they are holding today if they had been the product of the liberal approach they are forever advocating? Answer me that! Did you know that more than 85 per cent of school-leavers can read? Did you know that? And write! Did you know that Britain has the highest percentage of newspaper readers in the world? You didn't know that. Yes, you can sneer. They tell me that only 8 per cent of readers read the 'quality papers'. But who decides what is quality? Answer me that!

In spite of it all, we are still turning out an orderly mass of God-fearing and upright citizens, capable of conforming and thinking in a co-ordinated way – better still, leaving the thinking to those who have been destined to do so. We are producing loyal subjects prepared to follow, fight against all comers for the flag and our way of doing things; decent, hard-working citizens who appreciate the freedoms they have been given, exercise them responsibly, and respect those who are landed with the task of administering those freedoms and liberties.

Only in a vague way do children know that the more they take on board, the better are their chances later on. They don't realize how apparently useless information may well be of some value sometimes in the future. Facts such as, say, the importance of isthmuses. Where, for instance, would the Malayan peninsula be if it wasn't for the isthmus of Kra, pray tell. An island surrounded by water it would be, cut off from the Asiatic mainland it would be. Yes, you ought to know that!

Or take ruminants. They have five stomachs – or six – and humans have but one. How about that? And cockroaches have two. That puts ruminants into the top league. You didn't know that, did you?

Ruminants? All those that ruminate, of course. That's the truth.

Then there are the carbon chains to be consumed and stored. What chains? Carbon chains. The letter C, in groups of six written all over the blackboard, forming a meaningful pattern.

Then there is the Pythagorean theorem to be absorbed.

And did you know that $ax^2 + bx + c$, add up to nothing, zero to be exact. Isn't that interesting?

'We don't wanna HIN VESSI GATE,' a group of uninspired second- year boys say to me, telling me of their activities in the art department. Well, they may not have liked the artificiality of that requirement but they certainly had learned a new word.

'We got YOU MANA TEAS this afternoon,' they say with resignation. They had by now accepted the school and its way of life, as well as its idiosyncrasies and perplexities, with the stoicism of twelve- and thirteen- year olds.

'What's YOOMANITEES?' I enquire.

'I's about towns and places . . .'

'Yea an' the coastline an' things . . .'

'I's GEE O GRIPHY . . . like . . . like countries an' things.'

'. . . an ISTORY . . . King Alfred . . . an' things.'

More words absorbed.

'Why do we have to do metalwork?' they ask me.

'Because you may need it one day. You are learning many useful things to do with your hands.' I reply with lucidity.

Like a good and prudent gardener who cares for her – or indeed his – plants, propping them up, removing a leaf here, cropping a branch there, helping a growing bud to unfold, so in teaching we give support, redirecting growth as we deem necessary.

As in the development of a plant it is imperative to trim back unwanted growth, graft on, transplant, cross-fertilize and always nip in the bud undesirable tendencies. It is given to the teachers of this world to preserve the status quo ante.

With a strong emphasis on the ante.

Originality and a sense of innovation have their place, but it wouldn't get us very far if we were to give it free rein. We must not lose sight of our heritage and our traditions and our established values. And we must at all times aim for presentation and the good image.

The headmaster at Brooksmill Upper, was a pragmatist. 'If it looks good, then why worry?' he enunciated. 'If it doesn't, move it to the far end of the corridor or into the potting shed.'

'What the eye don't see,' the deputy would reinforce in his rendering of earthy Yorkshire, 'the mind don't grieve after.'

Just as plants must compete and the weak fall by the wayside so the good teacher encourages competition and the will and the drive to out-do the next guy. Co-operation has its place, certainly, but it does not build motorways and channel tunnels.

From an early age we must convey to our charges that simplistic notions such as 'Life is about living' do not work. Life is about meeting the demands and the challenges of this world, rising to the challenge society is making on us, giving service, being proud of one's traditions, and yes, laying down one's life for the fatherland or king and country or *la patrie* depending on what passport you happen to hold.

'We set their soft brains in cement,' enthused the headmaster. 'There is no other way. They'd be thinking in sixes and sevens otherwise, and industry wouldn't thank us for that, now would they? A child's mind wanders, it must be channelled. That's what it's all about.' He nodded and he winked.

'Children must be pointed in the right direction. They wouldn't know which way to turn otherwise.

This is our job in a nutshell: to impart to them what it is all about . . . to impress upon them the values we aim to instil, that's what it's all about. It is about moulding them into the required shape – round pegs into round holes – so they may fit into society, become fully contributing members of this great society in accordance with its requirements. That's what it is all about.'

He nodded vigorously and fell silent, leaning back with pride, pleased with his effort, almost waiting for applause but not quite expecting it, as it is not the custom at staff meetings.

Endgame

Unlike Richard Nixon, I cannot claim 'I am not a crook!' What I can say is this, 'I am a liar' and that's the truth.

F. P. in one of his assertive moods.

Oh Lord! Have mercy upon us. Temper our compassion, so that we may enjoy to the fullest this breakfast and the bounty thou hast given us. Amen.

Grace spoken in the 1990s at the point of ingesting the morning repast

The pheasant at the bottom of the garden has been mocking me again. 'Homo soppy,' he taunts, to the tune of 'Yoorra silly billy'. He allows me to get to within ten paces, pretending not to notice the stealthily approaching *Homo ineptus*, after which he deposits a dropping and withdraws lethargically. Should I start running, he would lift himself angrily over the hedge, swearing while airborne. This is my moment of triumph, for I have forced the creature to leave the ground. His kind are lazy; walkers by nature, they use their wings only as a last resort. He shows no appreciation, nor recognition for my position. He knows that I hold the deeds to this piece of land. So do the sparrows and the rooks, the hawthorns, the mosses, the pebbles and all the creepy crawlies. None of them show the slightest respect. The nettles display their acknowledgement by stroking me gently as I pass. There are even no-go areas. Oh yes! Interdicted by wild bees, whipping branches and prickly and noxious weeds; on my own property, would you believe.

The only friendly voice, in fact, comes from the young thrush who sits on my TV aerial calling 'Jine the libbril partioo libbril libbril tioo tioo trrrrrrrrrrrrrr!' She just loves to stir things up, seeking to create instability in the land.

In 1965, we discovered Highfield.

Highfield in the parish of Harlton. Hopefully the last stop. Enough of the wanderings, the travellings, the trains, the planes and the furniture vans. From the moment we saw this place, Jean and I couldn't tear ourselves away, although the house is unremarkable, built as it was in the undistinguished style of the cheerless mid-thirties, in the drab days of my apprenticeship.

Standing on one acre of ground, Highfield sprouted ideas of self-sufficiency and grand projects. It is situated at the edge of the village and there are cattle in the neighbouring field. A nameless hill, insignificant but prominent in this flatland, stretches along the back. Alas, no brook gurgles through, or alongside our domain. The green pastures . . .

OK. KLAUSNER
SELF-STYLED ICONOCLAST,
PURVEYOR OF PARADOXES AND CONUNDRUMS,
COME TO THE POINT.
SAY WHAT YOU HAVE TO SAY NOW
AND THEREAFTER HOLD YOUR PEACE.
THIS TIRADE WILL HAVE TO COME TO AN END
FOR THERE IS A PAPER SHORTAGE.
YOUR BOOK CONTRIBUTES TO THE ACCELERATING DEMISE
OF THE WORLD'S FORESTS.
EVERY PAGE UTTERED IN FRIVOLITY
IS A TREE LOST IN FUTILITY,
ANOTHER DEAD PAPAYA
FLOATING POINTLESSLY
DOWN THE ORINOCO.

In common with most of the villages around Cambridge, Harlton acquires its character from a picturesque mix of managing directors, retired colonels, regional sales reps and the inevitable academic,

275

along with a sprinkling of locals who have managed to cling on. These are the remnants of the families who have been here for generations, who now live in rented accommodation and who earn extra money by weeding and digging the gardens of the ever-changing influx of head teachers, chief accountants and city wallahs. They make the beds and bed the marigolds of those blessed with purchasing power.

The descendants of the builders of the thirteenth- and fourteenth-century churches go to the houses of the nouveaux riches and clean their toilets, vacuum their soft furnishings and carpets and admire the mediocre taste of their benefactors. They do the errands and generally relieve the overworked scholars and tireless civil servants of the chores these creative professionals simply cannot find time for. They complement one another and everyone is happy. It's the old Yin and Yang at work. The influxees, having secured all the select parcels of land and being providers of spare-time work, have the clout to successfully oppose all further housing development needed for the young people. Thus they preserve what rurality there is left to enjoy.

This arcadian suburbia finds itself cocooned from the discordant regime of the 'market forces' and the brutal economic and social realities of the 1990s.

The focal points in this elliptical confinement are the church and the inn. On Sunday mornings the congregation gathers in that Gothic edifice built for continuity, singing hymns to all things bright and beautiful and to the glory of their achievements. They rely upon their vicar to adapt Christianity to the rigours of the present condition, and to unburden them of the teachings of him who taught sacrifice by example. Invigorated, they return to their homes behind treble-locked doors and burglar alarms, confident that professing to this demanding creed is, if nothing else, a celestial insurance policy.

God helps them that help themselves!

Their need for further congregation is being met by the brewers and distillers in unassuming, purpose-built structures designed to generate jollity and conviviality. Social intercourse, therefore, is closely entwined with the consumption of fermented juices, and the inhalation of tar-laden fumes of smouldering weeds, backed by the euphony of soft music and the thudding sound of darts missing the board. Mind-clouding alcoholoids and nicotinates provide the necessary relaxants for people of all walks of life, enabling them to unwind after a dispiriting day at the office, or the production line or the dole queue. Without the calming effects of these narcotics, how could we face the rigours and stresses and the boredom of the days and weeks and the years ahead? Answer me that!

In the scheme of things, the brewing establishment and those who command the distilling operations, discretely provide the leadership the country so badly needs at a time of constant social flux and instability. It is they who prudently underwrite the fight against indecency, leftwingism, and alien drug culture. Unobtrusively, they underpin the things we hold high, our tradition, our heritage and our established practices.

Status quo, as the Romans say.

On a more intimate level, dinner parties are held among like-minded people. At these, the cultural level of the formal epicurean event is governed by the strictness of adherence to rules of etiquette, based on eighteenth-century French court protocol. A variety of drinking vessels must be at hand to accommodate diverse beverages served. Crockery and cutlery must be of the right kind, in the right place, at the right time, and special instruments must be provided and removed with the Scampi à la Reggiana. Here again, varieties of brewed and distilled drinks and fermented juices of grapes are essential. Candles are lit. Soft nondescript tunes waft from inconspicuous hi-fi equipment. Respectability, quiet wit and warmth rebound from the walls and lend reassurance that all is for the best in the best of all possible worlds.

And while one half of the people on this earth are subjected to raw, chronic starvation, this half is suffering from the harmful effects of obesity.

We all carry one burden or another.

Here then, on this acre of Anglian land which belongs to me by virtue of having paid for it, I have the best of both worlds; urban rurality and rural urbanity. The beauty, the charm, the romanticism of the countryside and the comforts, amenities and solidity of the city; cow dung and computerized convenience you might say; social intercourse even.

Here, I can plant my celeriac, scorzonera, land cress and winter cherries, runner beans and parsley, and please myself as to when to mow the grass, if at all.

Here, I can lie me down in green pastures and delight in a summer's day with the wind rustling refreshingly over the tops of the ashes and sycamores, rejoice at seeing my children flourish, and lament the passing of the English elm.

Here, with the leaves turning rusty and fluttering to the ground, I can go over the top recording my memoirs, mixing metaphors, agonizing over idiom and struggling with syntax.

Here I can sit in one of the broken-down cars that clutter the back of the garden and watch the snow swirling, quietly settling and gently covering. And reminisce gleefully over the sinister forces who have slipped pursuing me through the valley of the shadow of death. And look back with nostalgia, gloating over those bloated baroque bastards who forever attempted at restricting my movement; at breaking my will.

Here comma bald-headed, barefaced and toothless, the features sagging, the pace slowing, hair growing from my ears and nostrils, I can meditate and contemplate and cogitate, ponder and reflect and thank my lucky stars, or the powers that be, or whosoever it is who is giving me this day my daily bread and forgives my trespasses and delivers milk to the door.

Here, people are broadminded and tolerant and don't resent the odd oddball in their midst. They show forbearance towards radicals and other misfits.

Since this oddball has no hope of beating them, maybe it is time he should join them?

Why not?

FRED KLAUSNER,
INTROSPECTIVE EXHIBITIONIST,
BITER OF THE HAND THAT FEEDS HIM,
RETURN TO THE FOLD.
SUBMERGE IN THE TENDER FLUIDS OF THE GREAT WOMB.
GIVE UP YOUR SELF-RESPECT AND BECOME RESPECTABLE.
CONFORM DAMN YOU!
IT WON'T HURT.

Well basically, what is there to say? I mean, personally speaking, how much longer have I got to play the maverick? Let others carry the torch, I am too old, quite frankly, to bang my head against the wall. I mean listen, I'll be seventy-three and a half in two years' time, in case you've forgotten.

To be perfectly honest with you; what has individualism ever done for me? Answer me that. I mean basically . . . in the final analysis, what has my self-esteem ever given me? Answer me that. How much have my principles *per se* . . . I mean, at the end of the day, how much have they added to my wealth? Explain me that if you can.

THAT'S IT FREDDO!
NOW YOU'RE TALKING POSITIVE.
THE WORLD BELONGS TO THE OPPORTUNIST.
GRASP THE NETTLE BY ITS HORNS WHILE THE IRON IS HOT.
THIS IS YOUR LAST CHANCE, DON'T BLOW IT, FREDDI.
DON'T BLOW IT NOW.

No, I won't. Not this time. How can I resist? I'm coming in . . . yes I'm coming in. Just give me time to put on my polka-dot bow-tie, readjust my ethics, and turn off the lights . . . hang on I'm coming.

I feel better already.

Thank you all for having me. Thank you, thank you, thank you, *mercie mille fois, muchas gracias, katal kherak, herzlichsten Dank, todah rhaba, balshoiye spaciva* and all that. IT HAS BEEN GREAT!

Farewell, farewell, farewell. Hurrah, farewell and thank you. I'm coming. . . I'm coming . . .

I'm coming . . .